Spilt Milk

Also by Sarah Steel

Correction Squad

Spilt Milk

Sarah Steel

Delta

Publisher's message

This novel creates an imaginary sexual world. In the real world,
readers are advised to have safe sex.

Copyright © 1999 Sarah Steel

The right of Sarah Steel to be identified as the Author
of the Work has been asserted by her in accordance with
the Copyright, Designs and Patents Act 1988.

First published in paperback in 1999 by
HEADLINE BOOK PUBLISHING

A HEADLINE DELTA paperback

10 9 8 7 6 5 4 3 2 1

ISBN 0 7472 6315 9

Typeset by CBS, Martlesham Heath, Ipswich, Suffolk
Printed and bound in Great Britain by
Mackays of Chatham PLC, Chatham, Kent

HEADLINE BOOK PUBLISHING
A division of Hodder Headline PLC
338 Euston Road, London NW1 3BH

Spilt Milk

Spilt Milk

Easing back a fraction, so that his weight rested on his heels, he viewed the colours swimming before his lust-narrowed eyes: the white, the cream and the tiny gleam of wet pink. Grunting, he closed his eyes and lunged. She screamed out in raw pleasure. He felt the soft weight of her buttocks rasping his pubic curls. Opening his eyes, he silently named the colours: the white of the breakfast bar; the cream of her smooth cheeks; the wet pink of her rosebud sphincter revealed by his controlling hands that gripped and prised apart her fleshy buttocks.

Housewives. She was his third this morning. A hot little strawberry blonde, provocatively pony-tailed, who liked it across the breakfast bar. No preliminaries, no chat. He just came in, nodded, reversed his blue and white striped apron and unzipped. She squealed her token protest but parted her thighs for him even before her breasts squashed down beneath her, forcing the nipples to kiss the cool melamine.

He caught the whiff of her willingness as he planted his right palm down against her proffered buttocks, using his thick thumb to explore her sticky cleft. Then, using both hands to talon and control the satin flesh, he drove his hardness into her. As he plunged, pumping rhythmically, his thumbtips opened her pliant cheeks, prising her shadowed cleft painfully apart.

By the time they glimpsed the anal whorl, his eyes would be slits of concentration. Writhing and drumming her fists down upon the white melamine, the willing blonde moaned. They had done this so often now, they were as good as any married couple – they just didn't know each other's names. Both held back until they sensed each other's climax: up on his toes, he buried himself deep inside her tight warmth. She came softly, mewing like a kitten at its cream. Exploding, he jerked his head back. As usual, the pencil stub slipped from behind his ear and rattled on the Italian mosaic kitchen floor.

He scooped up his pencil stub, licked the dull tip and bent across the breakfast bar, elbows splayed, totting up a column of figures in his well-thumbed book. The naked blonde, standing behind him, snaked her arms around his hips, burying her breasts and belly into his hard back.

'Six quid,' he muttered.

'Six?' she murmured dreamily, fingering his sticky shaft playfully.

'Gave you an extra quart of cream, Saturday. Remember?'

'Mm.' She remembered.

'Want any yoghurt?'

She shook her head, declining this week's special offer, as she dragged her juicy labia across his striped apron. She always dried her slit this way, finding the rough cotton stretched across his firm buttocks delicious against her wet, silken flesh.

'Zip me up, then.'

Murmuring her protest, she obeyed with reluctant fingers.

Pushing himself away from the breakfast bar, he stood up straight and deftly wrenched the milkman's apron around to cover the bulge in his denims. Winking, he lowered his face close to hers, licked her mouth with a slow, measured force, then slapped her naked left buttock sharply and strode out of the kitchen, leaving the pony-tailed blonde pressing an ice-cold pint to her left nipple – still peaking painfully after the milkman's delivery.

It protested with a shrill whine at its top speed of 8 m.p.h. and exposed him to frost, wind and rain – but he wouldn't swap his milk float for a chauffeur-driven Rolls. As milk rounds went, this one on the Beechwood Estate didn't earn much, he thought, nursing the sluggish float between a Volvo Estate and a lazily parked Merc. But the perks – he grinned and tossed his head back. All the husbands on the Beechwood had vanished on the 7.20 to Waterloo, leaving it all to him: like a fox in an unguarded henhouse. The husbands – big earners in the City – came back on the late train, richer but tireder men. Good luck to them. He wouldn't swap his milkman's apron for a striped shirt. He liked things they way they were. The Beechwood was an ideal hunting ground for a fit young man. All those young, neglected housewives.

Nosing the float out of the avenue, he stamped on the accelerator. The needle flickered to 6 m.p.h. as he cruised down the cul-de-sac. This was his favourite run. Ferndale Close. He thought of his four pairs of fresh boxer shorts nestling in the chilled box on the back of the float. He loved the kiss of cold cotton against his hot balls. He had five special deliveries to make in Ferndale Close – not on the same day. Not that he couldn't manage it: it was just that he liked to spread the pleasure. Tuesday was number six, the brunette. Blue-eyed, small-breasted but mad for it. He made her greet him naked except for a pair of black court shoes – sexily kitten-heeled with gold buckles across squared toes. He would deliver the two pints slowly, carefully – maddeningly slowly and carefully – as she shivered from both the cold, raw morning and her hot, raw arousal. Shivered, naked, in the open doorway, shielding her nipples and pubis from neighbouring windows. He liked that, making her stand and squeal in the cold. When he had stepped inside, she always slammed the mullioned glass front door with a gasp of relief, legs together, black court shoes pressed together, thrusting her buttocks up against the cold glass.

'Where?' he always asked.

She would point, in silence. Up the stairs, to the bathroom. Or straight into the dining room. Never, it suddenly came to him, the bedroom. He'd take the brunette in the bedroom one Tuesday. Soon. And pull out just in time to spurt all over the satin sheets. Then wipe her face in it.

Last week, it had been right then and there in the hall. Pinning her down firmly, her arms spread out across the carpet, he had ridden her with brutal relish, sinking down to mouth her apple breasts. Soon, her court shoes were raking his thighs as they had both come savagely. Before he had left, he'd ordered her to roll over. Intimately inspecting her reddened, carpet-burnt buttocks, he'd palmed the punished cheeks slowly, making her come again. She'd watched him go in sullen silence – but, as the left toe of her black court shoe ground down into the carpet, her sparkling blue eyes had blinked pure gratitude.

Number eight was kinky. Definitely kinky. He liked a bit of kinky, just like he enjoyed cold sliced beetroot with hot shepherd's pie. She always dragged him to the lounge and made him sit down in a large chair – a cream job with Suffolk roses. She would inch up her skirt and sit, stockinged legs astride, on his lap. Knickerless, she squirmed as she impaled herself on his throbbing shaft facing his feet. The TV would be on. Usually the weather on BBC1. She loved it that way. Gripping the sides of the chair with whitening knuckles, she rode him furiously while the isobars on the screen tightened into a vortex around the eye of a storm. Spasming, she would scream, the concentric lines on the TV weather map pulsing in time to the contractions of her muscled warmth around the thick hardness buried inside her.

Obeying her frantic instructions, he would whip it out just before orgasm – shuddering as the engorged knout swept up along the hot silk of her cleft – to splash her between the shoulder blades with gobbets of quicksilver. She would scream softly as he rained down upon her, quickly going down on all fours – just as the main news headlines flashed up – begging him to tongue her wet fig. He usually managed to lick her into ecstasy by the time the regional news bulletin came on, her groans of pleasure drowning out the traffic report.

Number Eleven was a riot. Ten minutes at each heavy breast – sucking and nibbling the hard nipples – then a brisk three-minute knuckling between her wet thighs and she would be purring like a Daimler – and revving like a Jag. She always kept her tights on. Dark, honey bronze with a glossy sheen. He loved rubbing his shaft against them. Especially the darker band stretched above her hips. Dark as chocolate. He called her his little Mars Bar as he sucked and bit. Sucked and bit gently at her tiny clitoris trapped behind the shining nylon that imprisoned her pubic nest. His little Mars Bar. She came silently. Never a murmur, but he always knew.

She would bury her naked breasts into his upturned face as, holding her nylon-sheathed buttocks, he hugged her to him like a prize.

Friday morning was number fourteen. Number fourteen liked it on her knees under the dining room table. He would shuffle up behind her and thumb her panties down, pausing to savour her swollen cheeks. That was exactly how she liked it. Kneeling, trapped under the dining room table. He would spank her bare bottom seven, maybe eight times, as he rode her. Clawing for the table leg, she would make a pretence of scrambling to escape – earning a second flurry of searing swipes across her reddening cheeks. The punishment stilled and silenced her – besides, trapped under the table, there was no way out. Restricted, spanked and helpless, she had to submit and surrender to him.

Today was Friday. He palmed his spanking hand into his milkman's striped apron. Suddenly he winced, remembering how, last week, he had almost done his shoulder in, lunging under the heavy oak tabletop. Silly bitch. He would redden her bare cheeks good and hard today. Why couldn't she have it on top of the table, or in the hall? Still, he grinned, drawing up to a gentle stop, there was nothing quite like giving it hot and strong to a freshly smacked backside. Yanking on the handbrake, he scooped up a bottle of gold top.

Stepping down from the float, the milkman shivered with pure delight. The wet asphalt felt soft beneath his trainers. Firm but pliant, like the bodies of the housewives in Ferndale Close. He strode along the pavement, his breath visible in the cold morning air. He strode with an unconscious swagger: cock of the walk.

The door to number nine inched open shyly, like the legs of a young music teacher on her honeymoon. He saw it open more boldly. He broke his cocksure stride and turned. Number nine – his was a black Lotus, hers a white Mondeo – didn't get their milk delivered. Probably did a big midweek shop out on the edge of town and stocked up the fridge. But the door was definitely open, and open for him.

He paused, turning towards the door. A mature woman, forty-

5

something – but, he thought appreciatively, as fit as she was luscious – beckoned to him. The gesture of invitation caused her white towelling robe to gape open, then part. He saw that she was naked underneath. His shaft stirred, thickened and rose to salute the heavy breasts, white belly and broad hips. He could certainly slip this a quick red top, he thought with a grin.

'Milkman.'

'That's me.'

'Can you spare me a moment? I don't like to ask, but—'

His eyes widened, then narrowed immediately, as she shrugged, her heavy breasts bouncing softly.

'My husband's gone.' Three words that spoke volumes.

'No problem. I'm your man.' He nodded curtly.

'How kind,' she murmured, allowing him a quick full-frontal before belatedly gathering her robe around her nakedness. 'Do come in.'

His pace – like his pulse – quickened. His brain spun, sending him almost tipsy with lustful anticipation. He'd give this beauty a right ride. Suddenly, he remembered his dad's Ford Zephyr. Big, brassy beast of a motor. Classy, though. Sensual upholstery to slide into, slick gears and plenty under the bonnet when the moment came. His palms were wet with excitement, he almost dropped his bottle despite his firm grip.

'Through here.' The plummy, modulated tones of middle class suburbia beckoned. 'You're just in time.'

He almost ran into the spacious kitchen, finding her naked, legs apart, her feet buried in the discarded robe. Her bottom – heavily swollen and ripely curved, the cleft gaping temptingly – caused his throat to tighten.

'I want you naked,' were her only words.

It was not, he sensed, an invitation: it was an instruction. His thickening shaft twitched, thrilling in response to her stern note of easy authority. Accustomed as he was to the young, submissive housewives he took in his arrogant stride, the presence of this dominant, mature nude electrified him. Tearing off his apron and kicking off his trainers, he knew he was in for the ride of the year.

'I want a pint,' she remarked.

'Can spare that,' he grunted, unbuckling his belt and dragging down his denims. 'Gold top?'

'Out of you, young man,' she warned, glancing down over her shoulder at his nodding spear. 'Not from your float.'

He tossed his head back – sending the stub of his pencil flying – and brayed his disbelief in nervous laughter, 'Nice one, lady. Like your style.'

'Oh but I mean it,' she whispered, turning to face him. He saw that she had donned yellow rubber gloves. The thumbs, tips just touching, rested deep in her pubic nest. She strummed her labia slowly, rhythmically.

'Hell, lady, have a heart. I'll do my best, but a full pint—'

'It's what I asked for and it is exactly what I'll get. Kneel,' she thundered, jabbing her finger to the floor.

He grinned, genuflecting. 'Like me to get you going, eh? Like a bit of mouth down south—'

'Kneel,' she ordered, her tone crisply severe.

Eager to taste the new delights of domination, the naked milkman sank down into the soft cork tiling.

'He's ready,' the heavily breasted nude called out, casually stroking her slit with a rubber-sheathed fingertip.

'What the hell—' he gasped.

Three naked matrons, superbly ripe in the full flowering of their forties, padded into the kitchen in silent menace. He staggered to his feet, suddenly self-conscious and slightly alarmed. He covered himself with cupped hands.

'Kneel, and get those hands behind your back. At once,' the nearest nude barked. She was blonde, grey-eyed, and generously bosomed. His nostrils caught her perfume – Orange Water. It failed to mask his own perspiring fear.

'That's right,' the grey-eyed blonde whispered as he obeyed. 'Struggle, and you'll get five years.'

He closed his eyes and groaned. What chance would a milkman have, found naked by the police, in a kitchenful of middle class crumpet, with all their money, brains and sharp barrister friends. Five would be a result – seven years would be more like it. He shuffled on the cork, pressing his knees together, wishing his proud cock would shrink.

They circled him, studying him intimately. 'Quite the little Samaritan, aren't you, milkman?' the woman who had enticed him in through the front door said softly, her mocking tone sugaring a darker note of malice. 'See to all the little needs of the pretty young housewives hereabouts, don't you?'

He bowed his head to avoid her piercing gaze and remained silent. She inched closer, planting her legs apart, bringing her nest three inches from his face. His mouth felt dry; he tried to swallow. He glanced up, his eyes sweeping over her rounded hips, flat belly and resting on the superb swell of her breasts.

'Don't you?' she insisted. Her breasts wobbled deliciously as she placed her rubber-gloved fingers under his chin and tilted his face up to meet her stern gaze.

He sensed the score. They were jealous. Jealous of the younger wives getting it regularly. They wanted some of the action themselves. He relaxed, grinning. 'I do my best to keep the customers satisfied.'

It was a mistake, that. Her angry eyes told him. His answer had been a mistake, And he knew it. The cock of the walk had just stumbled – crowing was not a good move.

'Oh, I am sure you do,' the naked beauty purred. 'We are mothers.'

His vanity still held the whip hand over common sense. The chicks have given me a great press to the mother hens, he thought. Now they'll all want servicing, too. Beechwood Estate was getting a bit too much. Especially Ferndale bloody Close. Look at the thighs on that one. Built like a Buick. And the grey-eyed blonde – ruddy chassis on her like a Volvo saloon. He swallowed as the ripe buttocks to his left joggled.

'Mothers-in-law. Mothers of the husbands,' his tormentress continued fingering his cheek with her rubbered finger, her words breaking into his whirling thoughts.

Husbands. His heart skipped a beat. Were there a couple of them waiting with baseball bats next door? Between clenched buttocks, he felt his anus shrivel and tighten.

'Mothers of the wronged husbands—'

'But—'

'Silence,' she snapped, stuffing three rubbered fingers in his mouth. 'In fact,' the dominant nude continued in a casual aside, 'you'd better gag and bind him. He'll probably squeal under the whip.'

The whip. He struggled up to his feet, swayed and was forced down by firm hands, one taloning set of long fingers cradling and squeezing his balls. They propelled him belly-down across a leather-topped stool, gagging his mouth and binding his wrists tightly together behind him. Heavy buttocks – the grey-eyed blonde – pinned him down as she straddled him. He shuddered, delighting in and yet dreading their soft warmth on his back.

'Warm him up,' the ringleader barked harshly.

The onlookers stepped back to observe his chastisement as the grey-eyed blonde, sliding her bottom towards his neck, lowered her breasts into him as she sank her face down to inspect his buttocks. He writhed as he felt her hands cup and spread his cheeks apart, felt her supple thumbs prising his cleft painfully wide. Despite his fear, his thick shaft dug into the leather stool. twitching and pulsing as her fingernails scraped his anal whorl. She sat upright – he felt the swell of her perched buttocks ripple – to accept a short leather belt from the brunette. He clenched his cheeks in a spasm of anguish as she dangled the tip of the belt across his rounded buttocks, dipping it into his cleft.

Crack, crack, crack. His upturned cheeks jerked in response to the withering lash. Crack, crack, crack. The grey-eyed blonde bounced as she delivered each stroke, her damp slit saluting him with a Judas kiss each time she plied the leather. Seven more times, in furious, merciless succession, the cruel length of hide cracked down, snapping onto his rump and blistering his cheeks. She drew the belt up to her lips to kiss and tongue it feverishly, then tossed it aside, returning her cruel hands to ravish his crimsoned flesh. He came, grunting thickly, as her nails raked the crown of each punished cheek.

'Watch him,' barked the dominant brunette, hauling the blonde away. 'Look.'

9

Sliding down from the stool, his belly smeared with his own sticky warmth, the milkman groaned softly as he saw the four faces peering down at the tell-tale sheen on the wet leather.

'I'm not going to get my full pint at this rate. Take his gag off and make him lick it up.'

A hand reached down, grabbed his hair, dragging his face into the warm silvery puddle. His gag was whipped away. He refused to lick.

'Use the belt.'

Whimpering slightly as another hand snatched up the belt and plied it across his defenceless buttocks four times, he lapped up his own warm mess.

'Now get me a bottle,' the brunette barked, flexing her yellow gloves impatiently, 'and put that gag back on.'

A willing pair of hands sprang to obey both commands. As the gag was roughly applied, he glimpsed the yellow rubber-sheathed fingers of the brunette's right hand closing around the empty milk bottle.

'Up,' she ordered.

He knelt up and shuffled back from the stool. She strode forward and sat upon it, her heavy bottom dimpling the shining leather. She nodded, parting her thighs. Two pairs of hands assisted him to his feet, pushed him towards her and guided him across her knees. He shuddered as the wet knout of his throbbing shaft grazed her inner thigh.

'Hold him down while I position the bottle.'

Pinned down, from his inverted viewpoint he saw her yellow-gloved hand guiding the empty milk bottle down the tip of his extended shaft. He grunted as she tried to sleeve him with the cold glass, writhing as she gave the bottle a deft twist.

'It's no good. He's too thick for a bottle. Pass me that jug,' the brunette instructed, retrieving the bottle.

A plastic jug from the food mixer was positioned on the cork tiles beneath her parted thighs. She scooped it up and placed it at his throbbing length, instructing a naked accomplice to kneel and hold it.

'And now we milk the milkman,' she laughed softly, taking

10

him firmly in her rubber-gloved hand. 'We shall get our pint.'

He closed his eyes and shuddered.

'Commence,' came the crisp command.

Opening his eyes in a reflex of alarm, he found himself staring directly into the bobbing breasts of a bending nude. The breasts were slightly pear-shaped, the flesh smooth and silky. The strip of neon up above illuminated the swollen outer curves deliciously and gave the deep cleavage an inviting shadow. Despite his fear, his erection twitched. The yellow rubber-sheathed fingers grasping it tightened their dominant grip.

'I am going to spank you,' the bending nude whispered, cupping and bunching her heavy bosom so that her peaked nipples brushed his perspiring face. 'I am going to spank your bare bottom very hard, you wicked young man. My daughter-in-law has confessed everything to me. And she too has been punished, although I intend to keep a very strict eye on her from now on. But this morning, it is time for you to suffer.'

His eyes flickered up, finding no mercy in her stern gaze. Rising, she briefly crushed her stubby nipples into his eyes. Seconds later, she was bending down over his upturned buttocks, her left hand pinning his neck firmly, her right hand palming his cheeks in preparation for the rain of pain to come. He tensed, squeezing his cheeks together tightly. The gloved fingers around his shaft responded painfully.

'Relax your buttocks, milkman,' the brunette controlling him across her lap instructed. 'My friend prefers to spank a soft bottom.'

He refused, keeping his cleft a tightened flesh-crease. The yellow glove released his shaft and, as it cupped his balls, slowly became a fist. He yelped and instantly surrendered his bottom up to its doom.

The flurry of harsh spanks rang out loudly against the shining tiled walls of the kitchen. The firm, flattened palm of the punishing hand swept down harder after the ninth searing swipe, and faster after the thirteenth. Grunting and cursing into his restricting gag – but rendered immobile by the rubber glove at his balls – the bare-buttocked milkman suffered severely as his reddening cheeks seethed.

11

'I'm milking him now,' his tormentress announced, her tone primly clinical.

He felt the rubber-gloved fingers encircling, then gripping, his massive length. The harsh staccato of the spanking hand continued to bark aloud across his crimson buttocks, and the gloved hand milked him rhythmically. Burning and squirming in his shame and pain, the milkman tensed and jerked his bottom up, as if desirous of harsher discipline. His neck strained against the hand that pinned it down and he squeezed his thighs together, screamed a smothered cry of anguished delight and came, squirting his liquid release noisily into the plastic jug.

Eager faces, their wide eyes sparkling with shocked delight, peered under his belly at his pulsing, glistening glans as five more savage spanks cracked down across his cheeks. His orgasm spasmed and ceased, though the edge of the plastic jug scraping across him to catch the last sticky pearl caused him to hammer his hips in helpless abandon.

'Not much from that one,' the grey-eyed blonde opined doubtfully, holding the jug aloft in triumph and squinting into it. 'I make it 8cc. It's going to be a long job getting the full pint.'

'We have all the time we need,' the cruel brunette whispered, absently plucking out a wiry black hair from his pink anus.

'No, please, I'm sorry. I'll do anything, anything—' His words, his pleas for pity were genuine. But they went unheard, being merely another muffled moan to the ears of his implacable punishers.

'Next,' the brunette commanded.

A faint trace of Orange Water announced his second punisher. It was the blonde, the grey-eyed blonde who had measured his first contribution to the plastic jug.

'I want him kneeling on the floor,' she announced.

Her victim was positioned, thighs slightly apart, to her satisfaction.

'Give him the jug. He can hold it himself, this time.'

The milkman, his hands released from their bondage, clasped the jug reluctantly at first, but an imperious tap from a warning fingertip had him angling it correctly so that it received his flaccid member.

Standing directly behind her kneeling victim, the blonde guided her left foot between his parted thighs and tapped his balls with her pink-varnished toenails. He clamped his thighs together, trapping her foot. She steadied herself; her left arm stretched out to grip his shoulder.

'Open up,' she snarled softly.

The jug trembled as he obeyed – and trembled again as she continued to toe his sac in slow, sweeping circles with her upraised foot. Peering briefly over his shoulder, she glimpsed his manhood thickening and arrowing into the waiting jug.

The other nudes watched, their eyes vicious slits of eager expectation. 'Keep going,' the brunette whispered, flexing her gloved fingers slowly. 'Almost there.'

The grey-eyed blonde suddenly withdrew her foot, knelt down behind her victim and called aloud for a wooden spoon.

'Butter the handle,' she instructed.

The pale pearwood spoon, its thick shaft glistening with a daub or butter, was supplied. The blonde brushed the concave bowl of the spoon against her slit, then returned the pale pearwood to her wet heat to bruise it deliberately, causing her to snarl in pleasurable pain.

'Don't spill a single drop, milkman,' her voice curdled. After a brief silence, the wooden spoon spoke, harshly swiping his right buttock. With her left hand still gripping his shoulder, she sensed his body tense, sensed his gathering climax and the approaching ejaculation.

Both in response to the swiping spoon across his rump – and the cool touch of dominance at his shoulder – his naked body spasmed in her absolute thrall. Judging him to be only seconds away from release, the blonde twirled the spoon deftly in her hand as she sank to her knees and rammed the buttered shaft in between his cheeks. Probing the anus, she pumped him wickedly. With a loud groan into the choking gag, he slumped, emptying himself with a splatter into the plastic jug. As his seed spurted, the wooden shaft pumped rhythmically. His buttocks clenched to trap and

13

contain it – but her skill with the buttered wood was too much for him.

'That gives us 17cc so far,' the brunette chuckled, holding up the jug and examining the clouded fluid. 'Give him a quick shower, some slow humiliation and half an hour's rest.'

They had been tenderly brutal with him in the shower. Bound at the wrists once more, he had been propelled by three of his four naked captors under a freezing sluice. The fourth, the grey-eyed blonde who had used the spoon so cunningly, knelt down by the bathtub, knees splayed, playing with herself until she had squealed her own climax loud and long.

Fingering the shower gel into his most secret places, they deliberately nannied him into utter humiliation – a humiliation completed when the yellow rubber gloves visited his foreskin with a fastidious sponge, and in between his cheeks with a cruel nailbrush at his cleft. Cursing into his tight gag as he twisted and writhed to avoid the nailbrush, he was forced to submit to their total domination. Roughly towelled and then intimately talcumed – the grey-eyed blonde splashing a cupped handful of stinging Orange Water into his sensitive cleft for good measure – he was tossed down onto a bed and allowed to drift off into a dream-crazed sleep.

They woke him with black coffee laced with brandy. His mouth was sore after the gag, and he had to work his lips for several moments before gulping down the welcome drink. Over the rim of the white mug, his eyes rose up sorrowfully to meet the brunette's stern gaze.

She launched into a harsh rebuke, pouring scorn on his assumed potency and mocking his reputed prowess, stinging him with her cruel taunts as sharply as the leather belt. Satisfied that she had made her point adequately – the giggled laughter of the others confirmed this – she warned him firmly off the young housewives and then produced the plastic jug with an ominous flourish. 'Still a long way to go,' she continued, adding, 'but we have the rest of the day. I'm sure they won't be missing you at the betting office.'

He looked up, frowning.

'Oh, we have been watching you very closely, milkman. We know every little thing you do.'

He lowered his head.

'Take today, for example. By now you would have parked the milk float behind that pub in Cross Street. After an hour or two in there, you would stagger over to the bookies. Nobody will miss you, milkman, and that makes you completely ours.'

They ordered him to kneel against the side of the bed. The grey-eyed blonde took control of the plastic jug and held it carefully between her thighs as she knelt upon the bed. Guiding his shaft into the jug, she buried his ungagged face into her soft bosom. 'Begin,' she murmured.

They caned him, the other three nudes stepping up in turn to swish-slice his bare bottom with whippy little garden canes.

'Suck,' she commanded, adding a stern caution not to bite.

Flinching under the welter of searing cane strokes as the supple bamboo lashed his cheeks, he obeyed her instruction, guzzling at the pebble-hard nipples and sucking upon them frenziedly. Transfixed in his pleasure-pain, the milkman's shaft became engorged: so stiff did the urgent spear grow that it raked up and threatened to dislodge the plastic jug. The grey-eyed blonde adjusted her posture and realigned the jug, smothering his face as she did so with her suffocating pillows of swollen satin flesh.

Swish, swipe. Swish, swipe. Relentlessly, though not with maximum savagery, the canes strokes impelled him towards the trembling brink of explosive release. Nuzzling the firm ripeness of the blonde's heavy breasts, he pumped his hips and cried out aloud as a vicious stroke lashed him instantly into a searing ecstasy. The squirt and sporadic splatter of his ejaculation was audible, despite his soft screams of delicious agony.

'26cc now,' he heard a distant voice say. 'Coming along nicely.'

He heard other vixen voices laughing. He opened his sweat-scalded eyes to see the plastic jug being passed around and held up for close scrutiny. It came to rest before the cool appraisal of the rubber-gloved brunette.

'Coming along,' she echoed, chuckling darkly.

15

Spreadeagled, his wrists and ankles were bound to the bedposts with nylon stockings. As he squirmed, the impromptu but effective bondage burnt. They mounted him, one at a time, kneeling down over – then onto – his helpless, upturned face. He spluttered and gasped as the first heavy bottom smothered him, subsiding into muted moaning as the hot, feral flesh above was expertly rasped across his mouth. His erection rose sluggishly in response to the first vigorous queening; straightened potently as the second wet slit and hot cleft raked his mouth; engorged painfully as the third nude rode him ruthlessly – squeezing her heavy buttocks into him punishingly – and exploded in a shimmering jet that rattled against the strategically positioned jug as the fourth Valkyrie straddled her helpless mount, demanding that he tongue her bittersweet sphincter.

'31cc and rising,' was the verdict from the brunette, who was carefully calibrating the contents of the plastic jug.

To his surprise, they did not loosen his bonds – nor did they produce a whip, crop or paddle. His bare buttocks, reddened and painfully scored with earlier punishments, escaped chastisement for the next ninety minutes. It was an hour and a half he would remember for the rest of his life.

They used little balls of cotton wool and feathersoft brushes. They used foundation cream, blusher, face-powder, eye-liner, lipstick, lip-gloss and an eyebrow pencil – giggling as they squashed nakedly around his prostrate body.

He resisted more vehemently than in his earlier attempts to escape the lash and the cane, twisting his face from side to side: but the cruel rubber glove at his balls quelled his frantic protests, forcing him to submit and surrender as they feminised him totally.

Burning with deep shame at the bizarre face staring back at him from the hand-held mirror, he felt tears trickling down to furrow the alien make-up. The sweetness of the lipstick on his mouth failed to mask the sour taste of haunting humiliation. Without using a single instrument of discipline or correction – or spilling a single drop of his semen – they broke the milkman as easily as he would smash a bottle on a concrete path.

'One last donation to the milk fund,' the brunette purred, untying his ankles as the others tackled the nylon stockings at his aching wrists.

Handing him two nylons as he sat on the edge of the bed, rubbing his freed wrists, the brunette ordered him to don them. He obeyed, palming them up his sinewy calves and fingering the darker bands stretching around his thighs.

'Turn over, face down,' the brunette continued, tapping the bed dominantly with a rubber-sheathed finger: though in a soothing, seductive voice.

Meekly, he obeyed, drawing his stockinged legs together. A dildo, wickedly curved at the glinting knout, was produced and lubricated with face-cream. The yellow-gloved hand teased his sphincter with it for several minutes before slipping it in between his parted cheeks. He sobbed softly as the supple wrist of the brunette pumped. Stiffening and arching his back seven minutes later, his shaft speared the duvet.

'Catch it,' the brunette cried, jabbing at the plastic jug.

The grey-eyed blonde giggled. 'Just in time.'

'That makes nearly half a pint,' the brunette whispered. 'You may go now, milkman, but we expect to see you here next week -' she tapped the jug '- for the rest of your delivery.'

The cock of the walk, now a capon, grunted softly and nodded.

The brunette tapped his nose with the sticky tip of the dildo. 'We thought you would,' she smirked.

Servile Maid

Tuppence opened her eyes – and smiled as she suddenly remembered. The shrill whistle that had just woken her must be the early morning market train bound for Much Wenlock. It was Lammas Eve. Every chocolate-coloured third-class carriage would be full of fat farmers and their fatter wives struggling with dressed poultry, eggs, rounds of dark yellow cheese and baskets of flowers.

Lammas Eve. Tomorrow, all the surrounding Shropshire countryside would be bringing in the harvest. Tomorrow night, lusty farm lads would chase wanton girls around – and then into – the haystacks. Tuppence smiled sleepily, her fingertips dabbling at her nipples lazily, as she imagined bare-breasted girls plucking straw out of their tousled hair beneath the big harvest moon. Bare-breasted girls wiping their wet bellies and thighs dry with the sleeves of their ripped gowns, drying the sticky seed sown by the lusty harvesters.

Up in her attic bedroom, with no warmth other than a single blanket, it was chilly. Tuppence wriggled and snuggled down into her narrow bed. Soon it would be time to rise, light the candle and don her maid's uniform. The four sisters who resided at The Birches insisted that their maid was neat and trim at all times – punishing Tuppence promptly for a wrinkled black stocking, stained apron or crooked lace cap.

A second train – an express – thundered by in the distance beyond Spinsters' Spinney. Tuppence knew that it would be a troop train, carrying the finest of the Shropshire Rifles away to fight the Boers. There would be sturdy young men in khaki and gallant officers in scarlet, black and gold. Tuppence eased her thighs apart and fingered her hot slit. Gallant officers, she murmured dreamily, with waxed moustaches and sinewy thighs sheathed in black breeches. Surrendering to her waking dream, she thumbed the outer lips apart and fingertip-teased the inner fleshfolds, deliberately strumming their wet warmth.

Still tipsy from the mug of stolen sherry last night, Tuppence ignored the small voice in her head urging her to rise, dress and go down to the kitchen to stoke the fires and boil the kettle for early morning tea. Silencing the voice of conscience and stern duty, she ground her buttocks into her bed and surrendered her nakedness up into the fierce embrace of a brown-eyed officer, imagining his hard mouth upon her parted lips and that the hands cupping and squeezing her breasts were not hers but his. Her nipples thickened within her slit-wet fingers. The feral tang of her own arousal perfumed her nostrils, maddening and exciting her.

As her fluttering belly tightened, she drew her knees up to her breasts and scrabbled for a thin crease of her blanket. Knuckling the fold into her cleft, she rasped the prickling fabric against the sensitive ribbon of velvety flesh between her cheeks, grunting softly as her inner thighs grew shiny with the scald of her excitement. Inching the blanket fold a fraction forward, Tuppence closed her eyes and punished herself with her knuckles, kneading the fabric into her hot hole. Bright lights flashed behind her eyes, the scarlet and gold more brilliant than that of the imagined officer's crisp uniform.

The door to her attic bedroom opened abruptly and a tall, stern-faced young lady – no more than five years older than Tuppence's twenty – strode across to the foot of the young maid's bed.

'Get up at once, you lazy girl. It's gone cock crow.'

Tuppence opened her eyes in alarm and shrank down behind her blanket, blushing deeply with shame. The muscles deep inside her were loosening and just about to melt, the rapidly spreading ripples of joy signalling her climax.

'Did you not hear me, girl? Up, this instant.'

'Sorry, Miss Emily,' Tuppence mumbled. 'I was asleep.' Tuppence clamped her cheeks and thighs together tightly to contain her urgent delight.

'Asleep? Nonsense, girl. And I can smell sherry. I can distinctly smell sherry.' Miss Emily, her firm breasts bulging within her tightly bound silk kimono, snatched up a white mug from a small bedside cabinet. Sniffing it suspiciously, she gasped in outrage. 'I thought so. Stealing sherry again. Up. Out of that bed,' she commanded, unfastening her kimono and rolling up her right sleeve. 'I'm going to punish you.'

Tuppence clutched the blanket with both hands and drew it up to her chin. Miss Emily's eyes narrowed. Like a heron spearing a trout, her fist flashed down and taloned Tuppence by the wrist. Inclining her head so that her golden curls tumbled freely, Miss Emily sniffed the maid's wet knuckles.

'So,' she whispered, 'not only do I smell sherry, I smell the taint of wickedness, the very perfume of sin.'

'No, Miss, please, Miss—'

'Idle hands tempt the devil, Tuppence. Did you not learn that lesson at Sunday school? Idle hands must be punished. Hold them up.'

'But Miss—'

'At once, girl. No, stay as you are,' Miss Emily ordered, briskly dragging the blanket down to the shivering maid's belly. 'Hold your hands out, palms up, for the strap.'

The strap, sixteen inches of supple hide from the local tannery, was affixed to a nail on the back of the bedroom door – just like the strap hanging from every maid's attic bedroom door throughout the land. Miss Emily snatched it down, snapped it twice savagely and returned to the cowering maid's bedside.

'Idle hands tempt the devil, girl,' Miss Emily hissed, whipping the strap down across the upturned palms.

Tuppence squealed, but was too terrified to flinch or withdraw her hands from the fierce lash: to do so would have exposed her quivering breasts to the harsh kiss of the hide. Miss Emily administered four blistering strokes to each pink palm, then snatched up the blanket and tossed it aside. Tuppence attempted to cover her nakedness with her throbbing hands.

'Hands away, girl,' Miss Emily barked. 'I am now going to punish the devil.'

Tuppence whimpered as she struggled to obey Miss Emily's

21

instruction to ease herself up from the mattress. With her thighs parted, Tuppence offered herself up for the leather. Both mistress and maid gazed down at the dark snatch of wet pubic curls. The devil.

'Open your legs wider, you little whore.'

Timorously, and burning with shame, Tuppence thrust her hips and thighs up and forced them wider apart: not for pleasure, this time, but for pain. The strap cracked down six times in rapid succession. Twice against the soft flesh of each inner thigh and then twice – searingly – across her pubic mound.

'Stop snivelling, girl. Get washed, dressed and downstairs,' Miss Emily ordered, fingering the wet tip of the strap where it had kissed the maid's splayed labia. 'My sisters and I await our early morning tea.'

'Another financial scandal in the City,' Miss Edwina remarked, rustling her copy of *The Times*. 'Thank goodness we put our capital into Treasury Bonds.'

Tuppence served the austere spinster with kippers and retreated to the sideboard, where jars of quince and Seville marmalade required her attention.

'News from Paris,' Miss Edwina continued after a forkful of buttered kipper. 'Oscar Wilde arrived on the boat train the day before yesterday, after being released from Reading gaol.'

Miss Edwina, the oldest of the four spinster sisters residing at The Birches, made it her custom to inform and educate the breakfast table every morning with snippets from *The Times*. Her sisters sat in silence, taking in the random paragraphs with their cold ham, poached eggs and thinly sliced bread and butter.

'The Boers are in disarray,' the oldest sister announced with every evidence of relish – then launched into a colourful account of a young chap called Churchill who had covered himself with glory.

Heads bowed, Miss Edwina's three sisters busied themselves with their breakfasts. Tuppence, still sore from the strap, squeezed the cold flannel between her thighs and sighed softly. Bringing a second silver teapot to the table, she wondered what Miss Emily had thought as she had plied the strap earlier that morning. The cruel leather had licked the maid's pubis harshly, unleashing Tuppence's pent-up orgasm almost immediately. What the naughty maid's nimble fingers had begun beneath the blanket the strap's lash had brought to fruition. Tuppence had moaned and climaxed openly as the leather burned her thighs: jerking her hips and slamming her buttocks into the mattress shamelessly. Tuppence could not quite remember, but she could have sworn that she had seen her stern mistress kiss, then surreptitiously lick, the leather.

'More milk, I think,' Miss Victoria commanded.

'One moment, my dear,' Miss Edwina intervened, holding her hand up imperiously. Without turning to address Tuppence directly, she continued in a solemn tone. 'I am informed that fortified spirits were purloined from the pantry, last night. Sherry, no less.'

The matter was discussed briefly and it was the opinion of the breakfast table that such an outrage merited punishment. Tuppence fiddled with the hem of her white apron nervously. She had hoped that Miss Emily would have forgotten her other misdemeanours, but the younger sister had not overlooked the matter of the stolen sherry – and had placed the matter into her sister's capable hands.

'Across my knee, Tuppence,' Miss Edwina ordered, letting *The Times* slither down to the carpet as she spread her thighs apart to receive the bending maid.

The three other sisters wiped their lips delicately with white napkins and craned across the table to witness the baring of the maid's delightfully pert bottom. Tuppence's soft cheeks wobbled deliciously as Miss Edwina caressed them firmly with her flattened palm. Shrinking from the dominant touch of the spanking hand at her peaches, Tuppence clenched her buttocks tightly in fearful expectation.

The spanking was brisk but blistering. Sixteen harsh cracks of a very firm palm rang out, sweeping down mercilessly across the softness of the maid's perfectly poised cheeks. The punished buttocks blushed instantly, the deep pink quickly turning to an angrier shade of crimson.

Tuppence wriggled and squealed, then squirmed and sobbed,

but Miss Edwina was an accomplished chastiser and administered the discipline with consummate skill. Pinning Tuppence firmly at the neck, she spanked the bare-bottomed maid until every inch of the rounded cheeks burned bright with the scarlet of pain. After the last of the searing blows had echoed around the silent breakfast table, the three watching sisters rose up and gathered around to inspect the punished bottom, Miss Emily dimpling both reddened crowns of Tuppence's hot bottom with her straightened forefinger as she prodded the ravished rump.

A little later, Tuppence took the small pan and bristle brush to the white lawn tablecloth to sweep away the breakfast crumbs. Stooping to retrieve the napkins for the laundry, she noticed that one of them was quite damp. Raising it up to her nose, she sniffed the starched linen inquisitively. It had been used against wet lips – not to wipe away marmalade, Tuppence flushed as she realised her discovery, but to wipe away the excitement oozing from lips lower down, an excitement caused by witnessing the bare-bottomed spanking of the naughty maid. Tuppence grinned. It would be Miss Elizabeth's napkin. Miss Elizabeth, who always seemed to get more pleasure in watching than actually dispensing strict discipline. Tuppence gathered up the napkin in her fist, shuddering as the wet patch kissed her palm.

Inching her naked thighs back over the edge of the cold porcelain, Tuppence guided her hot bottom below the brass tap at the scullery sink. Pawing blindly behind her, Tuppence's fingers found the tap and twisted. The icy sluice brought instant balm and soothing relief to her spanked and scalded cheeks. Towelling her cool buttocks dry, she pulled up her cami-knickers and adjusted her trim uniform, taking pains to retie her apron neatly.

Pausing to feast upon ripe greengages – plucked earlier from the hot house and destined as delicacies for the fierce sisters' dinner table – Tuppence relished the juices of the fleshy fruit running down over her chin.

Still burning with shame after her bare-bottomed spanking, she tiptoed down the stone steps into the dark cellar and selected a pint bottle of champagne. Back up in the scullery, she paused, straining to hear the sound of an approaching predatory sister. All was quiet. Tuppence uncorked the champagne, using a tea towel to muffle the 'pop', then quaffed the stolen pleasure quickly. Dizzy and slightly astounded at her own audacity – the discovery of her crime would surely mean nothing less than a strict, slow caning – Tuppence hid the empty champagne bottle and collected a zinc bucket and scrubbing brush.

'I trust you have been diligent in your duties, Tuppence. Have you done the passage thoroughly, girl?' Miss Victoria demanded, standing in the open doorway, her hands on her hips, her elbows angled.

Tuppence, kneeling on the flagstone floor, looked up anxiously.

'I dread the possibility of mice,' Miss Victoria observed. 'Mice will only flourish where there is dirt. Dirt will only flourish where there is a lazy maid.'

Easing back so that her buttocks sank down onto her heels, Tuppence surveyed the stone floor of the narrow passage she had just scrubbed.

'Well, girl? Have you been thorough?'

'Oh, yes, Miss Victoria,' Tuppence murmured, rising up from the floor and picking up her bucket and scrubbing brush.

'We shall see,' the severely cropped ash-blonde replied doubtfully, and managing to weave a thread of menace into her tone.

Tuppence shivered. Miss Victoria was always hounding her in her daily chores, and punishing her ruthlessly when all was not strictly as it should be. Tuppence watched, her heart thumping rapidly, as Miss Victoria strode down along the passage towards the pantry, her tightly laced brogues echoing on the hard stone floor. Pausing at a basket brimming with apples, the narrow-waisted young woman bent and lifted the wicker basket up by the handles. A large Sweet Susan – a local variety of Shropshire pippin – spilt out from the basket and rolled along the floor. It came to rest at the maid's feet, presenting Tuppence with its ripe redness – just as she had presented her spanked bottom for inspection at the breakfast table that morning.

'Just as I suspected,' Miss Victoria snarled. 'Come here, you wretched girl.'

Tuppence approached, her throat tightening with apprehension.

'See?' the angry woman hissed triumphantly. 'I sprinkled borax under the apple basket. A diligent maid would have lifted the basket and scrubbed. Only a lazy maid would fail to do this. You are a lazy maid, Tuppence. And what happens to lazy maids?'

Tuppence remained silent and gazed down at the floor.

'Well, girl? Speak up?'

'Lazy maids are punished, Miss Victoria.'

'Precisely, Tuppence. They are punished. Lift up your dress.'

Tuppence obeyed, dreading the impending pain that would soon be visiting her bared bottom. Miss Victoria, she knew, had a partiality for whippy bamboo.

'No: bare-bottomed, girl. I want you bare-bottomed for the wood.'

The wood. Tuppence imagined the thin yellow cane and shivered.

'Hurry up,' Miss Victoria snapped waspishly.

Tuppence stepped out of her cami-knickers and shivered again.

'Bend over.'

As the maid obeyed the command of her mistress, the carriage clock in the hall struck ten. The tinkling Cambridge chimes filled the air with a pleasing music. Behind tightly closed eyes, Tuppence knew that the song of the swishing bamboo would fill the air with notes of suffering.

'This apple is bruised,' Miss Victoria announced, scrutinising the Sweet Susan that she had retrieved from the stone floor. 'It is no longer fit for the table but I shall find a good use for it. Waste not, want not,' she added, piously observing the virtue of thrift. 'Part your legs for me, girl. No, a little wider, if you please.'

The maid's trembling thighs parted, allowing Miss Victoria a glimpse of the pubic bush and labia as the stern spinster gazed down at the upturned buttocks she proposed to beat.

Tuppence gasped aloud and struggled to steady herself as she felt the firm apple being thrust up between her thighs – and grunted as she felt the polished skin of the Sweet Susan pressed against her own secret flesh.

'Kneel,' Miss Victoria instructed, slapping Tuppence's left buttock sharply.

Tuppence sank down, wincing as her knees kissed the stone floor in submissive obedience.

'Be careful to hold that apple in place as you scrub the entire passage floor once again, girl. Should it fall from where I have lodged it, you will feel the sharpness of my cane.'

Clamping her thighs tightly, Tuppence shuffled backwards to her bucket and scrubbing brush. Reaching out behind her, she grasped the square of soft hessian sacking and dragged it to her knees.

'No, girl,' Miss Victoria barked, returning down the passage with a length of yellow bamboo gripped in her right hand. 'No pad for your knees. You will scrub without the sacking. Penitence is not meant to be comfortable,' she whispered, tracing the swollen curve of the maid's left buttock. 'Now scrub.'

Tuppence bowed down to her work, painfully hampered by the Sweet Susan held between her upper thighs. She scrubbed furiously, eager to win the cruel spinster's clemency. As her bare bottom swayed with the scrubbing, the cane flickered and rose up, erect and alert in the tightened grip of her punisher.

The zinc bucket scraped noisily on the flagstones as Tuppence reached out to drag it towards her. As she dipped her brush into the water, the bucket tilted. Tuppence strained to catch and steady it, and the apple fell from her warmth down onto the wet stone floor. Miss Victoria trapped the rolling Sweet Susan with the tip of her cane, then lashed the upturned buttocks of the kneeling maid. Tuppence squealed aloud as the thin cane kissed her defenceless cheeks, bequeathing a scarlet stripe across their soft, rounded globes.

'Silence when being whipped,' the spinster snarled, dominating the bare bottom she had just caned with the tip of the cruel bamboo. The satin flesh of the left cheek dimpled beneath the imperious wood. Tuppence sank her head down. Her hair tumbled, fringing her tearful eyes. She whimpered softly as she felt the apple being

27

returned to the warmth between her thighs.

'Continue with your task, girl,' Miss Victoria commanded, taking up a stance directly behind the kneeling maid and playing the supple bamboo in between Tuppence's slightly parted cheeks so that the cane rasped at her yawning cleft.

Driven by a sense of delicious dread as the cane-tip worried her wet sphincter, Tuppence scrubbed frantically. Miss Victoria probed the rosebud of the anal whorl. The apple dropped to the floor as the bare-bottomed maid spasmed and shuddered. Miss Victoria lashed the proffered cheeks instantly. For Tuppence, the passage seemed to stretch out into a painful eternity.

The cruel young spinster had to replace the apple – and reward the naked cheeks with a punishing stroke – five times before the flagstone floor was scrubbed to her satisfaction.

'Give he the brush,' she instructed.

Tuppence surrendered the thickly bristled brush.

'In future, girl,' the tormentress whispered, dragging the narrow tip of the scrubbing brush down along the tormented maid's dark cleft, 'I trust you will be diligent in all your duties.'

Tuppence dipped her tummy and jerked her head back in a reflex of exquisite anguish as the bristles raked her sensitive flesh.

'Get up and get dressed, and let that be a lesson you never forget,' Miss Victoria hissed, tossing the brush into the bucket.

Tuppence staggered up from the floor. Shouldering her cane, the spinster bent down and plucked the apple from the maid's thighs. Tuppence blushed deeply – the Sweet Susan was quite wet and shiny with her sticky juices.

Miss Victoria turned and strode down the freshly scrubbed passage. Stooping to pull up her cami-knickers, Tuppence shuddered as she heard the firm mouth of her cruel mistress bite into the apple with a succulent crunch.

Despite their comfortable income, the four young spinsters at The Birches did not observe the prevailing conventions, eschewing the customary trappings of wealth by employing only one maid. Tuppence undertook all the daily tasks – and was frequently pressed into the service of attending their toilette.

28

Tuppence tapped politely upon Miss Elizabeth's boudoir door. The tallest of the four sisters, Miss Elizabeth had a graceful, slender figure and delightfully delicate hands. She seldom had occasion to chastise Tuppence, and the pert maid always enjoyed the intimate duties of dressing this gentle, almost submissive, mistress.

Miss Elizabeth sat naked at her dressing table, her auburn tresses spilling down over her white shoulders in customary disarray.

Tuppence picked up the solid silver hairbrush and started to carefully disentangle the rebellious locks, administering a succession of firm strokes to the tresses. In the looking glass, Tuppence caught a glimpse of her seated mistress. Eyes closed, lips slightly parted, her face tilted upwards, Miss Elizabeth was relishing the sweeping strokes of the hairbrush. Reflected in the glass, the bare bosom rose and fell voluptuously. Tightening her grip, Tuppence dragged the brush down hard. In the glass, the swell of the heaving bosom quickened. As the mistress grew more submissive, the maid grew bolder.

Watching the dark nipples thicken and noting how they grew erect as she plied the hair brush more dominantly, Tuppence placed her left hand down upon Miss Elizabeth's naked shoulder. The seated nude shuddered. Tuppence accidentally allowed the stiffly bristled brush down the nude's spine. It was a calculated and deliberate mistake. Tuppence watched as, in the glass, the face of her mistress gasped with delight – and gasped again as her naked body buckled beneath the cruel brush against her flesh.

'Sorry,' Tuppence whispered.

'No matter, child. No matter,' Miss Elizabeth's lips murmured as they parted wider in ecstasy. 'Accidents will happen.'

Emboldened, Tuppence stood alongside her seated mistress and brushed the tresses fiercely so that they fell down over the white shoulder to fringe the swell of Miss Elizabeth's right breast. Following the auburn cascade dutifully, the bristles began to dimple the upper slope of the naked breast. The fifth firm stroke dragged the brush down over the peaked nipple. The nude grunted thickly and clutched the edge of her chair. Tuppence noted the whitening knuckles. The bristles kissed the tormented nipple once more. Fiercely. Miss Elizabeth squirmed, grinding her heavy buttocks

29

into the satin cushion seat of her chair. Her hands flew up and fluttered helplessly in the air.

Tuppence suppressed her naughty grin. She knew, with all the sly cunning of a wanton, that the nude at the dressing table wanted to – ached to – cup and crush her tormented breast.

'Minx,' Miss Elizabeth hissed. The tone attempted was asperity, but being thickened with lust proved unconvincingly severe. 'Be more careful with that brush, child.'

'Very well, Miss Elizabeth,' Tuppence lied.

After dressing and fixing the nude's glorious auburn hair, the maid prepared to dress the mistress. The elegant, passive young spinster selected a lace corset in cream silk and satin, fingering the deep cups meditatively before passing it to Tuppence. The maid, standing behind her naked mistress, drew the open corset in towards the nude and sheathed the breasts and belly in its cool embrace before bringing the two sides together along the line of Miss Elizabeth's dimpled spine.

'Tie me tightly, child. Be sure to tie me tightly.'

'Yes, miss,' Tuppence grinned, thrilling slightly to the urgent whisper.

'Tightly, mind.'

Tuppence raised her right knee up and positioned it between the bare buttocks to obtain a better purchase. Lodging her knee in the cleft, she shivered briefly as she felt the heat. Gripping the laces, and kneeing the soft cheeks deeply, she tugged. The spinster sighed deeply as her breasts bulged in their sudden and delicious bondage – and moaned softly at the knee pressed up into her splayed cheeks.

'Tighter,' she hissed. It was a soft command, a stern entreaty.

Tuppence obliged.

'Leave me, child. I will finish dressing alone,' Miss Elizabeth murmured, steadying herself against the bedpost. 'Open that drawer.' She pointed. 'No, the second one.'

Tuppence discovered a beautiful pair of ivory kid gloves.

'A little present for Lammas Eve, child. Let it be our secret, mind.'

Tuppence was suitably grateful. She was always polite and thankful when receiving little kindnesses from Miss Elizabeth. Last week it had been a box of chocolates. On Sunday, after assisting her mistress in the bath, it had been a pair of silk stockings. Miss Elizabeth was extremely appreciative and always rewarded her little minx.

'Run along, child.'

Yes, miss. Thank you, miss.' Tuppence withdrew from the boudoir. She closed the door gently behind her, instantly dropping down to her knees, her eye to the keyhole.

In the boudoir, hairbrush in her clenched fist, Miss Elizabeth was kneeling at her bedside – breasts buried in the silk eiderdown – and was rasping the bristles savagely up between her parted thighs against her pubic mound.

Tuppence would have to pluck the auburn coils from the hairbrush later, unobserved, when the boudoir was empty. She felt her nipples tighten and her slit prickle with arousal as she spied upon her mistress ravishing herself. Tuppence noted that the tightly laced corset caused the kneeling woman's bosom and bottom to wobble and bulge, and that the bite of the bristles at her wet heat caused Miss Elizabeth's hips to jerk vigorously, so lewdly – so unfittingly for a lady.

A soft cry filled the boudoir. Tuppence held her breath. Would her mistress bury her face down into the silk and muffle her delight as she came? Would she use the hairbrush as she had done last week – to spank her breasts as, down below, her taut buttocks loosened in orgasm?

Through the keyhole, Tuppence saw Miss Elizabeth buckling under her approaching climax. Sweeping the hairbrush down against her left buttock, reddening the creamy flesh instantly with crimson blotches, the mistress spanked herself eight times then quickly inserted the thick silver handle up between her thighs into her gaping wetness.

Pressed against the door, and breathing heavily, Tuppence felt her hot trickle of arousal bubble then burst against the tight stretch of her cami-knickers as, inside the boudoir, the kneeling spinster came with a soft scream.

31

Hurriedly donning the supple leather gloves, Tuppence dragged up her maid's uniform apron and black skirt, then impatiently peeled her cami-knickers down over her plump buttocks. Before the screams of her mistress had died away, the maid's fingertips were busy, the leather of the gloves already stained.

It was a hot afternoon. Tuppence trod the cinder path down through the neat beds of the kitchen garden. She paused by the rows of beans and read the faded white card. *Aquadulce Claudia*. The beans were all shrivelled now after the long summer, wilting as they clung to the line of thin bamboo canes. Tuppence hated the beans – a succulent white variety which the four spinsters enjoyed when served with a moist gammon – hated them because they needed the bamboo frame to climb. Tuppence shivered at the bamboo glinting in the sunlight – bamboo which was collected before the first autumn frost and stored in the scullery for use on her bare bottom throughout the winter months. Hurrying by quickly, Tuppence came to the pea patch and, stooping down with her large bowl cradled to her bosom, plucked the pods that would accompany the saddle of mutton and redcurrant jelly for dinner that evening.

Pausing in the heat of the sun to wipe her moist brow, Tuppence split a pod open with her thumbtip – just as expertly as she would split herself open under the blanket at night – and dribbled the line of peas into her open mouth. They were sweet but left her very thirsty.

Back in the cool of the kitchen, Tuppence poured herself a glass of iced lemonade then rinsed the empty glass – drained gratefully in one go – under the tap. The cold water splashed her wrists. Dare she? Should she? The maid was strictly forbidden to wash herself at the kitchen sink but, on such a hot day as this, Tuppence decided to take the risk. It would only take a minute or two to strip, splash herself with the refreshing cold water – towel her breasts and belly dry – and struggle back into her maid's uniform.

Almost naked, and just as she was stepping out of her black stockings, the little brass bell on the kitchen board rattled imperiously. It was a summons from the drawing room. They would be ringing for afternoon tea. Let them wait.

Bending, her breasts spilling loosely in their freedom, Tuppence turned on the tap and, capturing the icy stream in her cupped hands, splashed her face, neck and breasts repeatedly. The naked maid had to suppress her squeals of delight as the silver droplets sprinkled her bosom with sparkling diamonds of ice.

'Wretched girl,' the stern voice of Miss Emily rasped.

Tuppence scrabbled to turn off the tap and reached out for her towel.

'Did you not hear the bell? Lady Draco has been out riding on her new hunter and is desirous of tea. Do you hear me, girl?' Miss Emily chivvied feverishly, her snobbery battling with her temper. 'Lady Draco awaits her tea. And you will be whipped, wretch. Soundly whipped. Bathing in these quarters is forbidden to you, as well you know.'

Tuppence, whose groping hand had managed to secure a towel from the back of a kitchen chair, was hurriedly dabbing her breasts. Miss Emily's eyes narrowed hungrily as she saw the maid's soft bosoms bulge beneath the towelling.

'What's the delay?' Miss Victoria inquired anxiously, entering the kitchen in haste. 'Lady Draco—' The stern spinster, joining her sister in the quest for tea, paused. 'Tuppence,' she thundered. 'You wicked girl. How dare you bathe in the kitchen!'

'We will deal with her presently,' Miss Emily hissed. 'Get dressed and serve tea in the drawing room instantly. Every minute's delay will earn your bare bottom an extra stroke. Understand? '

The rich hunting voice of Lady Draco echoed along the passage. The two sisters paled.

'Any tea this afternoon, girls? Simply dying of thirst. Ah, here you all are,' she concluded, entering the kitchen. 'Thought I'd take pot luck below stairs. Don't mind roughing it, if it means I get a dish of tea. Hello. Who's the pretty filly, what?' Lady Draco purred, appreciating Tuppence's squirming nakedness.

Miss Victoria signalled frantically to her sister to escort Lady Draco back upstairs to the drawing room. 'A trivial domestic problem, Lady Draco. We will deal with it later.'

'Deal with her now, my dear girl,' the huntswoman thundered, refusing to be expelled from the kitchen. 'Only way to settle the damned servant problem. Punish 'em on the spot. Pretty little thing. Wouldn't mind chastisin' her myself. Run and get me my riding crop.'

Miss Emily, bewildered by the turn of events, looked blankly at their visitor.

'Tally ho, girl. Left me crop and gloves up in the hall. Fetch 'em, will you? Thank you kindly.'

'But Lady Draco,' Miss Victoria protested, her face pink with the social disgrace of entertaining the queen of the county set below stairs, 'I'm sure you would rather take tea in the—'

'Tea be blowed. Ah, thank you,' Lady Draco boomed, accepting her crop from Miss Emily. 'Now, get that minx across the kitchen table.' She flexed her crop, then thrummed it twice. It sang a cruel note in ode to the promise of pain. 'Come along, come along. Tails up.'

Tuppence, who had only managed to don her black stockings, was seized and held face-down across the large scrubbed table, the stern sisters cupping a breast fiercely and grasping a wrist apiece.

'A stinging six?' Lady Draco demanded rhetorically, easing off her black velvet riding jacket and unbuttoning the cuff at her right sleeve.

Slightly overwhelmed by events, the two sisters merely nodded in silent unison.

'Six it is, then,' the huntswoman grunted, swishing the crisp crop down across the maid's bare bottom.

Tuppence, writhing in the pinioning grip of the two spinsters, jerked as the crop cut across her proffered cheeks – and squealed aloud as the two sisters squeezed her breasts within their controlling grasp. The second and then the third searing slice of crop across naked rump followed quickly upon the first, scalding the maid's soft bottom with red weals of livid pain.

'Fetching little piece,' Lady Draco murmured softly, dropping down on one knee in a genuflection to de Sade to inspect the whipped cheeks.

34

Tuppence whimpered aloud as she felt the fingers that had gripped the leather-sheathed crop now splaying across the curve of her hot buttock, to talon and torment the flesh of the punished cheek. The maid wriggled and squirmed to escape the tormenting hand but the two sisters held her firmly in their dominant thrall. Tuppence slumped down submissively as Lady Draco's straightened forefinger slowly traced the three stinging stripes that the crop had blazed across her bare buttocks.

'Hold her down, my dears,' the punisher demanded, rising up and swishing the crop ominously. 'Three strokes received and three strokes to come.'

Tuppence squealed aloud as the whippy crop sliced down, planting the three Judas kisses in rapid succession.

'Excellent,' Miss Emily hissed. 'A capital whipping.' She furtively rubbed her pubis against the corner of the kitchen table, raking the lips of her wet plum down over the angle of wood.

Tuppence, stilled pinned down at the nape of her neck by the strong hands of Miss Victoria, froze as she sensed Lady Draco kneeling once more, and shuddered as she felt her chastiser's warm breath at her exposed slit.

'That's the only way to deal with the servant problem, my dears,' the huntswoman chuckled. 'Now, how about some tea, what? Thirsty work, punishment.'

'Seed cake?' Miss Victoria inquired politely, desperate in her attempt to re-establish a drawing-room decorum.

'Seed cake? That's for family solicitors and stable boys,' Lady Draco retorted dismissively, palming Tuppence's striped cheeks rhythmically with her broad palm.

'Perhaps a finger of ginger sponge,' Miss Emily grunted softly, recovering herself after coming against the table. 'It's deliciously moist.'

Lady Draco, sucking on the tip of the crop, chuckled and nodded her assent to the suggestion of ginger cake. 'I think I could be tempted by a moist finger.'

Tuppence clenched her thighs together tightly, retracting her sphincter so that it was a stubbornly closed rosebud. Lady Draco worried the anal whorl teasingly with her finger tip and chuckled softly.

Being Lammas Eve, Miss Edwina was in her study settling up the household accounts. In between sips of a warming amontillado, she scribbled in the totals beneath the spidery columns of figures. When summoned by the tinkling bell to do so, Tuppence entered the study and presented Miss Edwina with the kitchen books – one each for the cellar, the pantry and the dairy. Miss Edwina retained the books for the fishmonger and the butcher, doubting not the maid's honesty but more her ability to be the judge of a fresh salmon or a well-hung sirloin.

Tuppence stood in respectful silence as the mistress of The Birches balanced the books. At length, Miss Edwina handed them back to her maid.

'All is in order. And now,' she murmured, opening a desk drawer and extracting a thin ledger bound in green leather, 'one more book to balance.'

Tuppence winced. It was the punishment book, into which details of all the maid's misdemeanours were solemnly entered – together with the punishments such mischief had been deemed to merit. For Tuppence, this ritual was as shaming as a bare-bottomed spanking.

'Well, girl?' Miss Edwina demanded briskly, her pen poised expectantly.

Tuppence admitted to her sins – and the catalogue of painful retribution. 'I was abed, miss. Doing wicked things with my person. Miss Emily caught me—'

'And?'

'Ten strokes, miss. With the strap.'

'Ah, the devil to pay,' Miss Edwina chuckled, entering a neat record of the maid's offence and punishment into the ledger. 'And?'

'Then you spanked me, Miss Edwina.'

'So I did. For stealing sherry, was it not?'

'Yes, miss.'

The crime, and the penalty, were carefully recorded.

'And?'

'Miss Victoria punished me for not scrubbing the passage floor properly.

'Cane?'

'Yes, miss,' Tuppence whispered, adding softly, 'and an apple.'

'An apple?' The inked nib paused above the ledger. 'Pray explain yourself, girl.'

Blushing, Tuppence reluctantly stumbled through a confused account of how Miss Victoria had employed the Sweet Susan while caning the kneeling maid's bare buttocks.

'We may omit the apple and record it simply as a caning. How many strokes?'

Tuppence supplied the answer. It was entered into the punishment book.

'Such an eventful day, my girl. Surely that is all?'

Tuppence recounted her memorable encounter with Lady Draco. Miss Edwina noted it all down.

'Sign here, girl.'

Tuppence stepped up to the desk and picked up the pen. The pages of the punishment book were of a creamy ivory colour – not unlike the flesh of an unpunished young woman's bottom. The golden nib – a shade deeper than that of a whippy cane – left a thin line of red ink as Tuppence hurriedly scribbled her signature. Gazing down, she shivered at the sight of the thin red line of ink across the unblemished cream: it was just like gazing into the looking glass to glimpse her own striped cheeks after chastisement. Above her signature, the thin red lines left a record of the day's pain.

Miss Edwina blotted the page carefully and closed the book. 'Off with you to bed, girl. No, wait a moment.'

Tuppence paused, her hand upon the door handle.

'We received a note this evening from Draco Hall. Her ladyship has requested your presence there for the weekend. Be sure to take your best maid's uniform, Tuppence, and a decent pair of shoes.'

'Yes, Miss Edwina. Is there to be a Hunt Ball?' she asked

brightly, her head swimming with the prospect of music, dancing and stolen champagne.

'No, my girl. Her ladyship will, I believe, be quite alone during the weekend. She merely wishes to use you as her personal maid.'

Closing the study door behind her, Tuppence felt her heart hammering rapidly. The memory of Lady Draco's riding crop across her bare bottom burnt as hotly as her whipped cheeks had done during the chastisement across the kitchen table. The memory of Lady Draco's breath against her buttocks caused her to shiver.

Miss Edwina's words flooded back to haunt her. To use you as her personal maid. The words filled Tuppence with a delicious dread – just as Lady Draco's tongue would no doubt fill her wet heat before the weekend at Draco Hall was over.

Across the woods and fields, the distant church clock in Wenlock Parva struck nine. Tuppence was abed. She counted the nine chiming strokes as they broke the silence of the darkening summer night. An owl in nearby Spinsters' Spinney hooted softly. Farther afield, prowling the corn stubble for rabbits, a vixen barked. Fretting about her impending weekend at Draco Hall, Tuppence could not sleep. She struggled to sit up in her narrow bed, and realised that she was hungry.

Minutes later, the maid was tiptoeing out of the pantry, clutching a glass of milk and two ginger sponge fingers. As silent as her own shadow, she mounted the stairs, treading carefully to avoid the steps that creaked treacherously. Just as she reached the turn at the landing, the yellow light of a lamp shone from an opening door. Tuppence froze, her abrupt halt so violent it caused some of the milk in the glass she was clutching to spill and splash the bosom of her cotton shift. She rubbed the wet breast with her wrist, thickening and peaking the nipple.

In the gloom of the landing, she peered to discern which of the stern sisters approached behind the glare of the lamp. If it was Miss Edwina, she would be taken up to her bedroom for a harsh spanking. Tuppence crammed a whole finger of moist ginger cake into her mouth and swallowed painfully. If it was Miss Victoria, she would be marched down to the pantry, stripped naked and given a severe caning. Forcing the rest of the incriminating ginger cake into her mouth, Tuppence ate it greedily and swallowed her milk. If it was Miss Emily, she would be strapped mercilessly across the bare buttocks right then and there on the landing.

It was, Tuppence sighed with relief, Miss Elizabeth.

'Naughty Tuppence,' the gentle sister said mildly. 'Out of bed?'

'Just checking that the pantry window was fast, miss.'

'And helping yourself to milk and cake, I see,' Miss Elizabeth remarked, holding the lamp up high to inspect the crumbs of ginger cake adhering to the maid's wet breast.

Tuppence was surprised to see that Miss Elizabeth was carrying the green ledger – the punishment book – under her left arm.

'I read with interest that Lady Draco had occasion to use the crop this afternoon, Tuppence.'

The maid merely nodded silently.

'Turn and face the wall and raise up your shift. I wish to inspect your bottom.'

'But—'

'At once, Tuppence. Be a good, obedient girl and do as you are told.'

Slowly, Tuppence turned to face the wall. Pressing her head against the flock wallpaper, she inched up her thin cotton shift until it rode over her hips and buttocks.

Miss Elizabeth peered at the maid's exposed bottom in the lamp light. Tuppence flinched anxiously as her mistress picked up the lamp and brought it closer to her buttocks, worrying if the brightly burning globe would touch and scald her own globes. She clenched her cheeks together tightly as she felt the heat approach her naked flesh.

'Please keep still, Tuppence,' Miss Elizabeth whispered, kneeling.

Down in the hall, the pendulum clock ticked quietly, counting off the minutes slowly. Tuppence lost all sense of time. With her arms just beginning to ache, she remained facing the wall, exposing her bottom to her kneeling mistress.

Soft sounds – a liquid lapping – filled the silence of the night. Tuppence shuffled uncomfortably. Her toes stubbed the green

39

leather punishment book where Miss Elizabeth had put it down on the carpet. Gazing down to her feet, Tuppence caught a glimpse of the flickering shadow on the wallpaper.

'Head up, Tuppence. Keep your eyes closed.'

Tuppence obeyed her mistress instantly. Behind her closed eyes, the image continued vividly. Tuppence could hear, could smell – and had briefly glimpsed the shadowplay of – Miss Elizabeth playing with herself. After inspecting and perusing the six stripes bequeathed by Lady Draco's crop across the maid's bottom, Miss Elizabeth was now fingering herself furiously.

Tuppence stiffened as, suddenly, her mistress slumped forward, burying her face into the bottom before her. Tuppence grunted as Miss Elizabeth's nose delved deeply into her cleft and shuddered as her mistress, spasming in her climax, dragged her open mouth across the maid's cheeks. Soon Tuppence felt the tongue and then the teeth of her orgasming mistress at her bare buttocks. Two trembling hands, the fingertips wet and sticky, alighted against Tuppence's cheeks, framing and controlling the deliciously rounded bottom. Tuppence pressed her face into the flock wallpaper, flattening her tongue against its velvety surface, as the nuzzling face of the kneeling woman buried itself deeper into the maid's soft warmth.

Later, silence reigned. Tuppence could only hear the rush of blood singing in her ears. Miss Elizabeth rose briskly and arranged her skirts. Leaving the lamp on the carpet, she struggled to open her small reticule.

'Straight to bed with you, my girl.'

'Yes, Miss Elizabeth,' Tuppence whispered, accepting the silver shilling her mistress pressed into her hand.

'And be sure to come and see me directly you return from Lady Draco. I want to see your bottom after a weekend at Draco Hall.'

'Yes, Miss Elizabeth.'

Strapping Muscles

From his desk at the bay window, Dr Breunig watched the setting sun glinting on the Mercedes in the distance. His leather gloves closed into tight fists as his artificial hands clenched at the sharp horn blaring impatiently as the speeding car tore up the narrow driveway. He sighed aloud at the sound of squealing tyres on loose gravel.

Rising slowly from his desk, he crossed his study, dragging his smashed leg behind him. Wincing as the Mercedes scrunched to a halt outside – Dr Breunig hated fast cars since his accident, nine years ago – he prepared to meet the Cabinet Minister.

'Your son missed Oxford by a whisker?'

'Corpus Christi. And by a little more than that. Rollo got in with a bad set. Gambling. And worse. Missed the scholarship by a mile.'

'Any official difficulties?' Dr Breunig asked delicately, avoiding any direct reference to MI5.

'Squared the Chief Constable but the damn tabloids are sniffing around. Need to get him out of the limelight and back to his studies.'

'Ah, the tabloids.' Dr Breunig nodded sympathetically. 'Chersey Manor is certainly out of the limelight, Minister. We are, as you see, well off the beaten track. And we will offer your son every opportunity to focus on his scholarship,' he continued, purring reassuringly.

'Offer him?' the Cabinet Minister spluttered, purpling. 'The hound wants strict supervision and firm discipline. Can you manage that?' The Cabinet Minister's tone was doubtful.

'Most certainly.' Dr Breunig nodded emphatically.

The anxious parent eyed the crippled, gloved hands even more doubtfully. 'Are you—' he hesitated. 'Are your staff quite up to it?'

'Chersey Manor is not a crammer for duffers,' Dr Breunig countered suavely. 'We have a unique regime here. Give Rollo to us and I assure you he will be very glad to go up to Oxford after the summer. Very grateful indeed.'

'You sound so certain—'

'I am. The curriculum is particularly suited to bringing out the best in obdurate young men. Eighteen?'

'Just. Well, he's in the car with his bags. I'd better send him in.'

'One moment, Minister. You have been fully briefed, I trust? Should you decide to entrust your son to our absolute care, there must be no contact. We run a spartan routine here: no frills or fripperies. No half day visits into the village, hampers from daddy or phone calls from mummy.'

'Splendid,' the Cabinet Minister beamed. 'Glad to get the young blighter out of my hair for a couple of months.'

'So long as that is understood. Bring him in, then. He's just in time for gym.'

'Gym? Hope you're not going to waste time—'

'Rest assured, Minister, exposure to the rigours of physical education and training are exactly what young Rollo needs at this crucial stage in his development.'

'*Mens sana in corpore sano*?'

'As you say, Minister. I shall be assigning Rollo to Miss Pringle. She is perfectly capable of taking the young man in hand, believe me. Former Olympic bronze medallist. Takes a very firm line.'

'Gets results?'

'Three of her former charges are in the F.O. and I believe a fourth currently meddles with the base rates at the Treasury.'

Suitably impressed with these credentials, the Cabinet Minister gingerly shook Dr Breunig's crippled right hand and strode out to where Rollo sat yawning in the chauffeur-driven Mercedes.

* * *

Rollo, a gaunt, dark-haired Adonis, stood languidly in the large reception room, waiting for a servant to collect his three cases. Brisk footsteps approached. It must be the maid, Rollo presumed. Quite tasty, he thought. Good breasts and amazing legs. Those black lycra leggings showed every smooth curve of her thighs and buttocks. His cock thickened and twitched. She'll probably come to my room after lights out for a couple of tenners.

Taking his hands slowly out of his pockets, he gestured to his luggage. 'Get these to my rooms,' he drawled, his youthful voice already carrying the assured tone of money and privilege.

'Rooms?' snapped the athletic blonde in the lemon sleeveless vest and tight leggings. 'No rooms here, laddie. Room. You get a room.'

The 'laddie' annoyed him almost as much as her brisk Scottish accent. He scowled.

'Room. Which you will do well to keep neat and tidy at all times—'

'I say, girl,' Rollo drawled dismissively, 'just get my cases—'

'Miss Pringle, laddie. Don't you dare "girl" me. Pick them up yourself. Come along. At once.'

Rollo tossed his head back and snorted angrily. He was about to deliver a withering rebuke when the stern blonde, ten years his senior, pounced. Before he knew it, she had grappled him face-down across an oak table and was deftly yanking down his designer jeans and blue boxer shorts.

'Listen, laddie, and listen carefully,' she snarled, fishing out a small leather belt from her cleavage and unfurling it with a snap. 'From now on, you only speak when spoken to and you obey every order instantly. Understand?'

Rollo, struggling to get free from the armlock pinning him face-down into the table, writhed in vain. She released him but kept him prostrate by grasping the nape of his neck.

'Hands together, out on the table,' she barked.

He refused. The short strap cracked down viciously across his bare buttocks. He yelped – and obeyed, stretching his hands out across the sheen of the polished wood.

'Palms together.'

His left hand found its partner.

'Like your saying your prayers,' she whispered, adding darkly, 'you'll need them, laddie, you'll need them.'

The strap that had seared his rump was quickly wrapped around his wrists, pinioning them in severe bondage. He splayed his fingers in a reflex of fear. Suddenly rolling and twisting, he made a bid to escape. The blonde laughed harshly and reached down, almost leisurely, to cup and squeeze his balls. Rollo froze instantly into a statue of meek obedience.

Releasing his balls, she thumbed his cleft. 'Spread 'em,' she commanded, palming his upper thighs apart. 'Perfectly still, mind, during punishment.'

The bare-bottomed Adonis, stripped of his boxer shorts and air of easy arrogance, slumped across the broad oak table, his hot breath clouding its polished surface. Flexing her right knee up into his buttocks, the blonde reached down and unlaced her white pump. Slipping it off, she caught it deftly and planted the rubber sole across the swell of his left cheek.

'You are here for the next seven weeks, laddie. You will be under my control every moment. You, and your bottom, are utterly and absolutely mine to punish as I please. Work hard, very hard, and you might just avoid too much pain.'

'Bitch—'

The supple pump swished down five times, reddening his cheeks mercilessly. He grunted and squirmed, his fingers splaying out in anguish.

'We can do this two ways, laddie. There is the hard way, or there is the very hard way. I am now going to give you a taste of what you will receive if you even dare to think of disobeying me. Do you understand?'

Rollo mouthed a soft obscenity.

Swipe. The rubber sole cracked venomously down, searing his buttock's swell with a scarlet kiss. Rollo yelped. The blonde gripped the pump tightly and swiped it down nine more times – slowly, deliberately and very painfully. The punishment left his buttocks burning. The blonde paused, wedging her lycra-sheathed thigh against his left buttock. The crimson globe wobbled gently

as the shiny black thigh nestled into its hot flesh.

'Now, laddie,' Miss Pringle purred, resting the sole of the pump down upon the bottom it had just blistered, 'we're getting to know each other properly. It's really quite simple. Just listen and obey.'

'My father—'

'Is paying good money to have you straightened out and fit for Oxford. No problem. You're just over-privileged and under-disciplined. Nothing that a spell of intensive corrective training cannot fix—'

'No, do carry on, Miss Pringle. I trust you are treating our new arrival to Chersey Manor to the customary welcome?' Dr Breunig enthused.

Miss Pringle turned and saluted him with the upraised pump.

'Pray continue, and let the welcome be memorable, if you please.'

The pump cracked down with renewed vigour four times in savage succession. The witness to the onslaught rubbed his gloved hands feverishly as Miss Pringle positioned the rubber sole across the crown of the punished cheeks and dragged it slowly across the ravaged flesh.

'You will address me as Miss, and only Miss, at all times,' she said sternly. 'Even under your breath; even,' she whispered, 'in your dreams.'

Rollo whimpered.

Crack. The pump spoke harshly. As did the punisher: 'Understand?'

'Yes,' Rollo replied, sullenly.

Crack. 'Yes, what?'

'Yes, Miss.'

Dr Breunig shook his head sadly. 'Goodness me, a slow learner, Miss Pringle. Do you think we'll ever get him into Corpus Christi?'

'He'll learn,' she murmured.

'I'm sure he will, under your strict tutelage.' Dr Breunig beamed as he departed.

Miss Pringle tossed the pump down onto the carpet and trod her right foot into it. Raising her leg up, she planted her foot down dominantly upon the punished cheeks to tie up the laces. Stooping,

45

she yanked away the penitent's jeans, shorts, socks and shoes, rendering him utterly naked from the waist down.

'Pick up your cases,' she commanded, quickly undoing the strap at his wrists and curling it affectionately, 'and follow me.'

Rollo blushed deeply as he rose from the table, struggling in vain to cover and shield his gathering erection. He rubbed his wrists and folded his hands together at the base of his belly.

'Cases,' she commanded, perusing his erection as he juggled with his baggage – one in each hand, the third under his arm. The case under his arm slipped. Stepping up to reposition it, Miss Pringle felt the tip of his thick penis prod her belly. Rollo shuddered and averted his gaze. She caught his chin in a fierce grip and gazed directly into his eyes.

'You are a very impertinent young man. Cocksure, hm? There are ways of dealing with cocksure young men,' she purred, unfurling the leather strap so that it brushed the twitching shaft. 'Painful but effective ways.'

Rollo groaned and trembled. Sensing his climax, she used the strap to trap his cock against his belly. He came, suddenly, with a soft moan.

'You need a shower,' Miss Pringle remarked, her tone crisply clinical. 'Which means of course that you will miss tea. Turn around,' she instructed.

Obedient to her command, he turned. The leather strap flickered across his already reddened buttocks.

'Proceed.'

Head bowed, and flinching from the cruel kiss of the strap, Rollo stumbled towards the door.

She monitored his shower, making sure that the water was little more than lukewarm, and watched as he soaped and rinsed the semen from his belly.

'Wash your bottom, laddie. Get that soap right up between those cheeks.'

Rollo trod the tiles at his feet carefully as he turned to conceal his naked manhood from her intense gaze.

'No, laddie. Face me. You cannot hide from me. From now on,

46

I own and control you completely. Now get weaving with that soap.'

Half-heartedly, the young man lathered the soap and washed his cleft. Miss Pringle snarled softly and pounced.

'When I give you an instruction, laddie, I expect to be obeyed.'

Spinning him around, she grabbed a rough flannel and ravaged his cleft with it brutally for a full three minutes. Rollo cried out, begging for mercy. Ignoring him, the stern blonde stepped out of the shower, twisting the tap to cold. The naked boy gasped as he stood, transfixed, beneath the icy deluge. Teeth chattering and eyes tightly shut, he stumbled blindly out into the towel she swathed him with.

At first, she dried him almost tenderly, but as the soft white towelling reached his balls her hand grew firm.

'Time for bed,' she announced. It was only seven-twenty. Rollo glanced at her sulkily. 'Six-thirty rise tomorrow. We'll start with a couple of hours in the gym before breakfast.'

He followed her meekly to the dormitory block. The blonde opened a door and jerked her head towards the bedroom. As Rollo passed through the doorway, she spanked his bottom harshly.

'You're probably thinking of running away,' she remarked briskly, entering behind him.

Rollo turned, guiltily blushing as red as his bottom at how easily she had read his thoughts.

'You'll not get very far. Not without shoes. For the length of your stay at Chersey Manor, you will go barefoot. At all times. And there must be no contact with any of the other residents – not that there'll be much time or opportunity for that. Now get into bed.'

The naked young man slipped thankfully between the cold sheets and curled up in the bed.

'Your studies won't begin until I'm satisfied that I have taken you completely in hand, laddie. Forget about books and exams for now. I'll be training you in more fundamental areas, to begin with. A complete change of attitude is required. Understand?'

Rollo nodded, but his perplexed frown was evident.

'It's all about attitude, laddie. You are here to make up for lost time. And wasted opportunities. You need to shape up. I want you in peak condition, so we'll be spending the first week or so together down in the gym. Keep your hands out on the blanket, laddie. No playing with yourself. Lights out in five minutes. Goodnight.'

'Goodnight, Miss.'

Dr Breunig's leather-gloved hand pushed the plate of lobster away and stretched for the bottle of chilled Chablis. Miss Pringle, who had finished her raspberries and cream, stood up from the dining table. 'Dessert?' she whispered.

The frosted glass in the clenched glove trembled as Dr Breunig nodded eagerly.

Plucking teasingly at the silk belt of her kimono, the blonde wriggled and let her garment gape wide. Rippling her shoulders sensuously, she shrugged the silk kimono off. It fell silently to her feet. Dr Breunig's eyes narrowed. He grunted as the blonde, naked except for her white, underwired bra, trod the carpet softly towards his chair. He lurched forward, his gloved fist stabbing gently at her blonde pubic nest.

'No,' she murmured, brushing his hand aside. She wagged her finger at him, skimming the tip of his nose. 'You know the rules. You know what you must do if you want to play with pussy. We agreed the programme.'

'Please,' he whined, thumbing her mons veneris feverishly.

Miss Pringle took a tantalising step back – just out of his frantic reach. 'You must take your physiotherapy seriously. Use your fingers properly to undo the clasp of my bra – no teeth, mind – and you can have my bare breasts. Do the task quickly, using your thumbs as well, and you can have pussy to play with.'

Breunig smashed his fist down on the table in a fury of frustrated lust.

'Temper, temper,' she chided, purring softly. 'We agreed the programme. I want those hands working again. Properly. Try. You must try. Think what you will be able to do when you regain full use of them. Why, in a month or so, you could be spanking my bare bottom. I know you want to.'

He nodded and beckoned her back to him. She relented, bending her superb breasts down to him, their warm weigh bulging invitingly in their underwired bondage. He pawed them, dimpling the swollen curves, then squeezed and squashed their soft ripeness. Inching closer, she parted her thighs and steadied herself – arms reaching out to the back of his chair – and buried his upturned face in her dominating bosom.

Gasping aloud, Breunig jabbed his gloved finger down to his bulging crotch.

'No, not yet,' she murmured. 'I won't let him out to play until you've done your physio.'

Turning, she sat down on his lap, shuddering as his fierce erection raked the cleft between her splayed buttocks; and, reaching out behind, caught his smashed hands and guided them to the clasp of her bra.

'Concentrate, doctor. Like I taught you. Slowly and methodically. You can do it. And just think of the prize.' She wriggled her bare bottom down onto his thick shaft. He swore softly and moaned. 'Try.'

The erection at her cleft throbbed excitedly as the leather-sheathed fingers fumbled with her stubborn clasp. Easing herself back slightly, she trapped then rode the trousered cock teasingly, all the time urging the crippled fingers to undo the clasp. Suddenly, the bra straps at her shoulders shrivelled and the underwired cups fell free.

'Good,' she cried enthusiastically, joggling her buttocks. 'You are making progress.'

The gloved hands encircled her nakedness. She gasped and writhed as they sought and found, cupped and squeezed, her bare breasts. The trembling fingertips struggled – but failed – to pincer and pleasure the stubby nipples. Extricating herself sinuously, Miss Pringle rose and turned, planting her breasts down upon Breunig's face. His head jerked as he tried to suck and bite.

'Patience,' she whispered, guiding the dark, thickened nipples into his eyes. 'I promised to reward you and I shall – but no biting.'

Whimpering softly, he nodded obediently, eager for her soft bosom. She cradled him tenderly, breast feeding him with a tender dominance. He sucked contentedly, greedy at the swollen breast. His crotch bulged painfully.

'Can I play with pussy?' he begged, mouthing the words into her warm, silken flesh.

'You've been very good. Very good indeed. At this rate of rehabilitation, you'll be spanking my poor little bare bottom sooner than you think.'

He tensed and spasmed, his leather-gloved fists beating the sides of his chair.

Miss Pringle stood up, peeling her bosom from his upturned face. Fingering her berry-dark nipple, she gazed down at him, jerking and twisting in his chair. He was coming – violently.

'Oh dear,' she murmured, gazing down at the wet stain spreading at his crotch. 'You really shouldn't get overexcited.'

'Pussy,' he snarled, stretching out the twisted fingers of his right hand.

'No,' she replied in a tone of mock severity. 'Enough excitement for this evening, I think.' She took a step back and turned, offering her heavy cheeks to him. 'You've done well tonight, though. I'll let you look at my bottom for a spell. And you can tell me everything you want to do to it when it is, one day, all yours.'

Rollo gasped as the blanket was dragged down to the end of the narrow bed.

'It's six-thirty-seven. Get up, laddie, you're late already.'

Blinking in the sudden blaze of the harsh electric light, Rollo stretched and staggered up out of his bed. Through the window which she had just pushed wide open, he glimpsed the violet light of dawn.

Miss Pringle tossed him a white vest and a pair of black shorts. 'That's all you'll need today,' she barked. 'Wait. Don't get dressed until I've examined that bed.'

Rollo clutched the vest and shorts to his nakedness as he shivered in the spartan bedroom. The blonde peered down to examine the sheet intimately.

'No semen stains,' she observed, delicately brushing away a coil of his black pubic hair. 'Good. You obeyed. Now get dressed.'

He did so, immediately, the ferocity of her punishing strap across his bottom last night as vivid in his memory as it had been across his cheeks.

She escorted him down to the refectory. He found fourteen other residents there before him, their seats spaced wide apart, eating in silence. Nobody risked even a furtive glance. Rollo sat down opposite a beautiful Greek girl. Surely he knew her? Yes. Out at a private rave in Hendon. Her father was in shipping. The girl's large almond eyes rose up sorrowfully over her yoghurt. Rollo ached to speak – to find out what had brought her to Chersey Manor – but the ever vigilant Miss Pringle, together with the eyes and ears of six other female trainers, kept him in check.

As he ate his meagre breakfast – nothing like the sumptuous fare he usually enjoyed – he longed for the answers to other questions teeming in his brain. Was the fierce blonde, Miss Pringle, the Greek girl's trainer? Did Miss Pringle discipline the almond-eyed young beauty with that cruel strap? Bare-bottomed? Did those almond eyes – Rollo's tongue thickened and he swallowed with difficulty – blink penitent tears under the lash?

'Hurry up,' Miss Pringle snapped. 'As a newcomer, you have a different schedule. No studies for you, laddie. Not yet. Not until you are ready. It's down to the gym today.'

Across the table, the almond eyes widened – and gazed upon Rollo with unfathomable pity.

It was chilly in the deserted, echoing gym. Miss Pringle's white pumps squeaked on the polished wooden floor. Rollo trod across the prickling matting gingerly and picked up the medicine ball as instructed.

'Four laps, and keep that ball up high,' the stern blonde commanded, pacing over to the brick wall and taking down a fierce-looking strap.

Rollo shivered as he saw her lithe, muscled arm stretch up to grasp the length of leather – and shivered again as the blonde's firm hand tightened around the supple hide.

Miss Pringle snapped the strap. Its bark was savage – with the promise of a blistering bite. Rollo held the heavy ball up and commenced to jog around the perimeter of the gym. At the end of his first lap, his arms ached and his shoulders sagged.

The strap whip-cracked angrily. 'Don't slacken, laddie,' Miss Pringle shouted. 'Keep up the pace.' Her cherry-red leather strap – four feet long and three inches wide – dangled down at her right thigh and leg, hugging the shapely contours. 'Faster.' The snapping strap echoed twice more.

Rollo closed his eyes and redoubled his efforts. Two laps completed and two to do. The medicine ball grew unbearably heavy between his sweating hands. His forearms grew numb and a burning pain seared his shoulders.

'Come on. You can do better than that.' The curt instruction to jog faster was punctuated by another double snap-crack of the strap.

Rollo, lunging forward into the final lap, stumbled. The ball slipped from his fingers, thudding down without bouncing onto the polished wooden floor.

'Halt.'

Rollo skidded to a halt, stubbing his unprotected toes. Gasping, he nursed his left foot in his right hand and hopped inelegantly around the inert ball.

'Stand still, laddie,' the blonde tormentress snarled, approaching with soft steps of menace. 'Shorts off. Belly down across the ball.'

Uncertain, Rollo hesitated.

Crack. The strap flickered out to its full length, lashing his left buttock with unerring accuracy. Rollo yelped and dropped the bruised foot down.

'Stop clowning around. I said shorts down, laddie, and across that ball.'

Before she had fully refurled the length of cherry-red leather, Rollo was bare-bottomed and belly-down across the surface of the heavy ball, hugging the dull hide with both arms. Thrust out behind, his straightened legs were pressed tightly together. His toes whitened as they dug into the polished wood of the gym floor.

'Stamina, laddie. Stamina and self-discipline. That is what you lack and that is what I am going to instil in you. Especially the self-discipline. Of course –' she chuckled darkly '– before there is self-discipline. there must be discipline itself.'

Crack. She swiped his proffered buttocks with the strap.

'Please—' Rollo whimpered.

'All that wasted opportunity. Gambling and drinking, so your father said. Once I get you licked into shape, we'll tackle your neglected studies. But you must be fit. Fit, receptive and obedient before we embark on any intellectual rigours. Bottom up.'

Rollo, closing his eyes, inched his scalded cheeks up a fraction.

'No, laddie. I'm going to strap it, not powder it. Get it right up. I want it big and round.'

Dreading the strap that was about to bark across his defenceless buttocks, Rollo peeled his thighs away from the soft hide of the ball and proffered his bottom. In his burning pain and shame, a sudden confusion imploded in the belly of his brain. His cock had sprung up, the wet snout of the glistening glans nuzzling the medicine ball.

Crack. The leather strap exploded across his clenched cheeks, searing them with a crimson weal. His cock jerked, thrusting into the soft hide.

Behind his tightly shut eyes, Rollo pictured Miss Pringle's proud breasts thrusting as she bent down to flex the strap, then pictured them bouncing deliciously as she applied the punishing stroke. He imagined her superbly muscled arm, taut and supple. In the grip of her slender hand, the cherry-red leather length of leather. Red leather which left lines of angry crimson across his whipped bottom. His engorged cock pulsed, quickening as his climax tightened inside him.

Snap, crack. Snap, crack. The blonde lashed the bare bottom twice in a blistering staccato. Rollo squeezed the medicine ball tightly – and his punished cheeks together even more tightly. He trembled, on the brink of orgasm, as he waited for the next stroke.

'Up,' came the unexpected, confusing command.

The dark-haired Adonis scrambled to his feet, attempting to cover his red bottom by dragging down the hem of his white vest.

'Shorts on.'

Rollo stepped into the black shorts and drew them up over his sore buttocks.

'Now pick the medicine ball up,' his tormentress ordered, studying the proud erection piercing the front of his shorts. 'Two more laps,' she whispered. 'And laddie—'

'Yes, Miss?' Rollo swallowed anxiously.

'Don't spill any of that precious seed,' she purred, gently swinging the strap up to tap against his balls. 'You'll be needing every drop of it, presently.'

Miss Pringle, her strap around her neck so that the two leather tails fell down across the swell of each breast, held a short stick of yellow chalk between her fingers.

'The long jump,' she announced. 'The ultimate test. Once I have trained you successfully, you will, I think, be ready to undertake your studies.'

And once I get to my books – and study hard – I can earn my release from Chersey Manor, Rollo reasoned logically. Better do my best in this damn long jump event.

'Pay close attention, laddie. We'll be trying for three metres.'

But that's only nine feet or so. Rollo couldn't believe his luck. I can jump that easily, no sweat. He almost had to suppress his grin of relief. Then a cloud of anxiety dulled his eyes. Had the beautiful, strict blonde said high jump or long jump? Nine feet would be almost impossible for him to clear.

'The long jump—'

Rollo did not pay close attention as Miss Pringle praised the track event with unreserved gusto. Bending down and kneeling on one knee, she drew a thick yellow line with her stick of chalk across the polished wood.

Peeping furtively at the curve of her hip and thigh, Rollo thrilled to the feline grace of the mature blonde he had come to both dread and adore.

'And here, I think,' Miss Pringle grunted, squatting down three metres further along the floor and scoring the point with her yellow chalk. 'Shorts and vest off. Toes against the chalk line.'

So, there had to be a catch. Was it to be a standing-start jump?

That could be tough. Puzzled – and anxious – Rollo kicked off his shorts, peeled off his vest and inched his toes up to the jumping-off line.

'Start masturbating,' the blonde instructed, her tone brisk and cynical.

Rollo gulped. He looked at her, blushing furiously.

'Begin,' she barked harshly, retrieving her strap from its resting place against her bosom and snapping it ominously.

'I want you to come,' she instructed. 'This is the long jump. Now get your semen across that line,' she thundered, jabbing her straightened finger behind her down to the second yellow chalk line. She kissed her coiled strap lingeringly. 'I'll assist you,' she whispered into the cherry-red hide.

She positioned herself at right-angles next to him, her strap raised. Rollo reluctantly enclosed his fist around his shaft and started to pump rhythmically.

Crack. The searing stroke exploded across his cheeks. Rollo cried out in anguish as he rose up on his toes. Clenching his whipped cheeks together he pumped harder – faster. Crack. Crack. He came, his silver spurt splattering down a good half metre short of the prescribed mark.

'Kneel. Bow down your head and get your bottom up, laddie. I can see we've some ground to cover before you come up to the mark.'

Crack. Crack. The strap spoke viciously as the cruel blonde substituted searing strokes for her stinging words.

A little later, she dragged her fingernails across his nipples, peaking them up in pleasurable pain. A little later still, his flaccid length straightened and rose up.

'Up,' she instructed, flexing her strap and tapping the tip of his straining shaft with the cherry-red leather. 'Toes to the line, laddie. Let's see how you shape up this time.'

'At last, Minister. Your secretary guards you jealously. Quite difficult to reach you, even on this number.'

'You have to get past three of 'em, Breunig,' the minister chuckled into the phone. 'All well trained. Speaking of training, how is that son of mine progressing? I am particularly concerned with his Latin. Needs it for the scholarship. And maths. Geometry defeats him.'

'Rest assured, minister, your son is responding to Miss Pringle's strict training schedule.'

'Pringle, eh? That the bronze medallist you mentioned. Capable, I presume?'

'Quite capable, Minister. A fine, strapping young athletic type. Pushing Rollo very hard down in the gym, even as we speak.'

'Not much use him being in the damn gym, Breunig. It's Latin and geometry he needs.'

'Miss Pringle has her methods, Minister. I can vouch for them personally,' the doctor purred.

Rollo tossed feverishly in his bed. It was the end of his fifth day of nightmarish incarceration at Chersey Manor. Repeatedly punished and humiliated into abject submission, he lay awake in the narrow bed, frantically trying to work out how he could improve his 'long jump'. He had tried – and failed – several times, despite jerking his hips and thrusting them forward at the point of ejaculation. He had even scowled sullenly – deliberately – at the strap-wielding blonde, to earn a cutting stroke across his cheeks just as he came. But he could not reach the yellow chalk mark three metres away.

No. He'd never do it. And until he did, his books must remain closed and his revision studies neglected. Oxford seemed to slip away on the horizon: out of his reach like the yellow chalk line. Was he doomed to remain here at Chersey Manor for weeks? Months?

Rollo sat up in bed. What he needed was the right fantasy. If he could just conjure up the right images, the most exciting stimulus, he thought, he could fuel his orgasm and reach the target.

Miss Pringle. Now slavishly in her thrall, he found it difficult to trespass on her image. His mind wandered down along the corridors of his immediate surroundings, trying to escape from her dominating image. An image he now both feared and adored. Rollo wondered how the other young residents were progressing.

He saw them several times each day, dining in subdued silence. He found their wet towels in the showers, overheard their soft screams of torment as their trainers plied the crop and cane.

And what about the Greek girl, the girl with the frightened almond eyes? Did Miss Pringle punish her? Rollo lifted his sheet up and watched his shaft thicken and engorge. Yes. The Greek girl. Bare-bottomed and bending, proffering her peach cheeks up for the kiss of Miss Pringle's strap. Yes. Rollo grasped his hot erection and started to masturbate, slowly, luxuriating in the fantasy of the naked girl – in his mind, seeing her pinned across the stern blonde's lap, being strapped. He saw the girl's squirming buttocks reddening; heard her shrill squeals of suffering; relished the snap-cracking of the burning leather. Yes. This was it. This was the fantasy that would fuel a successful explosion of hot seed.

Out of bed, he stumbled to the wall, turned, and edged backwards until his buttocks crushed up against its cool stretch. Pumping fiercely all the time, he followed the delicious sequence of images behind his closed eyes. The almond eyes wide with fear, the perfect cheeks crimson with pain.

With his buttocks splayed against the cold wall, and his feet planted wide apart, he whispered aloud, providing a feverish soundtrack to the silent film flickering behind his eyes.

The Greek girl. Smooth-buttocked. Olive-skinned. Softly fleshed. The cherry-red leather. The strap. Crack. Crack. The kiss of the cruel strap. Jerking hips and writhing thighs. A shrill squeal. Miss Pringle, superbly dominant. Miss Pringle, thumbing the red weals of pain on the helpless cheeks of the girl she had just lashed . . .

Rollo slumped, grunting aloud, and collapsed against the wall. Arching his hips forwards, he came, a fat squirt of exquisite liquid release. Pitter pat. Pitter pat. Like the hot raindrops of a sudden summer shower, his semen rained down in the darkness before him.

Nine feet. Oh, please let it be at least nine feet, he whispered aloud, balancing unsteadily as he trod the bedroom floor – one foot in front of the other – measuring the distance to splashdown.

* * *

Miss Pringle pounced, dragging him from the toilet seat. It was Sunday evening. The rest of the residents were either being punished by their trainers or tackling a variety of humiliating household chores. Rollo had secreted himself in the loo with his Latin dictionary.

'I distinctly told you that you were not to read or study until I gave you permission to do so.'

Rollo hung his head down penitently – just as he had done when he had been caught by his nanny reading a copy of *Hide and Sleek*, his father's favourite journal of leatherwear.

'No studying until your initial training is complete. Come with me,' she said angrily, snatching up the Latin dictionary.

Moments later, they were in Dr Breunig's study.

'I found him disobeying clear instructions. I wish to dispense the maximum punishment. Have I your permission, Dr Breunig?'

The doctor's tongue darted out between thin lips, wetting them expectantly. The gloved hands twitched. He merely nodded his assent.

'Bend over, laddie. Bare-bottomed. Remain in the punishment position while I fetch my strap.'

Breunig picked up Rollo's copy of *Liber Linguae Latinae* and approached the bending youth. Thumbing the lexicon with his leather-gloved finger, he conducted a brief vocabulary drill.

'*Colaphus*?'

'A striking blow, or stroke,' Rollo murmured.

'*Flagello*?'

'To whip, to lash.'

'*Plausus*?'

'A smack, a spanking blow,' Rollo whispered.

'*Punio*,' Breunig countered quickly, his voice tightening with gathering excitement.

'I punish, I correct, I chastise.'

The pages rustled softly. Rollo tensed. The softly leathered knuckles of the crippled hand swept up fleetingly against the swell of his bare buttocks.

'*Punit*,' Breunig said softly, gulping on the word like a bulldog on a bone. '*Punit*. She punishes. She corrects. She chastises.'

58

Rollo gasped as the gloved knuckles – now a tight fist – dimpled his left buttock.

'*Flagrum*?'

'A whip, lash or strap,' Rollo hissed.

'Very good,' Breunig nodded, shutting the dictionary with a loud snap. 'A strap.'

Miss Pringle returned to the study, fingering her cherry-red leather.

'I think we should all retire down to the gym,' Dr Breunig remarked, his crippled hand gripping the dictionary fiercely.

Miss Pringle stripped off her tight vest and stood, bare-breasted and supremely dominant, over the bare bottom she was about to beat. The doctor sat some distance away, anxiously awaiting the punishment. Rollo, shivering, touched his toes and shrank before the promise of his impending pain.

The whipping with the strap was protracted – almost a leisurely affair. The crisp leather cracked down again and again: searing upturned buttocks with merciless accuracy. The silence in the gym was deafeningly loud, broken only by the soft grunt of the chastiser, the harsh snapping crack of the strap – and the sweet moan of the chastised.

Breunig was forgotten by both punisher and punished as they entered their private, intimate world of pleasurable pain and painful pleasure. But Breunig, avid voyeur, followed them intently, missing nothing of the drama of dominance and discipline as it unfolded before him.

Pausing to examine her writhing victim, Miss Pringle knelt down on one knee to peruse Rollo's whipped cheeks. She fingered them gently, tenderly tracing each scarlet weal, then suddenly taloned them in a fierce pincer.

Rollo screamed.

'Don't you dare come until I say so,' the blonde hissed, slapping her strap smartly up against Rollo's engorged shaft.

'Sorry, Miss,' he mumbled, cringing.

Rising up abruptly, Miss Pringle changed her mind. Anxious to display her prowess as an accomplished disciplinarian before her adoring employer, she tapped the strap dominantly against Rollo's buttocks. Driving him forward on awkwardly shuffling feet, she edged him onto the yellow chalk line.

'I have decided to let you try for the long jump, laddie, if you really think you've got it in you. But no silly thoughts of that stupid Greek bitch getting it hot and strong. I own your bottom, laddie, as I own your mind. You will think of me when you come – and you will only come when I give my permission. Understand?'

'Yes, Miss,' Rollo whimpered.

Crack. Crack. The remorseless strap lashed down. With the soft muscles of her punishing arm rippling, and her ripe breasts bouncing in their naked freedom, Miss Pringle striped the buttocks before her ruthlessly. Rollo's whipped cheeks tightened in response to his gathering orgasm.

'Wait laddie,' she purred, 'I haven't give you permission.'

Rollo whimpered.

'Kiss the strap,' she commanded.

Rollo tongued the cherry-red leather hungrily.

Crack. Crack. Bending down, the blonde crushed her naked breasts into the cheeks she had just lashed, dragging the erect nipples across the vivid weals, then bunching the cool satin globes of her bosom into the blistered buttocks. Rollo screamed piercingly - and ejaculated. His spurt flew over the second yellow chalk line, with several inches to spare.

'Excellent,' Miss Pringle cried triumphantly. 'You did it, laddie. I knew you had it in you.'

Rollo collapsed down onto the polished wood, sprawled at her feet, spent and exhausted. She trod down dominantly onto his striped bottom.

'Dr Breunig,' she called, turning proudly to celebrate her conquest. 'Dr Breunig—' she gasped, in a tone of dismay and delight.

Sitting a little distance away, the feverish voyeur had managed – for the first time in nine years – to undo his trousers with his crippled hands and was masturbating furiously: sheathing his stiff shaft in a soft leathered fist.

Miss Pringle, exultant at her twin triumph, knelt down and

gently cupped Rollo's left buttock.

'Tomorrow,' she murmured tenderly, 'we will commence with your studies. Latin with Dr Breunig and Euclidian geometry with me. We shall,' she purred, palming Rollo's captive cheek, 'start with the properties of the sphere.'

Sweet Misery

Ann Hunter woke up tired. Like all single City girls – Ann moved millions around the money markets at her desk every day – she slept with one eye open. What if the price of Brent crude dipped? Would the yen creep up overnight against the Euro?

In her shower, she offered her breasts up to the fierce drumming of the deliciously warm water. It hammered down upon her wet, shining bosom, stinging her nipples slightly and thickening them up into buds of pleasurable pain. Palming the aromatic gel down across her belly, she shuddered as her oiled fingertips stroked her pubic fringe. Probing deftly, she prised open the tulip of her sensitive labia, then strummed the fleshfolds rhythmically. She raided her memory for a fantasy – but, like her diary and her after-work schedule, it was blank. It would have to be raw masturbation – flesh punishing flesh – with no haunting images to fuel her liquid fire.

The phone rang. Ann paused, her thumb at her clitoris. Probably work. Some surge in the markets. Like a gazelle at a waterhole leaping at the shadow of a lion, she sprang from her shower, grabbed a robe and raced to pick up before the answering machine kicked in.

It was only her market sector manager, warning her that the dollar might come under pressure. Ann sighed. Her teletext had told her that shortly after midnight. She snarled softly as she replaced the phone, frustrated by the elusive orgasm abandoned in the shower.

At her breakfast bar, she heaped apricot conserve on fingers of golden toast. The lightly toasted bread sagged under the heavy burden of jam. After her toast was finished, she dug into the jar and took another mouthful neat, sucking hard on her spoon.

She disrobed in front of her mirror, brushed her short golden mane of hair briskly, then reached down into a drawer for a fresh bra. It was a white, cotton sports style – sensible rather than sensual – but Ann liked the crisp cotton cups at her bosom, relishing their firm control as they firmly moulded and mastered her heavy breasts.

Frowning, she fingered the white strap biting softly into her right shoulder. The bra, an expensive Swiss model, felt unusually tight. It bunched and squeezed her captive breasts. Ann gazed down at her cleavage and noticed the prominent bulge. She unclasped and whipped the bra off so quickly it swept down and lashed her hip and right buttock. Ann, now utterly naked before the mirror, shut her eyes tightly and inched up on her toes. The bra had striped her hard. Her punished cheek blazed. Turning, she peered down over her shoulder at the reflection of the deep pink stripe across her swollen buttock. Her throat tightened. She found the fleeting pain quite pleasurable. She found the thin whiplash across the curve of her exposed cheek curiously, deliciously, disturbing.

The climax she had sought – and had lost – in the shower reignited, prickling her moist pussy. But there was no time. The dollar could sink as soon as trading commenced. She had to get to her City desk. Turning back towards the mirror, she bent down, steadying herself by planting her hands down on the dressing table. Inching her breasts into the cold glass, she examined their bunched flesh intimately. Was she putting on a little weight? She waggled her bottom. The soft cheeks jiggled, their fleshy wobble suggesting some weight gain. Her nipples rebelled at the kiss of the cold glass, peaking painfully. Dragging her breasts away, she frowned once more, making a mental note to slip into Knickerbox at Liverpool Street Station and buy a size 36C.

Her office was open plan. At the next desk but one, Hazel was sending suggestive e-mail to potential one-night stands. Ann gazed around the busy dealing room. The men were young, softly scented and sharply groomed. Public school types who ran in a braying pack from work to the squash courts and then on to the wine bar. Ann either despised them, or simply dismissed them from her mind. Pampered and privileged, they held no challenge for her. She yearned for cruder, rougher pleasures, seeking a touch of dominance rather than their timid deference. Like an exquisite butterfly haunted by its inevitable doom, Ann Hunter quivered at the thought of being pinned down, splayed and displayed for the cruel pleasure of her captor. But none of these striped shirts with their hundred-pound haircuts held such menacing promise. She'd often overheard them all giggling in the wine bar – at how they would come at the thought of Nanny. And she knew that they could only manage a Christmas call-girl in pairs.

There were other men. Men with reddish brown London clay on their broad hands, or hands black with oil from throbbing engines. Men, stripped to the waist, clambering the spider's web of steel scaffolding spun around City developments. Ann often wondered what it would be like with these men, who shouted down appreciatively to her as she skipped along the lunchtime pavements below in search of sugared doughnuts. She wondered how it would feel to have their stale breath at her mouth, their soiled hands at her white breasts, their contemptuous splash of semen in her upturned face. Such thoughts left her wet. There were tissues, applied surreptitiously to her pussy when Helen wasn't looking, for that. But even as she dabbed her moist pubic fringe dry, Ann knew that she was destined never to know. They travelled into the City at 5am, huddled in mud-splattered Transits. She drove her sleek Audi in at eight. Only their eyes ever met.

After work – a busy day chasing the spiralling dollar – Ann went to the health spa for a swim. Sitting at the café-bar after five lazy lengths, she sipped her hot, creamy chocolate. From time to time, she thumbed her bikini bottom; it seemed to be biting into her deep cleft. She was putting on extra pounds.

A brochure at the counter caught her eye. The de Stael clinic. Ann made a snap decision. Fishing out her mobile, she made an appointment for the following evening. She really must watch her appetite, she decided firmly, signalling to the waiter and ordering a second slice of apple and cinnamon strudel drenched in double cream.

The de Stael clinic promised to help its clients lose pounds. Sterling, certainly, Ann thought as she surrendered her gold visa card to the receptionist, who sat at a desk of solid onyx.

After a brief wait, Ann was briskly greeted by a lithe, grey-eyed blonde. The badge at her bosom said 'Petra'. When the lipstick-free mouth spoke, the accent said German. Petra was a strawberry-blonde, paler than Ann's own honey-gold. The German wore her hair combed back into a severe bun.

In the private cubicle, behind opaque glass screens, Petra interrogated Ann crisply, recording intimate details of diet and lifestyle.

'Sugar? In your tea or coffee?'

Ann nodded. She found herself having to answer 'guilty' to all the incriminating questions.

'Sex?' Petra's silver pen remained poised for the response.

'No – not really,' Ann whispered.

'No orgasms?' The pen rose inquiringly, as if in disbelief.

'I – I – sometimes—' Ann mumbled, blushing deeply.

'Playing with yourself counts. A really strong climax, when you squeeze your thighs and bottom, you know?'

'I know,' Ann replied, managing a weak smile.

'Burns off several hundred calories.'

The probing questions continued. Fully clothed before the German blonde, Ann already felt stripped naked.

'Take off your clothes,' Petra instructed.

Ann looked up, and blinked.

'I need to examine you thoroughly,' the blonde replied, her grey eyes glinting as she snapped on a pair of clear plastic gloves.

Ann wriggled out of her clothing and presented herself, in her white bra and panties, for inspection.

'No, I want you naked,' Petra murmured, flexing her gloved right hand into a shining starfish of splayed fingers.

Ann brought her hands together up behind her back, finding it suddenly difficult to undo the clasp. Her fingers fumbled as Ann

66

shivered self-consciously under the unswerving grey-eyed gaze on her bouncing bosom. At last, the white bra fell free. Her liberated breasts joggled softly. Ann swiftly drew her arms to her sides – to palm her tight panties down – causing her breasts to squash together and burgeon.

'You are heavily breasted,' Petra purred, approaching. 'Let me feel.'

Before Ann had been able to tread out of her knickers – they hugged her, binding her knees together – the German had placed her gloved hands at each swollen breast, weighing their captive warmth on her plastic sheathed palms. Ann froze, closing her eyes. The sudden intimacy at her neglected body almost overwhelmed her. The pulse at her throat quickened urgently; at her pubis, a gentle plucking sensation caused her to cream imperceptibly at the top of her labial fold.

Blushing at her own arousal – would she weep? Would Petra's nostrils catch the whiff of excitement? Ann panicked; she opened her eyes to find the grey-eyed German studying her face intently. The hands at Ann's breasts cupped and contained them dominantly. The tingle at her slit forced Ann to clamp her soft thighs together tightly. Her left leg trembled uncontrollably; the white panties slid down to her ankles.

'They are quite firm. Good muscle tone. But a little heavy, no?' Petra pronounced. '36C?' It was not really a speculative guess. Petra spoke her size with unerring accuracy. 'Now I will examine your bottom.'

Ann, thrilling to the cool, clinical tone, surrendered her bare buttocks up to the strawberry-blonde's stern gaze.

'Part your thighs,' the German instructed.

Aware of the wet drizzle at her sticky pubic fringe, Ann shyly inched her thighs apart.

'Now together, please.'

Ann's superbly rounded cheeks bunched as she tightened them for the German's close examination.

'Yes,' Petra murmured. 'Again, evidence of good muscle tone, but you certainly are carrying surplus poundage.'

'Can you do anything for me?'

'I am perfectly able to get you to shed that unnecessary weight,' Petra replied, briefly knuckling the soft buttocks. 'Some exercise, I think, and certainly a strict diet regime. These you will observe between weekly visits to the clinic. I will weigh you accurately and monitor your progress. For now, I think, a massage.'

Ann stood up and turned, modestly covering her blonde pubic bush with cupped hands.

'Up onto the couch. Face down.'

Easing herself up onto the black leather couch, Ann flattened her nakedness down, thrilling to the sensation of crushing her breasts and pubic mound into the dark hide.

'I wear special gloves for the administration of the massage,' Petra explained, peeling off the transparent plastic gloves, binning them fastidiously and donning a pair of studded leather gauntlets. Ann, peeping curiously, saw that the tiny silver studs ran along the length of the fingers and across the inner palms. She clamped her thighs together expectantly, juicing quite freely now where her slit kissed the leather.

'Head down and remain perfectly still,' Petra instructed. 'It is the isodynamic principle that I employ,' she explained, sweeping her right hand fleetingly down Ann's dimpled spine, bringing it to rest upon the soft, upturned buttocks. 'The studs encounter and eliminate subcutaneous fat globules, if applied very firmly.' The gauntlet slid over the swell of the furthest cheek down onto Ann's outer thigh. Petra squeezed slightly, then gently punished the captive flesh.

Slowly, methodically, inch by naked inch, the stern, unsmiling strawberry-blonde applied the increasingly fierce massage, concentrating chiefly upon the bare buttocks before her. Ann mewed slightly, mouthing her delight into the leather at her lips.

The studded gauntlet paused, then the fingers suddenly gripped, taloning the fleshy buttock in its grasp. The second buttock was seized, and it too surrendered to the painful treatment. The rhythmical squeezing of the helpless cheeks caused the cleft to gape. Ann writhed, burning with shame at the thought of her anal rosebud being exposed to the ruthless gaze of the grey-eyed blonde.

Deeper down inside her spinning brain, another flame flickered, warming her gently with the dark thrill of knowing that Petra was utterly in control of her nakedness. Utterly in control, and inspecting her bare bottom intimately. The flame inside Ann's brain began to blaze.

'Your diet needs special attention and willpower, Ann,' Petra said in a slightly less severe tone, using her client's name for the first time in their encounter.

Ann slumped into the leather, crushing her heavy breasts down into its polished sheen. The sound of her name from Petra's lips as the strawberry-blonde punished – yes, punished – her bare bottom caused a silver bubble to emerge from Ann's labia.

'I shall be very disappointed if you do not make a supreme effort. Very disappointed. You won't disappoint me, will you?'

Both studded gauntlets squeezed viciously hard.

'No,' Ann squealed, threshing in a spasm of agony. 'No.'

'I am so very pleased to hear that,' Petra whispered. A studded fingertip swiftly raked the velvet ribbon of Ann's hot cleft. 'Should you fail to observe the strict régime, I shall be forced to take certain measures.' The studded fingertip tap-tapped at Ann's tight little sphincter. 'Yes,' Petra murmured, 'I shall take certain measures.'

After Ann had hurriedly dressed, snapping on her bra and panties with trembling hands, and had departed, the strawberry-blonde slowly drew her gauntlets off with her teeth. Bending to inspect the spot where Ann's wet pussy had pressed against the leather couch, the German smiled, her grey eyes widening as they gazed down at the tell-tale stain.

Ann knew that her next appointment at the de Stael clinic was not scheduled til next week. Three days – and three turbulent, dream-filled nights – after her first visit, she phoned.

The receptionist remained maddeningly polite but firm – as if reading from a script – as she countered Ann's insistence. No, it was not possible. Petra was quite strict on that point. No, Ann would have to wait until next week. 'I'm sorry,' the receptionist continued unapologetically. 'Petra makes the rules and is very firm.'

Ann tossed her mobile down onto her work desk angrily. She ached to hear the German's crisp voice, burned to feel the dominant touch of the strawberry-blonde upon her naked flesh. Work broke into her moody trance. Before her, three screens were flickering red. The franc was easing rapidly. Ann sold all her short-term holding and left her desk. Hazel, wrestling with her francs, looked up inquiringly.

'Got to pee,' Ann lied, explaining her trip to the loo.

Inside the cubicle, the words of the receptionist at the de Stael clinic echoed in Ann's head. Petra was quite strict. Ann yanked up her skirt and thumbed down her black tights. Petra made the rules and was very firm. Scrabbling to peel down her panties, she thrust her soft buttocks up against the cold white tiles and splayed her thighs.

Petra. Strict. Very firm. Ann's fingertips flew down to her pussy and teased the sticky lips apart. The heat of her cleft clouded the cold white tiles as she ground her buttocks slowly against their hard sheen. Wet fingertips now teasingly punished her urgent slit. Petra. Strict and firm. Ann's thumbtips strummed her clitoris savagely.

Petra. The studded gauntlets, dominantly squeezing her bare buttocks. Closing her eyes tightly, Ann conjured up images of her visit to the clinic – and the sensations of being ordered to strip naked and then examined by the strawberry-blonde. Arching violently as her climax gathered inside her, Ann remembered being face down on the leather couch, tonguing the dark hide as the cruel gauntlets punished her bare buttocks.

Another memory flooded in, taking Ann completely by surprise. The dorm prefect at her boarding school. Yes. Ann examined the fantasy greedily, thrilling to this buried treasure unearthed from her mind after seven – no, eight years. The dorm prefect. They had both shared a jealous 'pash' for Emily, the economics mistress. Yes. And the dorm prefect had taken her revenge.

Ann succumbed to her climax as it imploded down at the base of her tightened belly. She saw it all clearly. That Thursday afternoon in the deserted dorm. The dorm prefect had entered to discover Ann applying pink lipstick – strictly forbidden at the school. Pouncing, the prefect had exercised her legitimate right to punish, seizing the opportunity to unleash her jealous fury across Ann's navy-knickered buttocks with a slipper. Halfway through the harsh slippering, the dorm prefect had – against the rules – dragged down Ann's navy knickers and reddened the defenceless cheeks of her squealing victim mercilessly.

Ann started to come again, the wet heat pulsing and scalding the three fingers wedged up inside her tightly muscled warmth. Behind closed eyes, with her bottom hammering into the white tiles, she relished and rejoiced in the exquisite memory of dominance and discipline, crying out aloud at the sudden memory of having her bare bottom spanked severely with the leather-soled slipper.

Ann, her brain melting as her third – then fourth – orgasm ravished her, tried to recall what the dorm prefect had looked like. She willed the half-forgotten images to return, then saw them as clearly as a sharp black and white snapshot.

She saw the dorm, with its long line of lonely beds. Rain was splattering against the high windows. The green blanket on the bed. Her snow-white teddy bear. The blue uniform of the dorm prefect, the red-and-yellow tie, pleated skirt, white socks and polished black shoes. Her ponytail swishing as she bent down to scoop up the cruel slipper. Ann now across the prefect's thighs, thighs firm and bronzed on the hockey field. Warm thighs. A strong feral whiff of female arousal. Her skirt being flipped up to expose her tight knickers. The crack of the slipper. The sweet pain. Her blue knickers being savagely peeled down. Her hot bottom exposed, wriggling under the swish, swipe of the burning slipper strokes. Ann remembered being punished on the bare bottom by the jealous dorm prefect. Remembered squealing aloud, begging for the beating to cease. Remembered twisting round to see her chastiser through tear-filled eyes.

Ann froze – her fingers still thrust up her contracting pussy – as one image superimposed itself upon another. She staggered slightly and moaned, her hot juice dripping down onto her panties stretched between her quivering knees. In the dorm, on the bed, spanking the bare bottom – images which had detonated five furious orgasms – was Petra, the stern strawberry blonde.

Pulling up her panties and tights, after drying herself with toilet paper, Ann unlocked the cubicle door and headed for the sink to rinse her sticky fingers.

Hazel, applying a dab of 'emergency slap', eyed Ann intently. 'Nice pee?' she murmured laconically.

Eleven minutes before the appointed hour, Ann sat by the onyx desk. The receptionist, head bowed, tapped her keyboard sporadically, occasionally looking up to gaze into the ghostly blue screen. Ann silently recounted her forbidden calories, cursing every one. She squirmed in her chrome chair, squirmed with both delicious expectation and dread. She had broken the strict diet régime several times. Cake had been taken to bed along with her print-outs of the latest Tiger economies analysis. Low-fat sandwiches had been avoided at lunchtimes in preference for baps bulging with mayo. Lean fish or veal suppers had been skipped, guiltily replaced by fattening risotto or juicy thick steaks.

The receptionist motioned Ann to go in. In the cubicle, Ann stripped before being instructed to do so. Under Petra's grey eyes, the naked City girl stepped up onto the scales.

'Weight gain,' the German pronounced tersely. 'Put on that robe and sit down over there.'

Somewhat conscious of an anti-climax, of her sense of disappointment, Ann obeyed. She had, she quietly acknowledged, hoped to be thrilled by a sterner response. She had been wicked – yes, very wicked – eating all those forbidden foods. And wickedness must be punished.

Petra produced a mini-cassette and clicked it on.

'Speak into it here.' She pointed to the small mike. 'I want you to confess. To confess openly to all the forbidden things you have eaten in the past week.'

Ann took a deep breath. Naming each day of the previous week, she whispered her sins softly into the whirring machine. When she had finished, Petra picked up the cassette and clicked the rewind, her thumb poised upon the play button.

'Disrobe, Ann,' the strawberry blonde instructed.

The white towelling slithered to the floor. Ann, utterly naked, stepped aside.

'I am very disappointed. And I did warn you that I would be forced to take—'

'Certain measures,' Ann whispered huskily. 'Yes. I was warned.'

'Mount,' Petra ordered, dominantly slapping the leather couch.

Ann obeyed instantly, her tongue thickening in her dry mouth. This is it, she thought excitedly. The moment has come. Petra is going to punish me.

Petra stood alongside the couch, a whippy length of red rubber enema tubing gripped tightly in her right hand. Ann eyed it with dismay, shuddering as she imagined the probing rubber up between her buttocks, pumping warm water into her distended colon.

'When you eat inappropriately, Ann, the resultant fat tends to accumulate here –' she whipped the tubing down across Ann's upper thighs '– and here –' the rubber lashed against the curve of the nude's hip 'and here.' Petra whipped the red enema tube harshly down across the bare, upturned bottom.

Ann grunted softly and nestled her pubis into the leather. Dipping her tummy a fraction, she unconsciously eased her hips from the hide, offering her buttocks up to the lash. Petra trailed the tip of the tube across the striped cheeks, teasing their smooth curves.

'I am going to discipline you, Ann. I believe it is the only way to teach you to exercise the self-control weight-loss requires. With such self-discipline, in time, you will be able to avoid indulging in those pleasures which only lead to pain.'

Ann squeezed her buttocks expectantly, desiring yet dreading the impending lash. Instead of the snap-crack of the whippy rubber, she was startled to hear the sound of her own voice. Petra had switched the cassette on.

'Each time I hear you confess to eating a forbidden item, I am going to whip your naughty, fat bottom. Understand?'

'Yes,' Ann hissed, her tone more eager than penitent.

'The punishment will tone and tighten your buttocks and burn away several hundred calories.'

'I understand.'

Ann's voice from the tape announced the consumption of chocolate fudge cake.

'Forbidden,' Petra snarled. Swish, swipe. The red rubber whipped down, kissing the creamy cheeks and leaving a redder line of pain across their quivering globes. Ann squealed, her knuckles whitening as the gripped the sides of the black leather couch.

'Fried bacon and sausages,' her voice announced as her taped confession continued.

'Forbidden,' replied Petra briskly, whipping the rubber tubing down once more to lash the bare buttocks savagely.

For six and a half long, agonising minutes, Ann's detailed account of her wilful disobedience to the strict diet filled the air. No less than nine times did Petra have to bring the rubber down to swipe-stripe the nude's ravished cheeks.

The following week, a fault in the steam room left all the cubicles moist and sweltering. Petra had stripped down to a black mesh bodystocking, stretched tightly over her firm breasts and supple thighs. Ann glimpsed the pert little nipples straining at the black fabric. Her own buds rose up in response. The heat became oppressive. By the time Ann had been stripped naked, weighed and then intimately inspected, Petra had discarded the mesh bodystocking, and turned to her client wearing only a stern smile.

'Good. Only a slight weight gain. I think we had better deal with that at once. Come here, over my knee.'

Ann, thrilling to the stern command, bowed her head and eased herself across the thighs of the seated strawberry-blonde. As her naked breasts brushed against Petra's thighs, her nipples grazed their mulberry peaks into the German's oiled flesh. Ann shivered pleasurably. A firm, controlling hand alighted at her nape; a firmer hand began to massage her proffered buttocks. Ann snuggled down, eager for her bottom to be deliciously blistered.

'I am going to spank you, Ann. Spank you very hard. I will not cease until you have achieved orgasm,' the weight-specialist pronounced in a clinical tone. 'Orgasm is an excellent method of reducing surplus weight. All this wicked eating of yours is, I believe, symptomatic of a deeper craving. It is that craving I must seek to satisfy. But more of that, later,' she whispered, palming the smooth buttocks urgently. 'We can discuss the matter in detail after your punishment.'

Digging her toes into the tiled floor, Ann squirmed until her rounded cheeks were poised perfectly for their pain. Submitting her buttocks up to her chastiser, she squeezed her thighs together until her cleft became a thin flesh-crease.

'Relax your buttocks. I want them soft for the spanking,' Petra commanded, then warned her naked victim to remain absolutely silent throughout the pain of punishment and the subsequent pleasure of her orgasm.

The spanking commenced: eight staccato slaps of firm palm down across soft flesh. Despite Petra's stern injunction, the brisk onslaught tore a soft scream from Ann's lips. The pace of the punishment slackened, the spanking being delivered more slowly but more stingingly. Ann writhed and squirmed, now anxious to escape the measured spanks raining crimson pain upon her helpless bottom, but Petra's grip tightened at the nape of the nude's neck and her spanking hand cracked down with increased ferocity.

Jerking her hips across her punisher's lap, Ann surrendered to the mounting sensation unfolding in both her belly and in her brain, the bittersweet delight of submitting utterly to the dominant strawberry-blonde. Crying out gently, Ann acknowledged the butterfly of pleasure-in-pain as it opened up its wings in her belly and fluttered down the walls of her spasming muscles below.

Spank. The ringing, stinging blow cracked down, rocketing her into a sudden release of liquid ecstasy. Juicing freely – Petra's thighs became slippery – Ann moaned and came.

'Excellent,' the German hissed, sensing the wet heat on her flesh. She paused, her spanking hand hovering above the cheeks rippling in orgasm.

Spank. Spank. Spank. Just as the first climax ebbed, Petra cracked her hand down harshly, relaunching her victim into a fresh paroxysm.

'Now it is time to speak more intimately of those cravings,

Ann. Cravings we must attempt to satisfy once and for all.'

Ann froze as she felt Petra's fingertip worrying her sticky anal whorl. Sinking down across the smooth, wet thighs, she unclenched her cheeks. The fingertip probed dominantly, slipping into Ann's heat. The finger between her cheeks launched Ann into another orgasm. Her third climax. Its removal, two minutes later, triggered off her fourth.

As Ann screamed softly, Petra bent her head down to kiss the punished cheeks.

Showered and towelled, her sore bottom was treated to the soothing balm of talc. Petra applied it to Ann's reddened cheeks with the palm of her spanking hand. Ann trembled with delight, relishing the notion that the hand which had brought a blaze of pain to her bare buttocks was now spreading the silky talc across the chastised flesh.

'Will-power is so important Ann,' Petra whispered, her lips a mere inch from the bare bottom. 'I will have to train you to resist. The training will be painful, but the results will be most satisfactory. I want you face-down upon the couch, please.'

Shivering with pleasurable anticipation, Ann mounted the stretch of polished hide, conscious of Petra's grey eyes at her cleft as it briefly parted wide. Face down, as instructed, she whimpered as she felt her wrists being drawn together above her buttocks. Petra bound them tightly together with a short length of waxed cord. Another length of cord bit into the soft flesh of her ankles as they, too, were tightly bound.

'Be silent,' Petra commanded, fingering the bondage to test it. 'Remember, the pain quickly ignites into a burning pleasure.'

Ann moaned into the leather.

'Do you like chocolate?'

The sudden question caught Ann completely by surprise. She answered with simple honesty, nodding vigorously.

'I thought as much. Here you are,' Petra said silkily, placing a delicious Nantes truffle – an epicurean favourite from the Kremlin to Kuwait – down upon the dark leather, eight inches from Ann's parted lips.

Twisting in her strict bondage, Ann strained to look up over her shoulder at the strawberry-blonde. For me? she asked silently through raised eyebrows of disbelief. For you, the slightly perspiring naked German nodded in silent reply.

Wriggling now to overcome the ropes at her wrists and ankles which hampered her considerably, Ann inched her nakedness towards the waiting Nantes truffle, dragging her bare breasts deliciously against the leather. Seven inches. She lunged, lips parted, nostrils flared. Five inches.

Snap, crack. Snap, crack. Petra lashed the swaying buttocks with a short strap. Ann shrieked and collapsed down into the polished hide.

'Move. Come on, piggy. Get your chocolate,' Petra barked.

Ann shrank back an inch or two in recoil from the glistening truffle. She shook her head, denying and disowning her desire for it.

Crack. Crack. The strap whistled down, snapping harshly across her bunched cheeks. Ann squealed aloud, her raw note of suffering echoing around the cubicle. The strap dangled over her whipped cheeks.

'Eat the truffle,' the German thundered. Then the strap spoke again. 'Eat.'

Ann pleaded aloud for mercy as a fifth and then a sixth red weal was planted by the cruel strap across her scalded bottom.

'Eat it,' Petra instructed, supremely dominant with her strap raised above the whipped cheeks.

Sobbing softly, Ann squirmed herself closer to the truffle. Crack. Above her punished cheeks, her bound wrists writhed. Crack. Her fingers splayed out in a reflex of pain. Crack. Her tongue flattened into the black leather surface of the couch. The truffle, aromatic and maddeningly desirable, lay an inch from her teeth. Crack. Driven on by the swiping, searing strap at her buttocks, she wriggled in renewed agony and strained forward, closing her mouth down over the exquisite morsel. Its creamy softness exploded in her mouth. Crack. The strap exploded across her ravished bottom. Trembling on the brink of a violent orgasm, she sank down like a stone into the depths of her sweet misery.

Chocolate melts at body heat. The truffle filled Ann's mouth, smothering her squeals. Crack. Her buttocks quivered and spasmed at the leather strap's lash. Face down into the black couch, she guzzled and dribbled, a spindle of chocolate-stained saliva oozing from her lips. Her belly tightened. She came. Further down the couch, at the warmth where her pubis kissed the hide, her other lips dribbled, a spindle of sticky quicksilver oozing out to smear the polished sheen.

At lunchtime, three days after Petra's aversion therapy based on the pleasure-pain principle, Ann left her work desk and, avoiding the express lift, took the eleven flights of stairs at the rear of the office block down to the busy street below. Along the street – past the deli, where Hazel was allowing her latest overnight conquest to buy her a hot salt beef on rye – and past the other sandwich bar was The Kiosk. Ann paused, gazing intently at the pyramids of crystallised ginger, chocolate fudge and Russian caramels.

She pressed against the plate glass, like a groom against his bride in their honeymoon bed. Her tongue peeped out between her lips as she espied the pyramid of pineapple and marzipan creams. A confusion of responses ravished her. As her mouth watered for the tempting confections, the muscles in her belly contracted, shooting darts of stabbing arousal down to her pussy. Suddenly, her bottom felt hot and raw, just like the salt beef Hazel was devouring twenty yards away. Hot and raw, as it had felt after the kiss of Petra's strap across its nakedness.

Ann felt slightly giddy. Steadying herself against the plate glass, she squeezed her thighs together. She was coming: right there in the busy lunchtime street. Jerking her face away from the tormenting display of delicious sweets and chocolates, she slumped heavily against the window, hammering her hips against the glass. She came with a squeal, stopping a dozen onlookers in their tracks, and ground her pubis into the hard glass. The paroxysms were so powerful, when she opened her lust-bleary eyes, the first thing they saw was the pyramid of Russian caramels tumbling down into the tissue below. The second thing they saw was Hazel, attentively escorted by her overnight conquest.

'Chocolates, darling?' he murmured. 'Which ones do you want?'

Hazel's eyes met Ann's in the reflecting glass.

'I want what she's having,' Hazel grinned.

'Good. Very good. Four pounds lighter,' Petra announced. 'And already looking – and certainly feeling – trimmer.' The grey eyed German's firm hands swept up along Ann's thighs and cupped, then squeezed, each naked buttock. 'Down from the scales. I propose to start a new programme with you this week.'

Ann dismounted and watched the digital reading revert to a line of blinking red zeros.

'New programme?' she echoed, her voice softly submissive.

'Come,' Petra beckoned, leading the nude across to a deserted corner of the nearby gym area. 'We will be alone here for the next hour. I arranged it this way. Over here.'

Ann followed the strawberry-blonde over to the wall bars, her naked feet padding silently upon the wooden floor.

'Turn and face the wall bars,' Petra instructed.

Ann turned. Her breasts collided with the horizontal bar. She inched away from it, peeling her heavy bosom from the shining wood.

'Arms up. No, a little higher than that. Now grasp the bar. Good,' Petra directed. 'Now climb. A good metre clear of the floor.'

Hanging down from the wall bar, her arms stretched and aching, Ann's breasts bumped against the wood, her toes pointing straight down like a ballerina. Her bunched buttocks, naked and beautifully rounded, hung like peaches ripening on the branch.

Petra mounted the wall bars, catlike, and stealthily stole up alongside the suspended nude. 'I am going to secure you, Ann. Do not be alarmed and do not struggle.'

Ann's tiny toes danced frantically in the empty air as handcuffs – two pairs, one at each wrist – were snapped into place.

'Close your eyes, my sweet,' Petra purred.

My sweet. The words exploded in Ann's brain. The dominant mistress was dispensing a touch of tenderness to her willing slave. Ann wriggled with pleasure, unaware of any latent irony in the words. For Ann, the lonely City girl, it was merely a term of intimate endearment.

A soft rustling filled the silence. Petra crushed up against her victim swinging gently in suspended bondage. Ann squirmed as she felt the strawberry-blonde's breath on her face. Something firm, cool and surprisingly solid was being pressed up against her lips.

'Open wide,' Petra commanded, her tone dominant once more.

What could it be? What manner of confection was shaped and fashioned like – like a lipstick? Or a fat bullet? Ann's mind whirled in a frenzy of anticipation.

'I said open your mouth,' the German hissed.

Pleasurably stung by the severity of the waspish instruction, Ann parted her lips – and moaned as the smooth phallus slid in to fill her wet warmth. It was, she realised without having to peep, an ivory dildo. The curved shaft played upon her flattened tongue, then teased the sensitive roof of her mouth. Ann jerked in her strict bondage as she sucked hard.

The dildo was slowly removed. Ann whimpered, mourning its loss. With it went Petra: Ann sensed the blonde's departure from the wall bars and heard her land softly down upon the gym floor.

A slow minute passed. Another. Soft grunts filled the silence. The sounds were unmistakable. Petra was using the dildo on herself. Ann thrilled to the image of the ivory nuzzling the stern blonde's pussy, then probing deeply. Petra gasped aloud and Ann writhed in response to the carnal moan, bucking in her bondage so that her breasts squashed into the hard wood at her nipples.

Was Petra kneeling, her thighs apart over the erect phallus? Ann burnt to risk a swift glimpse, but obeyed the stern injunction not to look. The image tormented her. How was Petra spearing herself with the wicked length? And where? Ann suddenly shuddered at the thought of the ivory inching up between the strawberry blonde's rippling buttocks.

A shrill scream filled the gym, then silence returned. A little later, Ann sensed – then felt – Petra's presence alongside her at the wall bars. A feral tang flooded Ann's nostrils. It was the haunting whiff of Petra's wet arousal. Ann mewed aloud as the tip of the dildo visited her mouth like a lipstick, pushing the top lip up with brutal tenderness.

'Lick,' Petra whispered.

Tongue flickering, Ann obeyed.

'Now open wide.'

Ann's tremulous lips parted to accept the probing shaft.

'Suck,' came the command.

Leaving her victim with the dildo firmly in her mouth, Petra dropped down onto the gym floor and scooped up a short whip. Planting her feet apart, she carefully judged the distance between herself and the bare buttocks above to within a centimetre.

Crack. Crack. The thin whip lashed up against the cheeks. Ann grunted, twisting in her bondage, her cry of pain smothered by the dildo deep in her mouth.

Eleven strokes later, Petra tossed the whip aside and sprang up the wall bars. Alongside her moaning victim, she slowly removed the hard, curved shaft.

'Open your eyes and look at me,' Petra whispered.

Ann turned her tear-filled eyes towards the dominant gaze of the grey eyed German. Inching closer, Petra kissed Ann's mouth firmly.

'From now on,' she whispered huskily, 'I am all the sweetness you desire. I will cure your craving.'

Their lips met hungrily.

'Yes,' Ann panted. 'Yes.'

Petra withdrew, smiling at Ann's sudden whimper for more.

'No,' the German said sternly. 'You will only get sweets if you are very, very good. Very good, very obedient and utterly mine.'

Ann nodded submissively, yearning for the sugared dominance of the strawberry-blonde's mouth upon her own. Petra, reading the signs of surrender, returned her lips to kiss Ann savagely – then drove her tongue deeply where the dildo had just been.

A rumour had swept Frankfurt at nine minutes past ten. By ten sixteen, all the screens on the trading floor were flickering red. For half an hour, the striped shirts battled over their banks of phones. The screens returned to blue.

Ann eased back in her chair and opened her drawer for a tissue to dry her damp palms.

'Hey,' Hazel called out, thinking the tissues to be sweets, 'give me one of those. My sugar level's as low as the lira.'

Ann tried to close her drawer but was to late to stop Hazel from swooping down behind the tissues and snatching up an ornate silver chocolate box.

'Wow. Fancy chocs,' Hazel pronounced, scanning the expensive Old Bond Street label.

Ann swivelled in her chair, her breasts bulging as she stretched up to retrieve the box.

'I'll only pinch one,' Hazel promised, stepping back and keeping the box aloft. She flipped the lid open. Her eyes grew wide as she gazed down at the contents. Suddenly she giggled. Her hand jerked and spilled the contents onto the grey carpet.

Several traders and a few brokers – who had gathered with amused tolerance to witness the horseplay – gasped aloud. Down on the carpet lay a smooth, nine-inch ivory dildo.

Hazel, affectionately known by the striped shirts as The Bike – all of them had ridden her – picked the dildo up. 'Now that's what I call a sweet tooth.'

Scandinavian Mischief

It was that time of the year again. Bad-tempered crowds in the shops. Tired old repeats on the yawning TV screens. Police vans prowling through the dirty slush, their stubby aerials trailing tinsel. Christmas.

Roy decided to give the works Christmas party a miss. Slade at sonic boom pitch, chicken in a basket and limitless lager. Just a rowdy 'Seventies night' with plastic mistletoe thrown in. As a security guard at the works, he was a loner anyway. Neither part of the management and definitely not one of the boys.

Sneaking out, he was cornered by a gaggle of tipsy girls from packing. After two hours in the pub across the road, they were unusually willing to let him frisk them – a task he always left to his more confident colleague. Breasts and thighs encircled him, crushing him up against the wall. Roy took the line of least resistance and slunk into the works canteen, merging into the shadows at a corner table.

The new canteen committee had made a bit of an effort. There were silver and purple balloons. A real tree: Roy caught the pungent whiff of crushed pine needles. The big rumour was that the committee had booked a hot act.

Roy went up to the bar. The two young barmaids – all thighs and eyes – were just about coping with the boisterous men crowding round the pumps. Up at his end of the bar, Roy waited patiently for the maturer blonde to serve him. She had a generous bosom, the deep cleavage displayed enticingly by the tight-fitting bodice of her black bustier. Roy furtively eyed it beneath the stretch of her straining silk blouse. She had broad, strong hands. Hands that excited him. He sensed their strength as she squeezed out a wet bar cloth. He briefly imagined them around his balls – squeezing, squeezing hard as she forced him to pay homage to her swollen breasts. His cock stirred and lengthened in his trousers as he waited for his drink.

She bent down to snap off the metal cap of a pineapple juice. Her bosom bulged, the satin globes rippling deliciously. Roy wanted to drown in them, to be smothered by their warm weight. His cock twitched and raked up inside his shorts as he appreciated her covertly. Indifferent to the two young lovelies further down the bar, he only had adoring eyes for the stern-faced, big-bosomed blonde. Her dark eyes were hard; the crimson lipstick gave her mouth a touch of cruelty. A woman to kneel down before and adore. A woman to worship on both knees, writhing in the cold heat of her supreme indifference. Roy sagged his knees and eased himself in against the bar, crushing the tip of his gathering erection into the hard wood.

'Yes?' she snapped. Roy thrilled to her white flash of teeth. The blonde was tired, her tone deliciously impatient.

Roy dithered, relishing her severity. He asked for a bottled beer, mumbling.

'What was that?' she snapped.

Roy repeated his order, took the bottle and glass and paid with a twenty.

'Nothing smaller?' she sighed, ill-concealing her exasperation.

Roy was in heaven. He closed his eyes as he waited for his change, briefly picturing the dominant bar maid pouring his drink into a large ashtray and making him go down before her on all fours to lap it up like a whipped cur. Whipped. He whimpered softly to himself. He opened his eyes to find the heaviness of nineteen pound coins weighing it down. The blonde's breasts bounced as she turned away angrily. Roy went back to his table deep in the shadows, thrilling to her dismissive scowl. As he sat, nursing his glass of pale ale and his painful erection, he examined and enjoyed every moment of his brief encounter with the dominant blonde barmaid. He had annoyed her. She had been brusque. It had been perfect.

Pulling the paper plate towards him, Roy mechanically ate cold chipolata sausages on sticks. There was no mustard or brown sauce handy – not without having to stand up and ask the giggling girls at the next table. Hating any unnecessary contact with such girls, he ate the sausages blandly unseasoned. Such girls always made him blush, but there was something about that big, busty barmaid. That stern-faced, plump blonde.

Peeping over to the bar from the safety of the shadows, Roy's eyes worshipped her ripely rounded breasts as she bent to pull pints. He dwelt on her deep cleavage, imagining its silky warmth as he buried his face into it, smothering and choking as she forced him to worship. Once more, he imagined himself kneeling down before her, trembling slightly, begging for permission to strain his mouth up to kiss them reverently. Permission denied, the red lips would snarl. Then her strong white hands – Roy was forced to open his eyes to glimpse them – would slowly unbutton his trousers and palm his engorged length. He opened his eyes once more – her right hand was gripping an erect pump handle and pulling it slowly – then shut them tight. He shivered as he thought of his cock in her hand, her thumbtip playing with his wet snout. Would she wank him slowly, dominantly, as she lowered her heavy breasts down over his upturned face?

Gulping greedily to rinse away the sour taste of arousal from his mouth, Roy drank his pale ale in one swallow. He remained in his seat, idling with the empty glass. He would not go for a refill just yet. He'd wait until it got busier, until the blonde was rushed off her feet. Then he'd go and find some way of deliberately making her angry – upsetting her to earn himself a delicious tongue-lashing.

The buzz in the centre of the canteen became audible. 'Stripper's here.' All heads turned to the double doors expectantly. There was a blast of taped drum-roll. A chorus of shouts and whistles. The excited hush as four young men, their naked torsos oiled and gleaming, their heads decked with green plastic antlers, entered the canteen. They each hauled on lengths of twisted red rope, dragging a semi-naked female Santa on her sleigh.

Another taped drum-roll. Fuzzy, not crisp. An echoing

announcement. 'Ladies and gentlemen –' the whine of feed-back '– all the way from the frozen North to melt the . . .' More feedback distortion.

Santa skipped off her sleigh and the human reindeer shuffled off, their PVC shorts shining, the little bells dangling between their thighs jingling faintly.

Santa was a heavy blonde thirty-something. A fit piece, Roy thought appreciatively – he couldn't go for anything younger than himself. He peeped at the little red tunic, his eyes bewitched by the white fur trim skirting her large bottom. Exactly the type of bottom he wet-dreamed about – heavily plump, superbly curved. A mature woman's buttocks. Her thighs were great, the black fishnets' stretchy sheen exquisite. Powerful thighs that would capture and grip a kneeling worshipper's eager face. Roy's throat tightened as he studied the black, knee-length leather boots and the elbow-length latex gloves. It was just like one of his special pictures – pictures he kept under his mattress – come to life. His pulse quickened and his cock rose up stiffly.

She had a little sack over her left shoulder. As she swung it down between the parted feet of her black boots, Roy glimpsed her white balconette bra. His favourite bondage for the female bosom. A balconette always denoted heavy breasts – swollen mounds of satin softness to drown in. A low-cut, half-cupped, delicious confection such as a balconette – his survey of lingerie brochures informed him – always meant a full, proud bosom. A bosom that demanded devotion.

Another taped drum-roll. The canteen lights dimmed and a spot-light raked the sea of sweaty, eager faces below. The spot picked out a young blonde who, fingered by the piercing beam, squirmed and giggled. Santa approached, dipped into her sack and drew out a short, rubber dildo. Raucous applause. The latex-gloved hand guided the rubber dildo down to the blonde's mouth. More applause, much of it obscene enthusiasm. Just as the spot swept away, Roy saw the blonde tucking her gift down into a red plastic handbag.

Another drum-roll – prolonged, to allow the spot-light to zig-zag teasingly. The blade of light stopped, quivering, freezing an elderly man in the act of eating a chicken leg. It was Stan from maintenance. Everyone laughed. His name was shouted out as Santa weaved between the crowded tables towards him. She produced a packet of coloured condoms. Stan gamely tried to inflate one, but his chicken-greasy lips failed him. Someone snatched down a silver balloon and patted it between his legs. More ribald laughter. The balloon burst. The spot died and Santa skipped away.

Roy stole a glance across at the big blonde behind the bar. She was repairing a broken red fingernail, filing it down in the half light of the tiny lights above the optics. He'd go now – go and interrupt her – and bask in her waspish anger.

Suddenly, just as Roy rose from his table, the drum-roll crashed and he blinked, blinded by the strong spot-light. Roy twisted to escape, hating being exposed to the crowded room. Santa streaked towards him like a torpedo. He was sunk. She was at his table. Roy could smell her body make-up, and the polished leather boots. She produced – to cheers – a short, supple whip and cracked it sharply. The cheers grew into a wall of sound. Tapping the table top sternly with a straightened, latex-sheathed index finger, Santa toyed with the little whip, playing its lash against Roy's belly.

Roy's knees buckled and his head swam. Laughing girls from adjoining tables pounced on him, pulling down his trousers and pants as they bent him over the table. Bare-bottomed, he lay sprawled beneath Santa's cruel whip. She tapped his bottom twice.

'Give it to him good and hard,' voices urged.

'Bastard security,' another yelled.

The cry was taken up. Santa turned to her audience in the darkness, and held up her latex finger to her red lips. They fell silent.

'Six of the worst?' she cried.

They brayed their coarse approval. Turning back to address Roy's buttocks, she lightly whipped him six times. He barely felt the sharp sting, but burnt with fierce shame. They all cheered and clapped. The spot-light swept away, leaving Roy belly down across the table, struggling to pull up his pants and uniform trousers. Santa strode away, her long leather boots creaking in the darkness.

She turned and dashed back to collect her sack abandoned on the floor by Roy's table. Bending down to retrieve it, she glanced up at Roy. Their eyes met. Briefly. Then she glimpsed his massive erection gouging into the paper plate that had held the chipolatas.

Romping away to handcuff a redhead caught in the spotlight – applying the plastic cuffs at the laughing woman's ankles – Santa left Roy whirling in delicious confusion. His brief sense of shame was now a burning bliss. He thrilled to the memory of the leather-booted Santa with the shining latex gloves. The short whip above his helpless buttocks. The stinging snap of the lash across his flesh. Trousered and back upon his chair, Roy could hardly sit straight, so painful was his engorged shaft.

His trembling fingertips brushed against his empty glass. Automatically, he looked across the bar. The busty blonde was eating salt and vinegar crisps. Roy sat enthralled as she twiddled her red-nailed fingertips after popping a yellow crisp in between her scarlet lips. She sucked on the damaged nail. Roy shuddered.

She has seen my bare bottom. My bare bottom – being whipped. The thought coursed through him like an electric shock, leaving his body stunned yet tingling. The dominant beauty behind the bar had leisurely witnessed his bottom being bared and lashed. The realisation tightened Roy's belly into a knot. He felt his balls contract, and the soft ache of his imminent orgasm.

The swollen-breasted, cruel-mouthed barmaid with the hard eyes had seen him being whipped – had witnessed his bare-bottomed humiliation. Roy shrank back in the shadows, desperately fishing out his swollen cock. Guiding into his empty half-pint beer glass beneath the table, he sat bolt upright as he stared adoringly at the blonde barmaid – and came violently.

Out in the raw night, Roy shivered beneath the unreal light of a sodium street lamp. He'd get a black taxi soon. One coming back along this road from the train station. All the mini-cab phones had been constantly engaged when he had tried in the canteen foyer.

A tiny orange light winked in the distance. Roy waved. The cab's black shiny nose swung in towards him in instant response. The cab pulled up with a squeak of brakes. The driver deftly swung his arm back outside to open the rear door. Footsteps scampered across the frozen slush. It was a woman, her breath a silver cloud at her red lips in the chill night air. She was swathed in a black, hooded cape.

'Go shares,' she pleaded, shivering.

Roy agreed – reluctantly, too shy to argue – and found they were both heading in the same direction. Sitting back in the weak yellow light in the rear of the cab, Roy stared fixedly out of his steamy window, dreading the moment when she might speak. Roy worshipped women – from afar. As the cab cornered, they rolled, thighs touching briefly. Roy shrank from the sudden intimacy of her animal warmth.

She stretched out a long leg. Tempted, Roy peeped down slyly. He saw the black, shiny boot. Glancing swiftly across at her, he met her smiling gaze. It was Santa. Roy's heart hammered.

'Enjoy yourself?' she murmured, shrugging off the heavy cape to reveal the skimpy red outfit trimmed with white fur high at her fish net meshed thigh.

Roy blushed furiously and squirmed in his seat. The movement of his lightly whipped buttocks against the leather reminded him of his delicious shame at her latex sheathed hands.

'I think you did,' she teased. 'I saw your cock.'

The cabbie's eyes flashed up into the mirror, scanning her face and then Roy's.

'So big,' she laughed. 'You naughty boy. And after only six strokes. Do you think it could stand another dozen?'

They both got out at Roy's flat. He tipped the grinning cabbie a fiver. He didn't mean to – anxious to escape the knowing leer, he simply didn't hang around for the change.

'No. You need not make me coffee just yet. I will tell you when to do so later,' Santa replied as Roy held up the jar of instant and shook it. 'I want to go to the loo.'

Reddening slightly, Roy nodded to a door at the end of the passage. Originally, it bore the sign 'Here it is'. She stomped back immediately, her pretty face a mask of severity.

'I can't use that. It isn't properly clean. Get in there and scrub it out this instant,' she barked.

Roy's heart thumped wildly, It had begun. He froze, like a child spinning out its delight by delaying the process of unwrapping a present. Slow down, he told himself. Slow down and luxuriate in every delicious moment of domination.

'This instant,' she snapped, her hands planted on her hips, her leather boots wide apart.

Roy nodded submissively.

'Wait. You'll serve me naked, my boy. Take off your clothes and show me your bottom. Then get down on your hands and knees and scrub that toilet floor. I'll be there, watching you, making sure you do a thorough job.'

With trembling hands, Roy tore off his clothes and bent over, touching his toes. His bare buttocks rose up for her intimate perusal. He felt her latexed fingertips skim across the tightened curves of his cheeks. His cock speared up, tapping his belly as it throbbed.

'Kneel.'

He knelt down before her, gazing up adoringly. Still dressed in her Santa costume of red tunic, black fishnets and boots – with the sinuous second skin of the elbow-length gloves – she looked magnificent. With her red pixie hood down, her golden curls tumbled in wanton disarray. Slowly, deliberately, she swept her hair up and fixed it into a severe ponytail. Her face was, Roy noticed, sharply featured with her hair up like that. Almost vixenish. The rosebud lips tight and cruel. His cock throbbed as it saluted her. Santa acknowledged the tribute, her eyes narrowing as she gazed down dominantly upon her naked slave.

'I know what you want for Christmas, my boy. And you shall most probably get it. If you obey me absolutely. First,' she continued crisply, adjusting the white cup of her balconette with black, latex-covered fingers, 'you will go in and scrub the toilet floor. In you go – no,' she barked. 'Keep down on all fours. I want to see you crawl.'

Roy shuffled happily along the lino, crawling submissively along the black and white diamonds of the loo floor.

'That's the way,' she murmured approvingly, propelling him along with a sharp toe in his left buttock. 'Santa's little helper.'

She issued him with a toothbrush, scouring powder and a stale, stiff flannel. 'Now scrub. When I inspect it, it will be spotless. If it is not, you will lick it clean.'

Roy trembled with delight. Bending down to his humiliating task, he scrubbed vigorously, thrilling in the knowledge that she was standing over him, her hard eyes glaring down upon his bare, vulnerable bottom. She withdrew – he heard her rustling about in the kitchen cupboards – and returned, eating a festive mince pie.

'Keep scrubbing,' she commanded, her mouth full, as she positioned the toe of her polished boot beneath his dangling sac, then tapping the leather up against his balls. 'I'm going into your bedroom now. I am going to search all your secret hiding places and expose all your wicked little secrets.'

Roy flushed, ashamed and confused, yet thrilled to the image of her peeling back his mattress to find the lingerie brochures and the underwear section torn carefully from mail order catalogues. A few dry, prickling crumbs dropped down from her lips onto his bottom, trickling down into his cleft. He clenched his cheeks as her shadow fell upon him. She bent down, her index finger firm, and swept the latexed tip dominantly down the length of his cleft, ridding his sensitive flesh of the irksome crumbs. Spank. Spank. He jerked in ecstasy as the punishing gloved palm cracked across his helpless cheeks.

'Keep scrubbing, slave. I can hear you from your bedroom.'

The boots returned, just as he had completed his menial duties with the toothbrush. Their measured tread, full of menacing promise, grew louder as Santa approached the toilet door.

'Very interesting little collection you've got. Boys like you who peep at such forbidden things deserve to be punished. Severely. And you do peep at those pictures, don't you?'

Quivering under the delicious interrogation, Roy raised his head to confess.

'Head down,' she snarled, instantly trapping his neck beneath her boot. 'I think I had better tell you that I haven't got the little whip.'

Roy slumped, signalling his disappointment.

'But I did find this,' she whispered. 'It will serve my purpose.'

What? What had she found in his bedroom to punish him with? A belt? He had no braces. A hairbrush? The supple plastic ruler from his desk?

'Bottom up, my boy.'

Eager for his pain, he inched his cheeks up. She tapped them with a wire coat-hanger gripped firmly in her gloved right hand. Roy swayed his hips invitingly. Santa whipped the coat-hanger down. He grunted aloud as it bit into him, right across the softest part of his curved cheeks. Swish, crack. Again, and then again. Pausing to inspect his thick shaft straining up against his belly, Santa resumed her dominant stance and swiped the wire coat-hanger down four more times across his buttocks, criss-crossing the suffering cheeks with deep pink lines of pain.

'I haven't got that little whip,' she repeated, standing back a little and planting the sole of her right boot down along his hot cleft. 'The barmaid, the big blonde with the blouse, bought it for a tenner.'

Roy whimpered with sheer delight, trembling on all fours as his imminent climax threatened to explode.

'But don't worry, my boy. She said she'd be putting it to good use,' Santa whispered, deftly treading the spiked heel of her boot into Roy's wet sphincter. 'She found your glass hidden under the table. The glass you spurted your naughty stickies into. Wicked boy,' she whispered, probing his anus with her cruel heel. 'That barmaid can't wait to meet you again. I hope Santa hasn't spoiled your surprise.'

Roy gasped aloud as he splattered his fierce ejaculation out across the toilet floor. It felt so thick and prolonged – as if some invisible hand was pulling a ball of twine down in his sac up through the core of his pulsing shaft. Panting, he wobbled on his aching arms and collapsed, face down into the plastic toilet seat, his arms encircled to embrace the stone cold bowl at his belly.

'Now look what you've done,' she rasped waspishly. 'I told you I'd make you lick it clean, and I meant it.'

In the bedroom, she tied his hands tightly behind his back.

Kneeling, he gazed at the three clothes pegs in the palm of her gloved hand levelled before his eyes.

They had just finished examining his collection of private pleasures. Pictures of shiny, stockinged legs; of heavily buttocked women in panti-girdles; of stern matrons in bathing costumes – and, most highly cherished of all, stern-faced models, large-bosomed, in a range of bras. Roy had cut them out from brochures and catalogues, using the ruler and craft knife on his desk, carefully mounting them with meticulous pains on blue squares of stiff card.

Santa had unearthed the treasure trove and spread them out across his bed. Roy had been forced to kneel at the bed and describe, in whispered tones of excitement, every picture in detail. Santa had spanked his bottom severely as he mumbled his words – seamed stockings; quarter-cups; lace trimming; silk gusset; peep-hole and suspender belt. Santa spanked him twice as he described each card. There were ten blue cards of A4 size and seventeen blue cards of the smaller A5 size. His bottom was very red. His bottom was very sore.

Santa made him bow down and kiss his favourite three pictures. Betraying his fantasies with Judas lips, Roy selected bra shots. Santa picked them up from the bed and spread them down before her kneeling slave. She knelt down alongside him. Enclosing her latex-gloved fingers firmly around his erection, she began to pump. Roy grunted as she gripped his hot spear and cried out with raw pleasure as she forced his spurting shaft down into the three blue cards – drenching the bewitchingly brassiered matrons with his wet joy.

The latex-gloved hand clenched. The clothes pegs disappeared beneath her shining fingers. She opened her hand. Roy whimpered with delicious dread.

He shrank back as the first plastic peg, a red one, pinched his left nipple.

'Don't be a baby,' she whispered. 'Submission to Santa must be total. Santa's little boy must be brave. There can be no true pleasure,' she reasoned patiently, as if with a child, 'without a little – or indeed a lot – of pain.' The second peg, a green one, snapped down over his right nipple.

Roy's cock twitched and nodded. His eyes flickered down to it, then flashed up fearfully at the third clothes peg.

'Now, where shall we put him?' Santa mused aloud, relishing his squirming terror.

Roy's hands writhed in their bondage. He inched away, shuffling backwards painfully, retreating from the horror of the nipping peg at his foreskin.

'Stay still,' Santa hissed vehemently. 'How dare you even think of attempting to defy me?'

'No – please—' he whimpered.

'Silence,' she interrupted sternly. Leaning forward, she tweaked the clothes peg open.

Roy, beads of sweat running into the corners of his eyes, groaned. He squeezed his eyes shut – then opened them wide as he felt the peg pinching his nostrils painfully. The terror left his eyes, instantly replaced with liquid adoration for the cruel tormentress in the red festive costume standing before him.

'You like the idea of being dominated by cruel matrons in their crisp, white underwear, don't you, my boy?' she teased.

Roy nodded, his face already hot and scarlet from the clothes peg at his nose. He was panting slightly.

'Can it really be true?' she wondered aloud, shrugging off her red fur-trimmed tunic to reveal the balconette binding her breasts. 'Would you really come if I were to simply subject you to my bosom? Let's see.'

She positioned him across the bed, face down. He started to splutter for air. Kneeling down behind him, she thrust her bosom up against his buttocks, then dragged her breasts down over his cheeks, before nipple-kissing their curves and then crushing the balconette's heavy, straining burden into his bottom. She kept up a clinical running commentary, describing each of her actions aloud. Roy responded so vigorously to the sound of her soft, stern voice that she told him a little Christmas story. About how she would masturbate him with a single red stiletto shoe, forcing his cock up into the narrow toe and jerking the high spiked heel until he flooded the supple leather with his pulsing quicksilver.

Roy almost came – but Santa pinched his wet snout together, denying him relief. He begged for another story. She took the clothes peg from his nose and fastened it to his foreskin. At his back, his bound hands jerked, the fingers splayed in delicious agony.

He pleaded for another story. Santa refused. He begged to be untied. To be punished. To be wanked. Anything but this exquisite limbo of torment.

Santa ignored him. In silence, she stood over him, rubbing the inner calf of her leather boot down between his cheeks and squashing his balls against the mattress. Grasping a fistful of his hair in her latex-gloved hand, she taloned him painfully and dominated him utterly. Reaching down, she curled the forefinger of her free hand in against her thumb, then flicked the clothes peg away. Roy came with a load moan, soaking the white sheet of his bed. Lifting her boot up, she kicked away the other two pegs from his nipples, then trod him down into the sheet, crushing his face into the warm semen.

She cooked beans on toast. Not very much in the Yuletide tradition, but she was hungry and ate them greedily. They sat at the kitchen table side by side, almost touching. Still naked, with his wrists bound behind his back, Roy had to watch his supper grow cold as Santa finished hers, then turned to feed him. She peppered and salted his beans vigorously. He grimaced as the first forkful skimmed his lips. Santa was stern. Roy swallowed them obediently but refused to open his mouth for any more.

'You will eat them, my boy. Every last one of them. I've cooked them specially for you. Now open wide.'

Roy shook his head vehemently and twisted his face away.

'Bad boy,' she snarled. Dragging her chair away from the table, she hauled him across her fishnet-sheathed thighs. The spanking was brisk and quite brutal, her black latexed hand leaving his helpless cheeks crimson after a relentless flurry of crisp swipes. He squirmed and bucked across her lap but Santa was very firm, pinning him down and showing no mercy to his bare bottom.

Twenty-six spanks later, she paused, fingering his hot cleft dominantly.

'Santa wants to know if her little man is hungry. Hm? Or does she have to make him really squeal for his supper?'

Broken, Roy sobbed his surrender. She guided the forkful to his lips and smiled as he swallowed obediently. She fed him until the plate was empty, then forced him to lick it clean. Still across her warm lap, he slumped in absolute submission.

'And don't you ever disobey Santa again,' she whispered, probing his sphincter with her index finger. 'I'm going to show you exactly what happens to naughty, disobedient little boys.'

Easing him down from her lap, she stood up, turned, then bent down to arrange him belly-down across the kitchen chair – making sure to trap his cock against the soft plastic seat. Dominating him – one gloved hand pinioning him down between his shoulder-blades – she spanked him again. The ringing blows echoed around the kitchen. She paused and stretched out for the condiments, then liberally sprinkled both black pepper and sea salt into his cleft. Writhing in renewed paroxysms of agony, Roy bellowed like a penned bull. The latex-gloved hand revisited his cheeks, swiftly delivering a final stinging salvo of a dozen harsh spanks.

With both buttocks blistered to her complete satisfaction, Santa mounted her weeping slave, kneeling on his back – a gloved hand taloning each shoulder – and trapping and squeezing his spanked cheeks between her leather boots. As the cool hide crushed his hot buttocks, she felt his naked body beneath her jerk and spasm across the kitchen chair. Riding him furiously, she pinned him ruthlessly until she sensed his body slacken, signalling the end of his agonisingly delicious ejaculation into the plastic seat. Dismounting, she grasped a handful of his hair and peeled him away from the chair, noting with satisfaction his wet belly and chest.

She watched late-night American football on Channel 5 while he slept. She wandered into his room and inspected him twice during the commercials as he lay naked and asleep. On her third visit, he stirred and gazed up at her, his eyes wide with servile adoration.

Santa raised her right leg up onto the bed, guiding the polished leather toe of her boot to his lips. Roy rose up eagerly to greet it, open-mouthed, but she trod his face down firmly into the pillow.

'Santa wants a little sleep,' she murmured.

Roy struggled free and pulled the duvet down, patting the sheet in a gesture of welcome.

'No,' she said sternly. 'I will take the bed; you can sleep on the floor.'

Moments later, she plumped the pillows and, sighing, peered down at her red-bottomed slave shivering on the carpet.

'Let me know if you are cold, won't you? Santa will soon find a way of warming you up.'

Roy shuddered – not from the cold, but from the promise of instant heat.

After he had brought her tea and toast, the following morning, she donned her red tunic, allowing him to finger it devotedly as he knelt down before her.

'Santa comes from Lapland,' she whispered, gently inching up the white fur-trimmed hem of her outfit. 'So lap.'

He shuffled forward on his knees and pressed his face into her exposed pubis, tonguing her nest and kiss-worshipping her pussy-lips through the stretch of her black fishnet tights. Closing his eyes, he inhaled deeply, snuffing up her feral scent.

'Lap,' she commanded, jerking her hips and smothering his face completely.

Roy whimpered, tormented by the sheen of the fishnets stretched across her hot sex. Maddened by the salty tang of her slit at his tongue tip, he longed to savour it raw. Devoting himself to the task of pleasing her – of pleasuring his strict Santa – he licked and sucked with increasing frenzy. Hampered by being bound by the wrists once more, he could not peel down the dark tights, or cup her soft buttocks and hug her to his face. Yearning to embrace her, and hold her tightly, his hands twisted in their tormenting bondage above his bare bottom. Soon, like a true slave, he found the suffering to be sweet – and thrilled to relish his desires being denied. Forced to kneel, naked and bound, he could only serve her with his lips and tongue.

Buckling slightly, Santa twisted her left boot inwards. Her polished leather boot grazed his cock. He spurted instantly, drenching her inner, upper thigh with his hot seed. The semen soaked into her fishnet mesh, causing it to glisten at her flesh.

'Naughty,' she whispered sternly, tapping his nose with her fingertip. 'Now look what you've done. I'm the one who's supposed to fill stockings. Not you mine.'

Pushing him aside disdainfully, she unzipped her boots, kicked them off and palmed down her sticky mesh tights. Presenting her hungry slit to his upturned face, she beckoned him dominantly with her curled index finger.

'Now get busy,' she ordered him, adding, 'there is a belt in the bedroom. If you need any encouragement, I will supply it.'

Two and a half minutes later, his chin was wet with her juice. Lapping, sucking and tonguing her savagely, he served her with submissive adoration.

Soon Santa was snarling softly. Rising up on her toes, she repeatedly wiped her labia down over his upturned face.

'Santa's coming,' she hissed, gripping her latexed fingers into him with vicious tenderness. 'You've been a good little boy. Santa always comes to good little boys.'

Silken Manacles

Safira had slept fitfully. In the distant blue hills surrounding her desert city, the jackals had cried all night. A lone silk merchant must have strayed from the track and perished. The jackals had been yapping as they quarrelled over his bones. Safira gazed from her narrow window, shading her eyes against the fierce sun. Yes. There in the haze, up in the azure sky, black specks betrayed the arrival of vultures, circling slowly over their skeletal feast in the rocks below.

Reaching out for her little brass bell, Safira shook it impatiently. The shrill tinkling brought a scamper of naked feet up the marble stairs. A soft tap on the cedar wood door was followed by the entrance of Nubia, Safira's slave girl.

'I will bathe,' the golden-limbed beauty announced, stretching her nakedness luxuriously in the milk-warm air. 'Be ready to oil and perfume me and dress me for the day.'

Safira, only daughter of the high priest, lived a life of absolute seclusion and was denied all companionship other than Nubia, her loyal slave. One day, soon, Safira would be anointed priestess to serve in the temple, alongside her father. The laws of the temple were strict. Safira must never know the company of men, or ever let her flesh be polluted by theirs.

In the secluded courtyard, behind the high walls which cast dark purple shadows even at noon, Safira bathed in the topaz waters of the small pool. Around the pool, green onyx frogs gazed unblinkingly through their diamond eyes. An ibis, the sacred bird, fashioned from beaten gold, kept evil spirits at bay.

Safira floated silently on the surface, her breasts proud and glistening. Her dark hair streamed out behind her. Between her parted thighs, her dark pubic nest spangled in the sunlight. Nubia knelt, head bowed, beside the pool while her mistress bathed. Only eighteen summers old, Nubia feared yet adored her older mistress – and felt a keen sorrow for Safira's exile from the teeming life beyond the high, imprisoning walls. Outside, in the bustling desert city, trade was brisk in slaves, silks, spices and gold. Whole oxen were roasted in the open market place, and bronzed men gambled and drank dark wine while beautiful girls baked fresh white bread. Lewd pipes and goatskin drums maddened the streets with sensual music – and the very air was delicious with perfume.

'The scent of sin,' Safira's father would warn his daughter solemnly. 'The stench of carnal pleasures. But you will never be sullied, Safira. You will remain pure and be fit to serve Aphrodite as her virgin priestess.'

Nubia recalled his many stern warnings and felt sad for her beautiful mistress, who was doomed to be forever denied all the pleasures of the flesh.

'Stop dreaming, girl. Night is the proper time for dreams,' Safira snapped, clapping her hands sharply. 'Bring me my towel.'

Nubia was at the edge of the topaz pool before her mistress, her golden nakedness gleaming, had risen from the dancing waters. The soft Egyptian towel embraced the dark-haired bather, clinging amorously to her ripely rounded breasts and heavy buttocks.

'Dry me, girl.'

Nubia patted the towel gently, drying the bather's breasts, belly and hips. Reaching out with encircling arms, she cupped Safira's swollen cheeks and dried them, parting the soft buttocks and driving the towel into the cleft with her fingertips. Safira grunted softly then parted her thighs.

'Dry me there,' she commanded. 'But be careful. I will be inspected by the elders in the temple before they anoint me. If that skein of silken skin that guards my maidenhead is damaged, they will cast me out from Aphrodite's hallowed ground.'

Nubia – who had been deliciously deflowered by a camel driver – gazed into the green eyes of her mistress and nodded. 'I will be careful, mistress.'

Kneeling, she peeled the towel away from Safira's naked body and, pinching up a corner of the exquisitely soft Egyptian cotton, dabbed it gently up between Safira's parted thighs. The green eyes widened and then closed tightly. Safira hissed and rose up on tiptoe, then reached out blindly to talon Nubia's hair as the towel kissed her pouting labia.

'Be more careful, wretched girl.'

Nubia squealed and squirmed as her mistress's hand punished her hair. Twisting to escape, she jerked the soft cotton upwards, rasping the tiny pink clitoris.

Safira moaned sweetly – a soft note from a song of sorrow. 'If you are not more careful, girl, I will take the whip to you.'

Stretched face-down on her damask divan, Safira ordered her slave girl to commence oiling her. Nubia knelt down alongside her mistress, her fingertips glistening with rose-scented oil. Working the unction into Safira's thighs, Nubia became absorbed in her task.

'You were outside the walls yesterday, in the city, girl.'

'Yes, mistress.'

'You went to the silver merchants, did you not?'

'Yes, mistress. Your father sent me to purchase two silver rings.'

'Did you get the rings?'

'No, mistress. The Persians, knowing I bore your father's purse, asked too much. I will return and beat them down to forty oblats.'

'You are wise for your years. You know much of the world.'

Nubia suddenly remembered the fierce breath of the camel driver at her lips – and his hands at her buttocks – and smiled.

'What was the city like? Busy?'

Nubia knew she was Safira's eyes, nostrils, mouth and ears. All the sights, tastes, sounds – were forbidden to the mistress but not to her slave-girl.

'There was trouble in the slave market,' Nubia replied, slowly palming the oil into Safira's buttocks.

'Trouble?' the mistress echoed, her voice sharp with interest.

'Two young slaves, brought in from beyond the Blue

Mountains, slipped their chains just as they were being auctioned. Money had been exchanged between the slave owner and their new mistress. The vizier was summoned to settle the dispute.'

'Who was found to be at fault?'

'The woman, the wife of the Sultan's bodyguard, petitioned the vizier, claiming that she should have her money returned.'

'And what did the vizier decide?' Safira murmured, offering her buttocks up to the firmly massaging hand.

'The slave owner kept her gold in his purse and said it was her misfortune that the two girls had escaped.'

'An interesting problem for the wise vizier,' Safira remarked.

'He ordered a search to be made. The runaways were quickly found and dragged back to the market place. As they were stripped naked, a wooden table from the wine house was brought out. The vizier ordered the naked slave girls to be forced across the table. The slave owner took his whip and gave them twenty lashes. They squealed and cried—'

'What kind of whip did he use to punish them with?' Safira demanded. 'A camel whip?'

'Yes, mistress. It snapped most cruelly across their buttocks, leaving its red mark across their dark flesh.'

'And?'

Nubia dragged her oiled fingertip slowly down Safira's cleft, thrilling to the touch of the silken buttocks as they tightened, trapping her finger between their swollen warmth. 'The vizier then took the camel whip and ordered the wife of the Sultan's bodyguard to flog the runaways. She was fierce, mistress,' Nubia whispered. 'The whipped girls squealed like suckling pigs under the sacrificial knife.'

Safira shivered and eased herself down into the divan. Her cheeks slackened. allowing Nubia's oiled fingertip to probe and enter her rosebud sphincter.

'All the music and laughter ceased. Even the jingling of the harnessed steeds fell silent. Only the brutal crack of the slicing whip and the squeals of the punished slaves could be heard throughout the market place.'

Nubia paused and slowly extracted her long finger. Dipping it into the pot of rose oil, she guided it back into Safira's sphincter, plunging it in deeply.

'Be careful, girl. Remember the whip.'

Nubia eased her finger out slowly and stroked Safira's cleft.

'And after the punishment of the slave girls, what was decided?' the mistress demanded.

'The vizier confiscated the money from the slave owner to pay into the city coffers and took the naked slave girls away with him.'

'For what purpose?'

'He led them away, red-bottomed and stumbling, proclaiming that he would enjoy them both before sunset.'

That night, the yapping of the jackals as they returned to their bleached bones drove sleep far from Safira's eyes. The air was warm and sticky. Restless, she tossed and twisted on her silken sheets, haunted by the memory of Nubia's account of the whipped slaves. Her yearning became like a hunger inside her. It was not the hunger of the belly that cold roasted fowls or sweet dates could assuage: it was a deeper craving, further down below her belly. An aching between her thighs.

She sipped some wine and nibbled at green grapes. But the thought of the whipping in the market place returned, causing her nipples to rise up and plague her with a pleasurable pain. Safira's wine-wet lips parted in a snarl. Inching her fingertips down to her dark pubic fringe, she gently strummed her outer labia, splaying the thick fleshy lips apart before raking her wet heat with a fingernail. Her hips jerked and her bottom pounded the silken sheets as her fingernail caught and rasped her exposed clitoris.

She knew she was on the very brink of danger. If she allowed her dabbling fingers to remain at her sex, she would tumble into the pit of shame – and exile from Aphrodite's temple. If her fingers probed her inner warmth, the badge of her honour would break, and her father's wrath would be extreme.

Scrambling across her silken bed, Safira snatched up the little brass bell and rattled it vigorously. Almost instantly, Nubia came into the bedchamber, her eyes wide with concern.

'Mistress?'

'I am lonely, girl. I would have company this night. Stay with me. Tell me more of the city. Talk to me of its delights until I fall asleep.'

'What of the city shall I speak?' Nubia murmured, sniffing the air of the bedchamber and shivering as her nostrils caught the odour of Safira's wet excitement. 'Mistress,' she whispered suddenly, 'you have not—'

'No, girl. But the temptation is almost too great. What is to be done?'

'Let me help, mistress,' the loyal slave girl replied. 'If I bind your hands together with manacles of silk, no harm can come to your maidenhead.'

'Wise words, girl. Let it be done.' Safira submitted her wrists up for their silken bondage, resting them together upon her naked bosom.

'No, mistress. Not there. Your fingers will stray to play with the buds of your breasts and be tempted – as the fingers of one walking through a ripening orchard are tempted to pluck the red cherry.'

'Can there be no relief for my torment tonight?' Safira wailed.

'Yes. Turn your face down into the silk, mistress.'

Safira obeyed, squashing her breasts into the stretched silk beneath. Nubia selected a length of raw silk, a cubit in width, six cubits long and, arranging Safira's hands above her buttocks, bound them tightly together at the wrists.

'Now, mistress,' she whispered, 'you are safe. And I will stay with you until you sleep. Perhaps I should tell of the men at their sport—'

'Yes,' her mistress hissed excitedly. 'Tell me of the young men at their lustful play.'

'Before sunset and the closure of the city gate, they race their steeds across the hot sands. Faster than the very wind—'

'No,' Safira barked. 'I do no wish to hear of their foolish acts of bravery. Tell me of their wanton sports. When they steal out at night, like cats do, to spill their seed.'

'I know little of that—'

'Liar. I'll whip you at sunrise, girl, if you deny me any more.

Tell me at once of the House of Pleasures.'

'I cannot, dare not do so—'

'No? Remember my whip, girl, and how it burns to kiss your soft buttocks.'

'Yes, mistress,' Nubia murmured, sliding alongside Safira on the cool silk bed. 'I will tell you of the House of Pleasures. Your hands are bound tightly. There can be no harm.'

Safira, her hands bound tightly out of temptation's way, eased her face down into her soft pillows. Nubia gazed up at the marble ceiling, studying the decoration of silver and gold stars. Their naked bodies touched as they nestled closely hip to hip, thigh pressing against soft thigh.

Nubia's velvety voice broke the silence:

'Before your father and the elders of the temple rescued me from my shame, I served wine to the visitors who came each night to the House of Pleasures. I came to know of their preferences, and how each man chose to indulge. Every month, on the night of the new moon, a Persian jade merchant would come to spill his liquid lust among the satin cushions. He cared not to mount and ride the girls as other men but would pay to watch two naked, perfumed girls punishing a third. The punished girl was drawn by a throw of the dice then forced to kneel, head bowed, and have her bottom caned. The nudes stood over her, one at either side, taking turns to stripe her slowly with golden rods of wood they call bamboo. It must surely be cut from an evil tree, so cruel is it upon a girl's bare flesh.

'The Persian would pull apart his robes and hold his manhood in his broad hand. It would grow and stand proud as he witnessed the canes lash the kneeling girl's buttocks. Then he would enclose his fist around his flesh-spear and urge the punishers to ply their whippy rods faster. Then his hand became busy at his lengthened manhood like the potter working at his column of wet clay. As the whipped girl began to squeal and whimper, he would fall down upon his knees and brush the canes aside. Shuffling up to her ravished buttocks, he would examine it closely, then bury his face into the striped cheeks – a choking cry in his own Persian tongue smothered by her punished flesh. Kissing and licking her bottom,

105

he would lean back and empty his hot seed over her. It would run in a silver stream down her arched spine and disappear in between her reddened cheeks. Drawing his hands together, like a sorcerer in his lair at some alchemical flask, the Persian would cup and squeeze her bottom until his seed ran out of her cleft.'

Nubia paused, and swallowed silently in the darkness.

'What a strange tale,' Safira murmured, her voice thick with excitement.

'It is a curious pleasure for a man, is it not, mistress, to watch a girl being caned severely, then use her hot cheeks for his dark pleasures?'

Safira, her face buried in the pillow, moaned sweetly. Behind her back, the fingers of her bound hands splayed out in mute ecstasy. 'Another story,' she hissed. 'Tell me more of the House of Pleasures.'

Nubia was silent for a moment, then spoke:

'The Janissaries were the most vigourous at their sport, and in truth the most generous afterwards. Also the most feared. When they rode the girls, it was always as the dusty lion takes the lioness – and always with whip in hand. They would mount the kneeling girl from behind. So excited were they that sometimes they would spear her in that place not fashioned for their manhoods—'

'You mean—'

'Yes, mistress. So blind in lust had they become, they did not care where they entered the girl's soft body. And they would use the whip to lash her thighs – or, most cruelly, her belly and even her bosom—'

In the darkness, Safira shivered and gasped aloud.

'The girls would scream softly but, from their shining eyes and twisted smiles, I knew that they took the pleasure well, often reaching paradise before those who rode them.'

Safira ground her breasts into the silk beneath, and tongued her satin pillow in muted anguish.

'There was one particular Janissary, I well remember, a fighter who had lost both arms against the fierce Mogul hordes. Several of the girls assisted him in his pleasure, helping him to perform the act. They would gently take his flesh out with their fingers,

106

but even as they did this kindness for him, he would shout out loud and splash their breasts, losing his seed before they could guide it into the waiting girl's open fig. At last, a solution to his torment was devised. It was decided that he should use the girl's mouth for his comfort. A girl with a wide smile was selected, and her lips were painted with deep red coral to entice him. Her hands were bound behind her back – just like yours, mistress –'

Safira cursed softly into the satin pillow at her lips.

'– so they were well matched for each other. She would curl up on the satin cushions and take his spear in between her reddened lips, and he would suck at her breasts and lick her belly, then bury his mouth into her wet heat. Much satisfaction was derived from this arrangement, mistress, although it is a custom and usage strange to these parts.'

Safira twisted and shivered in silence as Nubia continued recounting her memories from the House of Pleasures.

'The most curious practice I witnessed there was when a young man, one much given to astrology and music and who had no sign of any facial hair—'

'I have heard of him. His voice is like a girl's, when he is in song. What of him?'

'He would come to the House of Pleasures only to take fruit.'

'Fruit?' Safira echoed, wonderingly.

'From the thighs of a dark-eyed woman who is the eldest there.'

'I do not understand what you mean, girl.'

'I mean, mistress, that he would kneel before her and she, naked, would place ripe figs at her place of Venus. Straining his neck up, he would plant his lips upon the fruit and eat greedily, taking in some of her juices with the sweet flesh of the palm.'

Safira cried out like an owl at midnight.

'First, it would be a fig. Then the luscious dates. He would lap and suck as the camel does when coming upon an oasis after weeks in the waterless desert. Then there would follow several of the luscious, purple-skinned fruits the Ottomans call the bullaca and fair-faced foreigners from afar call the plum. Last of all, the dark-eyed woman of many summers would bring the feast to a conclusion with a succulent slice of melon, placing it deep up inside her and forcing him to use his tongue to dislodge it and eat it.'

Nubia, excited by this flow of wicked memories, was now furtively playing with herself. Her strong perfume of arousal flooded the darkened bedchamber. That, and her panting, betrayed her to her angry mistress.

'Girl?' Safira demanded, twisting round to her slave-girl. 'What are you doing?'

'Nothing, mistress,' came the whispered reply. Nubia shrank away from her stern bedfellow.

'Light the taper.'

Wiping her fingers dry on the silk sheets, Nubia scraped a flint and ignited the taper. Blowing gently on the red ember, she brought the flame to life.

'Untie me,' came the stern command from the bed of silk.

'But, mistress—'

'At once, wretch.'

Putting the taper's tiny flame to several oil-lamps, Nubia blew it out and then untied the silk binding the wrists of her mistress. Safira seized her slave girl and forced her face-down across the silken sheets.

'How dare you indulge in a pleasure you know is denied to me? And in my very own bed. How dare you?'

Nubia squealed as the rain of pain lashed down upon her upturned cheeks. Safira plied the fly-whisk expertly – an expertise gained through much usage – to sting and scald the slave girl's soft bottom. Fuelled by the venom of her frenzied frustration, the punishment was brief but blistering. Nubia cried out but her shrill squeals only increased the fervour of her punisher. The whipped girl wriggled and squirmed in her bid to escape the fifty short lengths of stinging cord. Again and again the fly-whisk lashed her bare buttocks, caressing their rounded curves with vicious tenderness. Nubia sobbed into the silk as her quivering buttocks blazed. The hand pinioning her neck relaxed its grip for an instant; Nubia broke free and, kneeling, raised her tear-stained face up to her stern mistress.

'Down across the bed,' Safira thundered. 'I have not finished with you, yet.' She lashed the silk sheet with the fly-whisk.

Nubia moaned. 'Please, mistress, don't—'

The fly-whisk punished the empty stretch of silk once more. Weeping gently, Nubia obeyed, submitting her whipped cheeks once more up to her angry mistress. She gasped aloud as Safira straddled her, trapping the slave girl's ravished cheeks between her golden thighs. Safira planted her wet sex down upon the crown of the curved cheeks beneath her, and began to ride them – raking them dominantly with her splayed labia.

'No, mistress, no,' Nubia gasped. 'Do not use me so. Not like that,' she warned – forgetting her own sorrow and protecting Safira's maidenhead. 'Remember the danger.'

'I remember,' the mistress snarled, easing herself up away from her slave girl's soft cheeks. Then a softer note stole into her stern voice. 'Sweet Nubia,' she whispered, fingering the girl's sticky cleft. 'Always so careful to protect me.' She bent down, crushing her swollen breasts into the slave-girl's bottom.

Nubia, alert to the thickened nipples at her hot flesh, murmured into the silk as the bunched breasts kissed her buttocks.

'Tomorrow, at dusk, I will leave my father's house—'

'Mistress,' Nubia squealed in alarm. 'What are you saying?'

'It must be so. I cannot bear this isolation any longer. Just for an hour or two. We—'

'We?' Nubia echoed, horrified – and mindful of Safira's angry father, whose prowess with the horse whip was legendary even beyond the Blue Mountains.

'We will go heavily veiled. You will be my guide. You will take me to some exciting place, some forbidden quarter of the city at nightfall—'

'The House of Pleasures?' Nubia gasped in horror.

'No. It must, of course, be a place where there are no men. I will wrap a band of silk around my thighs to protect me. I will return intact, of that you must have no fear. But I must go abroad into the city, at nightfall, to taste, to smell, to hear and see it all. No: be silent, girl. It is decided.'

Just before dusk, two sensually veiled figures threaded their way through the spice stalls, taking advantage of the lengthening shadows for protection against curious, prying eyes. The air was pungent with cinnamon, dried ginger, garlic, cloves and marjoram. Beyond the spice stalls, the two disguised women encountered a throng of flower sellers – Iqqabbi women from the south, whose faces were decorated with silver and lapis lazuli. A heavy perfume hung in the air; Safira and Nubia identified jasmine, wild roses, lilies and the elusive scent of the unnamed Blue Mountain blooms that flowered every decade. Nubia grew giddy; her heart hammered with fear. Safira kept halting suddenly to feast her deprived senses on the bustle and blaze of the city, increasing their chances of being discovered and punished.

'Come mistress,' she urged, as Safira stayed to watch a cock-fight. The black cockerels wore silver spurs. Droplets of crimson already speckled the sand beneath their dancing feet.

They were heading for the Pool of Desires, the sequestered bathing house reserved for the exclusive use of the city's maidens. Four eunuchs guarded the heavy wooden gate, their glinting spears crossed. Nubia whispered to them softly, slipping oblats into their soft, pale palms. The spears jerked apart. The heavy door yawned wide to admit them, creaking as it closed behind them.

'The Pool of Desires,' Nubia whispered. 'But we cannot stay long. Your father will be expecting you at the supper table, mistress.'

Safira nodded impatiently and swept Nubia aside. 'Come. Let us sit and watch the maidens.'

Nymphs, naked and utterly beautiful, their wet limbs shining, emerged from the heated waters of the pool. Others, who had bathed, stretched out on soft satin cushions, whispering and giggling as they traded secrets and revealed intimate desires.

A squabble erupted with shrill shrieks. Two delicious young women who had been grooming one another suddenly fell to blows. They rose, hissing and scratching. A chase ensued – a sudden dash to the safety of the pool. A splash as a naked girl tumbled into the water. She swam to the centre and trod water with her lithe, slender legs. The waters lapped at her swollen breasts, nuzzling the shadow at her deep cleavage. Another splash: her naked pursuer was swimming strongly through the water. They both made for the far side, touching the smooth marble edge of the pool together.

Nubia gazed across the pool at the two naked girls as they hauled themselves out of the pool. Her mistress followed her gaze, her green eyes narrowing into fierce slits as she perused the struggling girls' bare bottoms as they scrambled inelegantly up onto the marble. Breathless, they lay face-down upon the cool, polished stone, crushing their breasts into its hard surface. Silver water trickled from their dark clefts.

Nubia and her mistress watched, enthralled, as the dominant pursuer grappled her victim into submission, taloning the unhappy girl's hair as she marched her back to the satined cushions. There, taming and controlling her captive across her lap, she spanked the bare bottomed girl harshly, causing the creamy cheeks to crimson. Moments later, the two girls were wrestling playfully among the satin cushions, tumbling breast to breast, pubis to pubis, their shrieks of excitement splitting the air.

'Are you new?' a voice at Safira's side inquired.

Safira tightened her veil, her green eyes clouded with alarm.

'You are most welcome here,' the matron continued.

Nubia turned to see a proud face, a statuesque figure and a welcoming smile. The handsome matron was sheathed in pale purple. Her left breast, superbly ripe and heavy, was exposed. The nipple was pierced with a silver ring, denoting her noble lineage. The matron offered them refreshments.

'Please,' she encouraged, indicating an array of sweetmeats, sugared confections and delicious sherbets. 'Welcome to the Pool of Desires.'

Turning, the purple-robed matron clapped her hands twice. Her naked breast wobbled gently. Silence descended upon the naked nymphs gathered around the pool.

'Tonight is for pleasure but, first,' the Matron announced, 'we have a wrong to right.'

Nubia looked at her mistress. Safira gestured for silence.

'One of you has sinned and,' the matron continued, her voice a mere whisper, 'must be punished.'

The matron turned quickly and explained to the newcomers

111

that any maiden with a complaint could have the matter dealt with here, in privacy, away from the lewd laughter and coarse curiosity of the vizier's Court of Settlements. 'Fitting for the loss of six goats.' She smiled, adding, 'but we settle things our own way here.'

The naked women had gathered in a circle at the feet of the matron. Speaking tersely, she ordered one of their number to kneel, head bowed, while the accusation was made against her.

A tall, slender girl rose up and spoke. Her tone was bitter. Tears threatened her large, brown eyes as she spoke of her man's infidelity.

'Is this accusation true? Did you pleasure her betrothed?'

The kneeling penitent tossed her head back proudly and defiantly acknowledged the sin. 'If the honey at my hive is sweeter than hers, the man will seek it out—'

'Silence,' the matron thundered. 'You have just admitted your guilt. You spoke of honey and its sweetness, girl. I will bear your words in mind when determining your punishment. Honey comes from bees. And bees sting. Painfully. So does the lash. Twenty strokes.'

'No—' the kneeling girl protested hotly.

'Silence. Prepare her for the whip,' the matron ordered, cupping her bare breasts and squeezing them fiercely.

Willing hands seized the squealing penitent and dragged her to a marble column. The matron opened a sandalwood box and extracted a darkly hued, oiled whip. The handle was encrusted with mother-of-pearl, the gleaming lash – unfurled – tapered to a knotted tip.

Handing the whip to the aggrieved accuser, she pointed to the bare-bottomed penitent at the pillar. 'Take this and seek the satisfaction of revenge – but, in future, girl, be sure to pleasure your man properly, or else you will lose him to another.'

Those detailed to guard the accused dragged her arms around the smooth marble column. Her breasts crushed into its smoothness as her wrists were tightly bound. The girl with the oiled whip approached her rival in love and extended the whip out to the bound girl's face.

'Look at the lash,' she hissed, 'and remember it before you take another's love.'

The accused whimpered her sorrow for her sin, but the girl with the whip merely pressed the lash to the penitent's lips.

'Silence, or I will call upon Aphrodite herself to give strength to my arm.'

Crushing her breasts and belly up into the cold marble she was bound to, the nude rose up on her toes and clenched her buttocks. Taking two steps back, the punisher snapped the whip twice, then quickly flicked it across the bare bottom before her. The knotted lash caressed the rounded cheeks, leaving them jerking in anguish as a thin pink line deepened into an angrier crimson. Snap, crack. Snap, crack. The punishment had begun.

'That is how I will punish you, girl, the next time you deserve the whip,' Safira whispered into Nubia's ear.

'No, mistress, please—'

The purple-robed matron turned, frowning, and gestured for absolute silence. Nubia slipped her hand into Safira's and squeezed it gently. They nestled into each other, and, heads touching gently, gazed upon the whipped buttocks of the squealing nude.

Snap, crack. Snap, crack. The harsh strokes echoed across the Pool of Desires as the sounds of punishment and suffering filled the vaulted marble hall. Bound to her pillar of pain, the whipped nude writhed, grinding her hot sex into the cold stone. Her rounded buttocks were now criss-crossed with reddening weals of fire, her cleft a mere tightened flesh-crease as she squeezed her cheeks. Her low grunts became sorrow-sobs as her head lolled down in shame.

Snap, crack. Safira and Nubia watched enthralled as the whipper raised her arm up to administer the fourteenth stroke. Supple thighs astride, her heavy breasts rising up, she snarled softly as she brought the whip down yet again, searing the naked buttocks with another crimson weal. The punished nude cried out as she hammered her breasts into the marble and thrust her wet labia into its cold solidity.

'Enough,' the purple-robed matron announced, holding up her arm. 'She has suffered quite enough. Save the rest of the strokes

113

for the man who betrayed you. The woman who did so has had sufficient pain.'

All assembled nodded at these words of wisdom, as if the vizier himself had delivered judgement.

'It is time,' the matron said softly, 'to restore the loving friendship that binds each one of us to the other. After pain, there must be pleasure.'

The punished girl slumped at her knees and wept softly, her face pressed into the polished marble.

'You have punished her, now pleasure her,' the matron ordered.

The punisher knelt down and inspected the bottom she had just lashed. Tossing her whip aside, she raised her hands up and palmed the hot cheeks, cupping their softness and then spreading them gently apart. The bound nude screamed softly and jerked her hips. Picking the whip up tenderly, the kneeling nude inverted the mother-of-pearl handle and guided it up between her victim's parted thighs. A tense silence gripped all those watching as the thick whip-handle teased the penitent's wet fig before probing her glistening flesh lips.

'Delicious,' Safira whispered, squeezing Nubia's hand.

Bound to her pillar of marble, the nude tossed her head back and cried aloud – not in anguish, but in raw delight as the whip which had just punished her now pleasured her with the same merciless venom.

'I believe I know who you are,' the purple-robed matron whispered softly to Safira. 'I know those green eyes.'

Nubia let the little honey-cake slip from her fingers as her frightened eyes grew wide. She glanced at her mistress, holding her breath. Safira continued to sip her dark, aromatic coffee imperturbably.

'I feel sorrow for you, my child,' the matron murmured. 'How hard it must be to struggle against sweet temptations, to struggle and strive to keep your maidenhead intact. Of course, once the elders in the temple have inspected and examined you – and anointed you as priestess – there is nothing to stop you visiting us here at the Pool of Desires, when your urgent need proves overwhelming. We do not entertain men here, so there would be no scandal. And be assured,' the matron continued, 'a woman truly knows how to pleasure and delight another woman. Believe it, for it is true.'

Safira's green eyes sparkled. Nubia's quick little fingers retrieved her honey-cake from her lap and nibbled it in silence. Her mistress continued to sip her coffee.

'The day of your examination and anointment is still far off?'

'Yes. Another year, at least,' Safira told the matron.

'Many long days – and longer nights – of suffering,' the matron murmured.

Nubia felt her throat tighten, and had difficulty swallowing her cake.

'There is, perhaps, a remedy. One which will satisfy your needs and those elders in the temple who would have you remain intact. Come,' she beckoned as she rose from the satin cushion and ushered her guests through a velvet curtain into a side chamber. Safira and Nubia followed the purple-gowned matron in obedient silence. Inside the chamber, the velvet curtain was drawn, muffling the squeals and laughter outside at the pool. A carved cedar-wood couch, upholstered in zebra hide, almost filled the small room.

'I want you to stretch down, Safira,' the matron invited, patting the zebra skin gently. 'Girl,' she said, turning to Nubia, 'take the veils and robe from your mistress.'

'I must not lose my—' Safira whispered urgently.

'Be not afraid. I will show you how to obtain delight without any risk or danger. Trust me. You are at the Pool of Delights, where none are disappointed.'

Nubia disrobed and unveiled her mistress quickly, folding the silk carefully so that no unseemly creases would betray their forbidden excursion beyond the walls of Safira's prison-home. As the slave-girl attended to her mistress, the matron prised open the heavy lid of a golden chest and produced a short, curved length of white ivory.

'This tooth, or tusk, was taken from a strange beast found frozen in the ice high up in the Blue Mountains. The tip is smooth, the surface,' she purred, 'very sleek.' Offering her open palm to Safira,

115

she allowed the naked young woman to touch it with her quivering fingertip, 'Perfectly fashioned for pleasure, is it not? Take it. Hold it. Imagine it inside you.'

Safira accepted the ivory tooth and scrutinized it closely, her green eyes wide with wonder. 'But I cannot use this—'

'Be patient, girl,' the matron said, her tone soothing and unhurried. 'Girl,' she continued, speaking to Nubia, 'I want you to take these bands of silk and tie your mistress by her wrists to the edge of the couch. I always use silk,' she explained to Safira, 'not leather. It leaves no mark. Marks always seem to excite the suspicions of husbands, lovers and jealous fathers.'

The slave girl looked at her mistress for permission. Safira hesitated – then nodded and eased herself face down upon the zebra skin, offering her wrists up for bondage. Nubia took the short lengths of crimson silk and bound the proffered wrists tightly.

'Watch very carefully,' the matron instructed Nubia. Taking the curved phallus from Safira's clenched fist, she bent down over the bound nude's bare bottom and tapped the curved flesh of the swollen left cheek dominantly with the tip of the white tooth. 'Are you paying attention, girl?'

Nubia swallowed and nodded obediently.

'Do so, for you will have to perform this for your mistress from this night hence. And it must remain an absolute secret. Betray it to anyone, and you will walk in the shadow of the whip for the rest of your wretched years. Understand?'

Nubia, shivering, vowed solemnly to guard the secret closely. 'Watch.'

Prising Safira's buttocks apart, the matron quickly exposed the nude's tight little anal sphincter. 'See?' she tapped it firmly with the tip of the tooth. 'The door to paradise is firmly closed. Entrance, for the moment, is impossible.' She probed the rosebud with the phallus; Safira grunted her discomfort and jerked in her silken manacles.

'To open the door, to open it up wide,' the matron purred, 'we must use this.' She produced a short, thin strap cut from a strip of supple goat skin. 'I will lash this spot,' she continued, dangling the tip of the whip down at the dark cleft, 'until it becomes hot

116

and wet – and opens up willingly to receive and accept its delight.'

Safira moaned into the zebra hide at her lips. Spasming her buttocks, she tried to trap the supple whip between her heavy cheeks. The matron inched it up, letting it spindle tantalisingly as it skimmed the left buttock. 'Observe, girl. This will be your task tomorrow and thereafter.'

Guiding the phallus in between Safira's parted lips and lodging it firmly in the nude's mouth, the matron returned to the bare bottom, whip in hand. Mounting the couch – and the outstretched nude – the dominant matron straddled Safira, spreading the buttocks wide apart and trapping them with her knees. The exposed cleft yawned; the rosebud winked in the soft light of the oil lamps.

Nubia shivered as the supple whip lashed down, licking the parted cleft with a tongue of fire. Choking on the phallus filling her mouth, Safira squealed softly.

'After a dozen lashes, concentrate on the little pink door,' the matron explained, whipping the helpless nude methodically, each unerring stroke slicing down into the cleft between the pinioned, splayed cheeks.

Safira squirmed and writhed, but the matron rode her ruthlessly, aiming the goatskin whip repeatedly down between her buttocks. Nubia saw the little pink rosebud sparkle. After eleven strokes, the tight little whorl was glistening.

'The door is ajar,' the matron grunted, flicking the lash down directly onto the sphincter. 'Not yet open, but ajar.'

Nubia craned to glimpse the whipped cleft and the puffed, pouting crater of the anal whorl. Safira bucked and jerked in a frenzy to dislodge her tormentress, but the heavily buttocked matron straddled the nude between her thighs supremely, whip in hand.

'She is ready,' the punisher announced. 'Look closely, girl. You must flay her flesh until it softens and yields. See?'

Nubia stepped up to the edge of the couch and peered down at the cleft, and at the pouting sphincter within. She gasped.

'She is ready for her delight. Take the tusk from her mouth and use it. Bring delight to the mistress you serve.'

Moments later, Safira screamed softly – then cursed Nubia,

promising her slave girl the whip – then blessed Nubia, promising her slave girl oblats of gold.

'Ignore her,' the matron urged. 'Your mistress is in paradise. She is like a man in his wine. She knows not what she says.'

Nubia drove the wicked phallus in between Safira's plump buttocks with savage tenderness. Her own sex was hot and wet. Nubia rejoiced as her mistress choked aloud, drowning in her forbidden delight.

Sadean Methods

I The Outer Room

'Matthew, will you look at the three erotic prints on the wall behind you. Yes,' the attractive brunette added, 'that's right. Stand up and take a closer look.'

The young man rose from the leather sofa and dug his hands into the pockets of his dark brown moleskin trousers. As he gazed up at the three graphic prints from the notorious Regensburg collection, the marriage guidance counsellor absently scratched her light tan nylon stocking at the softest part of her inner thigh. Twelve years older than her client, she tolerated his shyness patiently.

'Which one,' she asked, after several minutes had elapsed, 'is the least appealing to you?'

Matthew shrugged. 'That one. The one on the left.'

The brunette uncrossed her legs. Her nylon stockings whispered as the sheen at her thighs kissed. She did not ask him to explain or elaborate. He had selected and dismissed the depiction of a lusty steel worker brutally enjoying his kneeling lover. The naked female was down on all fours, head bowed, her fingers splayed, as the sweating male speared her between the buttocks, his grimy hands gripping her wide, white hips. Her spilling breasts were grimy, betraying the squeeze of his large, fierce hands. It was a vivid portrayal of male dominance and female suffering and submission. She noted his choice carefully in the case notes.

'Tell me. Which is your favourite?'

Matthew raised his right hand and pointed immediately to the centre image. 'That one.'

'Describe it to me.'

There was a slight pause. 'It's just a picture of a young man sitting on a bed. He is undressed. There is a woman in the bedroom. She is clothed. And standing. Her arms are folded. I like it,' he added simply.

'Yes. They say, don't they, Matthew, that every picture tells a story? I want you to tell me a story. Tell me what is happening in that picture. What you see can be the beginning, or the end, of the story. And why is he naked? Why is she clothed?'

Matthew gazed for a full two minutes at the image on the wall and then resumed his seat on the leather sofa, burying his face in his hands.

The brunette did not hurry him. Glancing down at the case notes, gleaned from three previous encounters, she refreshed her memory. He was twenty-eight. Married – three years – no children. Farmed two and a half thousand acres of arable. Enjoyed riding and rough shooting. Plenty of money. County family background. Wife: twenty-eight, similar background, tastes and interests. No problems other than a cold marriage bed. She closed the file and looked up at him expectantly.

Given his monosyllabic responses up to that point, she was surprised at his sudden eloquence.

'They are on holiday. They had a decent hotel room but suddenly ran out of money. They are now *en pension* in the poorer quarter. He took a big risk at the casino. Lost the lot. She has discovered his foolishness. Of course, he lied at first. But she forced it out of him. She is making him confess. In a moment—'

'Yes?' the brunette prompted.

'In a moment, he will confess. He will kneel, naked, before her, and beg for forgiveness.'

'And,' she murmured, 'will she forgive him?'

'Yes. But only after . . .'

There was a long pause. The brunette did not speak. As an experienced marriage guidance counsellor, she knew that Matthew had to finish the story his way.

He looked up, his eyes shining excitedly. 'She will forgive him, but only after she has punished him severely.'

120

The blonde kept her gloves on. Her lips were blood-red.

'You do understand why I am seeing you separately?' the attractive brunette asked. 'In marriage guidance, it is important that I gain your trust. Especially when lifting up the duvet and peeping into the secrets of the marriage bed. I spoke with Matthew—'

'What did he say?' the blonde asked sharply.

'I spoke with Matthew the day before yesterday. Now it is your chance to confide in me. But first, Susan, I would like you to take a look at those three erotic prints on the wall behind you.'

Susan rejected – and then selected – the same prints her husband had done. Her story was quite different.

'She has just punished him. She spanked him with her hairbrush,' she said enthusiastically. 'It is a frequent love-game. It makes him very hard, very excited and very eager to please. Sometimes, she ties his wrists to his ankles with her stockings and then slowly canes his buttocks. This time,' she gestured to the erotic print, 'she forced him across her lap and used the hairbrush. We cannot see it but his bottom is very red.'

'And? What happens next?'

'They screw. Like rabbits. All night long.'

Susan had peeled both her gloves off and was twisting them savagely. The brunette noted the fact down quickly in the case notes.

'Thank you, Susan. You have been very frank. I find your story very revealing. And very helpful.'

At the next session, Matthew was content to remain silent as he sat on the leather sofa. The attractive brunette gently probed into his version of the failing marriage.

He shrugged. 'Don't quite know why,' he said guardedly, avoiding her searching gaze. 'We grew up as neighbours. Great childhood sweethearts, though she bullied me unmercifully. Great fun. We took names out of a book in her father's library. Arthurian legends. She was La Belle Dame Sans Merci, and I was her devoted courtly knight.'

The brunette nodded but remained silent.

'No money problems. We both love the country, hate the town. We're just not—' he faltered.

'Take off your clothes, Matthew,' she said, rising from her chair and walking slowly across the pale grey carpet to a table by the window. The curtains rasped as she drew them together.

'What did you say?' he stammered.

'I asked you to take off all your clothes. This is the Outer Room. This is where clients strip off all their defences, their masks. It helps to be naked, you'll find. No inhibitions as we work together towards the truth.'

'But—'

'I will take off my clothes, too. Naked, we can be completely honest with ourselves – and each other. If you are prepared to be honest with me, I may be able to salvage your marriage. And you do want to revive it, don't you?'

'Yes,' he nodded.

'Good. Just fold your clothes over that chair there.'

Turning, she took a glass and filled it with sherry from a decanter as he peeled off his clothes.

'All of them,' she instructed, noticing his hesitant hands hovering at the waistband of his boxer shorts. 'No secrets allowed in the Outer Room, Matthew.'

He dragged them down. Sipping her pale sherry, she perused his nakedness.

'Sherry?'

'No – Yes, please.'

She poured out a glassful and approached the leather sofa. As she handed it to him, she deliberately let the glass slip.

'Quick,' she snapped. 'Catch it in your hand.'

He juggled with the glass, his thighs and cock wet with sherry.

'That was very clumsy of you,' she continued, sustaining the sharp tone of asperity. 'Get a hanky before it stains the carpet.'

His cock thickened in response to her harsh tone. Scrambling across the leather sofa, he fished out a square of linen from his moleskin trousers and, kneeling, dabbed frantically at the carpet, mumbling an apology.

'Never mind that, now; the harm's done,' she replied acidly. She swallowed her sherry, kicked off her shoes and shrugged off her frock.

He gazed up at her as she stood before him, thighs parted, hands on her hips, superb in a black basque and sleek, seamed stockings. His eyes flickered down to feast at the dark tan material at her crimson-nailed toes. His erection twitched.

'I thought—'

'Thought what? That I would take all my clothes off? Are you sure you don't prefer to see me in this?'

He blushed and squirmed on the leather sofa.

'Now, Matthew,' she purred, arranging herself in her chair directly opposite him. 'I want you to tell me the fantasy you masturbate to. In the bathroom, when Susan isn't there.'

He crimsoned. 'I don't—'

'Now, you really mustn't lie to me. I know you masturbate. You do, don't you?'

He avoided her stern gaze.

'Don't you?'

'Yes, but—'

'Then tell me.'

Red-faced, he looked down to the spot where his whitening toes scrunched the carpet. It was, as she suspected, a punishment fantasy which fuelled his furtive masturbation.

He spoke rapidly. 'Then the two store detectives strike a deal. Punishment on the spot,' he whispered excitedly, 'and there'll be no need to bring the police in.'

Fingering the tight, stretchy basque cupping her breasts, the marriage guidance counsellor nodded sympathetically – noting how thick and engorged her young client's erection had become. 'Please continue, Matthew,' she murmured.

'They order me to take my trousers down,' he replied eagerly, 'and one of the store detectives—'

'A woman?'

'Yes – they are both women – one of them unbuttons her cardigan and orders me across her lap. I can feel her breasts upon my bottom. Then the other woman kneels down and spanks me.'

The brunette kept a cool, clinical note in her voice. 'Does she spank you very hard, Matthew?'

'Yes,' he hissed, closing his eyes.

'And does your bottom turn very red?'

'Yes. Very red and hot. They make me look at it in a small mirror. I have to twist my head around and look over my shoulder and see my red bottom in her small mirror.'

'And then?' she pressed, her voice a velvet whisper.

'He opened his eyes and shook his head like a schoolboy. 'Don't want to say.'

'Tell me, Matthew. I need to know.'

'No—'

'This is the Outer Room, Matthew. This is where we share our secrets. Do you come, Matthew, after being spanked?'

He nodded.

'You come across her lap, don't you? Her stockings are wet.'

'Yes. She places the cold mirror down on my hot bottom and I come at once. She wipes me dry with her cardigan sleeve. Then they use a slipper on me. I shout – it hurts – and they force the wet cardigan sleeve into my mouth. The slipper really hurts,' he gasped delightedly.

'Thank you for being honest with me—'

'There are others,' he broke in. 'Other fantasies.'

'Others?' she echoed. 'You mean you have several masturbatory fantasies?'

'Yes. There is a stern librarian. She wears her hair in a tight bun and has little gold spectacles on the tip of her nose. She is quite beautiful – in a severe sort of way, you know?'

'I know.'

'I return a book. It has been damaged – dropped in a puddle. She is very angry and brings me into her private office. She lectures me, calls me a barbarian for damaging her beautiful book. I try to offer money but this enrages her. I must be punished –'he clenched his hands together and spoke with increasing fervour '– with her leather belt. Twenty strokes. She counts each one out aloud. Each lash as it burns across my helpless buttocks—'

'Matthew—' she warned.

Suddenly, he slumped down onto his knees and gasped softly as he started to spasm and, hips jerking, come.

'Catch it in your hands,' she cried sternly, 'I shall be very cross if you splash it all over my nice grey carpet.'

Her anger sent him into a paroxysm of ecstasy. Fumbling blindly, he managed to cup his hands and capture some of his spurting seed.

As he knelt, groaning and spent, the brunette rose unhurriedly and approached him. She tilted his head up, her fingertips beneath his chin. He gazed up at her, his ejaculation over. She stroked his face three times with her fingernails.

'Thank you, Matthew. You have told me all I need to know.'

Susan took her gloves off, but kept them gripped tightly in her left hand – swishing them from time to time like an angry cat flicking its tail.

'Why do I what?' the brunette murmured, raising her head up from the case notes.

'Why do you call this the Outer Room?' the blonde repeated.

'Because,' the marriage guidance counsellor replied softly, 'this is where we take off all our outer defences, our pretences.'

'Is there an Inner Room?'

'All in good time. Not just yet. Matthew is ready to go in there, I think. I have to be absolutely sure. Take off your clothes, please.'

The gloves stopped twitching. Susan asked the brunette the purpose of getting undressed.

'So we can, together, get to the naked truth of your problems.'

'Unusual methods,' was all the blonde replied, standing up to kick off her kitten-heeled court shoes and unzip.

'But effective,' the brunette replied suavely, matching the blonde button for button.

Naked, they sat together, thighs slightly brushing, on the leather sofa. Susan, though younger, had heavier buttocks. Her bottom dimpled the soft hide more deeply than the brunette's.

'Sit back and try to relax. I want you to tell me what you think about – what images come to mind, as it were – when you play with yourself.'

125

Susan eased back into the soft leather and sighed. Turning to face the brunette, she whispered: 'How do you know I—'

'I just do,' came the reply. The brunette brushed her fingertips up along the blonde's thigh, resting her hand on the smooth, warm flesh an inch from the blonde pubic nest. 'I need to know.'

There was a full two and a half minutes silence.

'Trust me,' the marriage guidance counsellor murmured. 'Do not deny yourself this opportunity. We both know you have been denied enough. You have not known passion within your short marriage. Or excitement.'

Susan spoke. 'I'm in a school room. There are desks, small desks with ink-wells. You don't see them any more. Polished yellow wooden floorboards. Chalk dust dances in the sunbeams. And there is a smell of ripened apples. It is evening. The school room is deserted. A young man – handsome and sweating after a hard gallop across the fields on his stallion – enters. He has come for a private lesson. I am his teacher. He is afraid of me – but adores me. I have no panties on. I am wet. The lesson commences. I am a very strict teacher. He struggles to learn under the shadow of my cane—'

The marriage guidance counsellor watched the blonde. Eyes closed, Susan spread her thighs wide apart and wriggled her buttocks into the soft leather. She began to palm her belly rhythmically, her fingertips just teasing the fringe of her blonde, coiled nest.

'Put these on,' the brunette whispered, passing the leather gloves to the blonde beside her.

Susan, keeping her eyes closed, donned the gloves and splayed her fingers wide. The pungent scent of her increasing wetness perfumed the Outer Room.

'Please continue. It is a warm evening. You are in the school room with your eager pupil. You are the teacher. The strict teacher. You have a bamboo cane. Your young man needs to be taught a very painful lesson.'

'Yes,' Susan cried, her gloved fingertips strumming her wet slit. 'I take off my cotton print dress. I am not wearing panties. But I do wear a white girdle. It makes me appear maturer. Sterner.

126

My legs are sheathed in dark brown nylons. The suspenders draw the dark stocking tops up my thighs tightly. The girdle squeezes the cheeks of my bottom together. The young man at the desk begs for permission to kiss my bottom – to lick it and worship it. I refuse, and threaten him with my cane. It is bright yellow. I press it against my stockinged thigh. The girdle is squeezing my breasts and my bottom fiercely.'

Susan, thumbing her clitoris openly, jerked her hips. Her bare breasts bounced softly as she writhed on the leather, riding the soft hide spasmodically with her heavy cheeks. Her voice dropped to a feral whisper. She described how she bent her young man across the desk and slowly caned his bare buttocks. Slowly, dominantly, she sliced the whippy wood across his helpless cheeks, bequeathing red line after red line. Tossing the cane aside, she straddled his whipped bottom, crushing her wet heat into his punished flesh – just as he came onto the desk top.

The brunette gazed down at the blonde's gloved hands. The fingertips were stained darkly. 'Thank you, Susan. I believe I have the full picture now.'

II The Inner Room

Matthew entered the Inner Room hand in hand with the marriage guidance counsellor. She turned and locked the door. They were both naked, their clothes neatly folded on the leather sofa in the Outer Room beyond the locked door.

'Susan has gone down to London. I sent her on a shopping trip. Retail therapy, we call it.'

Matthew nodded in silence.

'Now that you have confided in me – told me more about your wants and desires than you probably realise – I can take certain measures to help you,' the brunette said, her tone crisp and imperious. 'I am confident in my methods. Up onto the table, Matthew.'

He looked at her anxiously. She patted his bare bottom with gentle firmness. 'Mount,' she ordered, propelling him to the table.

A black rubber sheet covered the entire surface of the waist-high table. Matthew climbed up as instructed and sat, marooned on the rubber, hugging his knees to his chest.

'Touch the rubber, Matthew. Feel it. You like it, don't you?'

His cock unfurled and straightened as he fingered, then palmed, the smooth expanse of soft rubber. Soon he was thumbing its dull sheen excitedly.

'Smell the rubber, Matthew,' she commanded. 'Press your face down into it and sniff.'

He obeyed. She saw his cock straining as it gouged into the dark surface.

'Kiss it, Matthew. Just like you would kiss the cane or strap that has just lashed your bare bottom. Kiss, then lick, the delicious rubber.'

Whimpering softly, the young man pressed his face into the dark rubber and parting his lips, worshipped it devotedly. The brunette saw his fingers grasping his cock, then raking its wet snout into the black sheen.

'No,' she commanded. 'Not yet.'

He twisted his face up to her, longingly. His eyes pleaded with her. She ordered him to place his hands, palms down, up by his face, where she could see them – but allowed him to wriggle, belly-down, and luxuriate in the clinging rubber surface. He flinched slightly as she rested her right hand down across his bare bottom. He twisted his face and gazed up at her.

'I know what you want, Matthew. You have already told me. And you know that I know. That is what makes it so exciting. Soon, we will let Susan know. Sharing the knowledge—'

'No—'

She spanked him firmly. 'Don't interrupt. I know what's best for you. Trust me. It should be a shared delight, discovering and meeting your mutual needs. You may kiss the rubber, Matthew, as I spank you. You may kiss the rubber – but do not dare to come.'

She spanked his upturned cheeks slowly, palming his reddening buttocks firmly, soothingly, between the sixth and the seventh blow. His thick cock gouged into the soft rubber as his jerking hips hammered down. Pausing after the fifteenth spank to inspect his hot bottom, the marriage guidance counsellor bent down and stroked his face.

'You would love it if Susan did this, wouldn't you?'

He screwed his eyes up tight and refused to reply.

She spanked him hard and then probed his anus with her thumbtip. 'Wouldn't you?' she insisted.

'Yes,' he confessed, his lips kissing the rubber sheet.

'But you dare not ask her, hm?'

His silence was an eloquent answer to her question.

'Kneel. I want you to kneel on the table.'

He obeyed, happy and unselfconscious as his erection jerked up to tap his belly.

'Head down. No, further,' she instructed.

His spanked bottom rose up submissively as he bent his head down obediently. Gripping his wrists, she dragged his hands down alongside his ankles. He whimpered.

'Grasp hold of each ankle, Matthew. I am going to tie your wrists to them in a moment. Tie them tightly with my dark, seamed stockings. The binding nylon will burn your flesh a little, but I know that you will find it a pleasurable pain. Then,' she whispered, dragging her straightened finger across his proffered cheeks, 'I am going to administer the cane.'

'No – Yes—'

'Silence. When I have you bound tightly in preparation for your punishment, I will let you see me put on my special rubber costume. It covers every inch of my nakedness. You want to see me put it on, don't you? Hm? See it squeeze my bottom and make my breasts bulge?'

'Yes. Yes, please,' he grunted.

'And for the time being, it must remain a strict secret. Our little secret. Later, when we tell Susan what you really want from her – what you really like—'

'No, I can't,' he cried.

'Oh but you can. And you will. Even if I have to make you kneel down naked before her and whip you until you confess.'

'I could never—'

'It will mean so much to her. And do so much for your marriage.

129

Trust me. I know. I have my methods.'

'But,' he whispered, 'to put it all into words. To try to express the inexpressible.'

'It can be done. You will be surprised how easy it will be, when the moment comes. When the time is ripe,' she said soothingly, binding his wrists to each ankle with her brown nylon stockings, then knotting them very, very tightly.

Matthew suddenly struggled in a bid for freedom but she had trussed and tied him expertly.

'Excellent,' the brunette pronounced, stepping back from the table to contemplate her naked, bound client – bare bottomed and perfectly positioned for his impending pain. She edged up to the table, sighing as the rubber grazed her thighs. Guiding her fingertip down the cleft between his tightened cheeks, she attempted to dominate him at his sphincter. The cleft tightened into a severe flesh-crease.

'Open up,' she commanded.

He whimpered softly but refused to relax his tightened cheeks.

'I said, open up,' she whispered sternly, spanking his bottom severely.

Matthew slumped face down into the rubber sheet. His muscles relaxed as he submitted to her will; her finger slid in between his softening buttocks. Reaching down, she pushed his head so that his face stared at his knees, pumping his sphincter dominantly until it was accepted meekly by the wet warmth. She bent down to inspect his erection: the straining shaft now pointed directly into his face.

'Kneel up and look at me,' she commanded.

Matthew struggled, twisting his face towards her. Rendered helpless by his bondage, it was impossible for him to raise his head up any higher.

'I am giving you permission to watch as I squeeze into my rubber outfit,' she murmured, 'but you will be blindfolded before being caned. It is not permitted to gaze upon the stern dominatrix when punishment is being dispensed.'

Stretched to its maximum length, his shaft twitched, threatening to explode.

'Look at me.' Naked, her soft breasts and buttocks rippling, she bent down over a chair in the corner of the Inner Room and reverently picked up a one-piece rubber cat suit. 'I do not wear cotton panties,' she explained, unzipping the rubber one-piece and shaking it out. 'I prefer to let my juices smear the softness at my slit.'

On the table, painfully trussed and bound, Matthew moaned gently, his fingers splaying out in an agony of frustration as they ached to grasp and deal with his swollen cock.

'It is important, however, to powder oneself,' the brunette continued, utterly ignoring his sweet torment and shaking talc upon her upturned palm. 'I always powder myself here –' she massaged her bosom slowly, generously, with her talced palm, '– and of course, here.' Her palm smoothed her rounded buttocks. 'My cleft gets so hot and sticky,' she murmured, 'when I use the cane.' She clapped her hands. The fine powder hung in the air, scenting it with a sweet menace. 'Now it is time to let my bare skin feel the delicious, tight rubber.'

Stepping into the left leg with a prinked foot – and then into the right – she eased the second skin up her sleek legs and thighs until the soft black material hugged her hips, squeezing her buttocks in its encircling grip. Palming it up over her hips, she let the sheath of tight rubber trap her heavy breasts.

'See how it moulds and clings to my thighs, and to my bottom,' she whispered, turning and displaying her cupped cheeks to his adoring gaze. 'And now my arms, and breasts.'

Turning to face him once more, she teasingly drew the zip up from her belly to her throat, trapping and squeezing her breasts beneath the stretchy rubber. The neon strip above shone down on the swell of her bosom and buttocks, enhancing and pronouncing their delicious curves.

'Do you like me in my rubber, Matthew?'

'Yes,' he hissed, tonguing the black softness at his lips.

'Head up,' she barked. 'Pay attention. I want you to watch me putting on my rubber gauntlets.'

She paced softly towards him, burying her hands deep down into the stretchy rubber. She extended her right hand out to his face, brushing his lips with her fingertips.

'Kiss,' she ordered. 'Kiss the fingers that will grip the yellow cane.'

He kissed and sucked at her fingertips feverishly.

'The cane,' she murmured. 'The yellow, bamboo cane. In this hand it will bestow such sweet pain.'

'Stripe me,' he pleaded huskily. 'Lash my bare bottom.'

'In a moment,' she replied sternly, as if he were a fractious child. 'First, I must go and don my rubber hood. When I wear it, you cannot see me. But I will see you, Matthew. I will see the red lines of my cane on your bare bottom. I will see the tears on your face. I will see you in your torment and in your ecstasy as you come, squirting you hot seed down onto the rubber sheet. Remember, Matthew. The dominatrix sees everything. There can be no hiding place whatsoever for her suffering slave.'

'Cane me, please—' he begged.

'My rubber hood makes me inscrutable,' she continued, ignoring his frantic pleading for pain. 'Inscrutable, severe and hauntingly mysterious as I chastise you. Just as you want it to be. Hmm?'

'Yes,' he groaned. 'Yes. You understand. You know—'

'I was taught by the master himself, Matthew. I was schooled by de Sade. I owe all my technique, my methods, to him and him alone.'

Matthew shivered, mouthing the words 'de Sade' in silent wonder.

'But now you must be silenced.' She bent down and brutally gagged him. Matthew's eyes bulged as the gag smothered his excited moans. 'And you must not be permitted to see your punisher,' she added, binding his eyes with a length of smooth velvet. 'The softness of this blindfold will absorb your tears,' she whispered.

He spasmed, almost coming.

'No,' she warned sternly. 'Not until I say so. Not until the bamboo bites.'

Matthew tensed as he heard the door to the Inner Room open and close once more and shivered in his helplessness as he heard the key click to lock the door. Two bolts were drawn, slowly. The deliciously slow dragging of the bolts quickened his imagination as he sensed his approaching doom.

The soft approach of his chastiser towards the table sent a trickle of icy quicksilver trickling down his spine. Between his clenched cheeks, his anal whorl tightened as a hot pulse plucked at the sensitive muscle. A maddening pulse of anticipation – a quickening pulse of delicious dread. Bound painfully, his head forced down between his knees, his unseeing eyes gazed blindly up at his throbbing shaft. The blood pounded as it sang loud in his ears; his heart hammered with excitement.

A soft thrum filled the taut silence. The thrum of a whippy cane being sliced down. He tensed – but it was only his beautiful dominatrix testing her bamboo for suppleness and satisfactory sting. A practice stroke.

A second thrum – this time, a note of venom in the slicing sound. Matthew gasped, his cry choking on the tight gag, as a flash of crimson exploded behind his eyes. The thin cane had lashed his bare bottom, searing it with a scarlet line of pain. Swish. Swish. Two more measured strokes kiss-striped his up-turned cheeks, biting them with savage tenderness. His balls tensed in his sac and his quivering shaft strained painfully for release.

Swish. Swish. Rocking gently on the rubber sheet, Matthew spasmed and grunted as the cane sliced down, the bamboo biting sharply again and again, biting his soft cheeks vehemently. He froze as he felt the tip of the cane tap-tapping the nape of his neck dominantly, then shuddered as it revisited his buttocks with another cutting slice.

He came with a sweet paroxysm, splashing his face with his own hot seed. Squirming in his bondage, his dark joy was suddenly intensified as his strict chastiser stood directly behind him, worrying his sphincter with the cruel tip of her whippy cane.

The utter domination of his helplessness in the eerie silence electrified him. He came again almost immediately. The stern disciplinarian, his rubber-clad tormentress, was now perusing him intimately. He shrank in delight from the rubbered fingers at his cleft, balls and shaft.

Then, the rubber fingers were pulling at his bonds, loosening and removing the restricting nylon stockings that welded his wrists to his aching ankles. He felt the rubber gloves pushing at him, rolling him over onto his back and stretching him out across the rubber sheet. A firm fingertip alighted upon his upturned face to trace the warm semen puddling his features. It dipped into the sticky sheen, tracing dominant arabesques, then rubbing the seed into his flesh. He writhed. Now the rubber-sheathed fingers were playing with his wet cock, contemptuously shaking the last remaining droplets of his ejaculation onto his belly. He ground his caned buttocks into the rubber sheet as his cock stiffened within the dominant fingers, pressing its length against the rubber palm that trapped it.

Then he gasped as he sensed his sweet tormentress mount him. He tried to picture the splendour of her easing herself down onto his face. Easing her rubber-sheathed, shining buttocks dominantly down onto his gagged, sightless helplessness. She was riding him now, the stretched rubber at her curved cheeks skimming his face. The gag was prised away from his mouth. He parted his aching lips and tongued at the softness above. The taste of warm rubber haunted him. He cried out aloud, proclaiming his delight.

Rubber fingers opened a flap between his chastiser's splayed thighs. Matthew's straining tongue suddenly tasted her wet tang – tasted the wet heat of the dominatrix who rode him. His engorged erection quivered. He heard the zip at her bosom slide down. Her breasts would be bulging. He gasped aloud in delight. She twisted and, turning deftly, knelt over him: just in time to catch his spurt in her deep cleavage as he came uncontrollably. Knowing that he was drenching her breasts intensified his release. His buttocks pounded the rubber sheet as he splashed her massively. Already, the hot seed was dripping down from her breasts, from her nipples, onto his own naked flesh below.

He was rolled over with a rough gesture of tenderness, the rubber gloves gently firm at his flesh. He moaned as his wet shaft was trapped against the rubber sheet. His sounds of joyful sorrow echoed eerily in the silent Inner Room. He cried out for mercy as the rubber gauntlet grasped the bamboo cane and sliced it down three – four – five – times across his proffered cheeks, and screamed gently as the cane was tossed aside and his tormentress crushed her wet breasts down onto his seething buttocks.

Matthew could not make out what was happening. She had positioned him, face down, into the rubber sheet. A satin cushion had been inserted between his semen-wet belly and the surface of the table. Something cool and hard – with a blunt, polished tip – was being dragged dominantly down along the length of his spine. He writhed and jerked his hips. It was a futile gesture, an attempt to rid himself of this unknown torment. The firm length of cold dominance swept down his spine once more, reminding him of his abject helplessness.

Wriggle and writhe as he might, the dominatrix was totally in control. The cold snout dimpled his left cheek as it traced the red cane-weals across the swell of the punished buttock. What was it? The stock of a whip? His mind became a frenzy of apprehension as it tried to identify the object. The thin handle of a spanking paddle? What was the delicious instrument of impending punishment being played upon his nakedness?

The tip of the cool length now explored his warm cleft. Matthew clenched his cheeks, resisting the insistent nuzzling at his sphincter. Tightening his buttocks, he tried to trap and contain it. Rubber fingertips expertly prised his buttocks apart. He squirmed – then cried out as a half-understood fear became a nightmare reality: she was using a dildo on him. She was committing the ultimate act of feminine dominance.

The ivory shaft slid in between his cheeks. Matthew wriggled his belly into the satin cushion so violently it slipped away, leaving his flesh against the warm rubber once more. A firm hand pinned him down at his neck as a firmer hand plied the cruel shaft.

He came, sobbing softly, the hot wet spurt sticking his belly to the rubber. His fingers groped back blindly to remove the dildo from his burning anal whorl. He begged – but firm hands rendered him immobile in his sweetly scalding shame.

* * *

The door was softly unlocked, the two bolts drawn. The click of the key exploded inside his brain. Who? Matthew threshed on his rubber sheet. The voice of the marriage guidance counsellor spoke softly. Yes. It was her voice – but speaking into the room as if she had just arrived.

'Take off his blindfold.'

He blinked, instantly dazzled by the neon above. Slowly, his eyes adjusted. The attractive brunette wore a rubber cat-suit, just as she had when his eyes submitted to the velvet blindfold. But she was not wearing a hood. The rubber-suited female by his table of shame was hooded.

'Now unmask,' the marriage guidance counsellor instructed the superb dominatrix. 'Let him know you as you really are.'

Matthew gazed in stunned silence as blonde hair tumbled from the black rubber hood as it was peeled away. His heart thumped – in a second, he would be face to face with the female who had pleasured him so utterly, so completely – so perfectly.

'Susan,' he whispered, scrambling to the edge of the table to kiss his wife's wet slit devotedly.

Stern Matron

When she glanced down and saw the photo in the newspaper – the photo snapped at a windswept Croydon aerodrome, the previous day – Matron knew that it would all happen just as the busy rumours predicted. There would be rationing and long queues for glutinous whalemeat and powdered eggs. Schoolchildren would be transformed into goggle-eyed frogs by gas masks. Guns would sprout in Hyde Park and fire watchers would prowl the midnight dome of St Paul's. Matron had served with the Red Cross in Spain, some years before. Then, scrambling through the rubble, she had seen the future of modern warfare.

Sitting up in bed, she gazed down at the front page of her *Daily Sketch*. Mr Chamberlain, tired and crumpled, smiled up at her. The smile was bleak – like the outlook for the peace he had just bargained for in Munich.

Naked before her full-length mirror, she gazed into her own stern face. War was coming. Matron did not flinch at the fact. She remembered the havoc dive-bombers from the dreaded Condor squadron had brought to Guernica. There would be bombers over London – already, the entrances to tube stations were being sand bagged. War meant casualties, and casualties needed nurses. Efficient, well-disciplined nurses.

Matron, a grey-eyed, broad-hipped brunette – just eighteen when the Great War had ground to a halt in the armistice mud – snapped her white suspender belt around her waist, relishing its crispness as it bit into her soft flesh. Carefully selecting and palming dark brown, seamed stockings, she prinked each foot in turn to accept their enveloping sheen. Smoothing each stocking up along her strong, slender legs, she trapped the darker bands of nylon at her thighs and secured them firmly. Turning her bare bottom towards the looking glass, she twisted her head and gazed down to inspect them. The nylon sheathing her left leg betrayed a twisted seam. Breasts bulging, she bent down and palmed it into place, the whispering sheen obedient between her strong hands. Straightening herself up, she inspected her stockings once more. Both seams were perfectly aligned, arrowing up unswervingly to the swell of her buttocks above.

Her pubic nest was quite pronounced, having a dark, luxuriant growth of matted coils. Matron drew her pale silk panties up, thumbing the soft silk from her cleft. In the looking glass, the pubic patch showed dark beneath the stretch of silk. She fingertip-tidied away stray pubic wisps where the edge of the taut silk creased her inner thighs. Easing her ripe breasts into the waiting cups of her bra, she grunted softly as her bosom surrendered to its controlling embrace. Adjusting the white strap at her left shoulder, she paused to appreciate her deep cleavage.

The clock in the bell tower dominating the hospital courtyard began to strike eight. Before the sixth echoing chime, Matron had donned her starched white blouse and was deftly buttoning it up over the swell of her bondaged bosom. Her uniform skirt – royal blue, with severe pleats – swished softly as its hem rasped at the curves of her stockinged calves. Black polished brogues, a wide leather belt, starched cuffs and a crisp lace cap completed her formidable ensemble.

She turned and, picking up her gloves, glanced around her quarters. A maid would be in at ten to dust and tidy. Matron strode across to her unmade bed. The sheet was stained where she had ravished herself last night, her strong fingers busy at her wet slit. Taloning the sheet up in her gloved fist, she dragged it from the mattress and deposited the evidence of her private pleasures in the wicker laundry basket.

Down in the nurses' refectory, the tables were crowded with chattering young girls in their pale blue and white striped uniforms. Freshly scrubbed faces glowed, freshly groomed hair gleamed. Silly, twittering girls, Matron thought. As annoying as the dawn chorus of town sparrows that woke her at six. The talk was of film stars and new lipsticks in Woolworths. Didn't they realise there was a war looming? How she'd like to spank their girlish bottoms. Instead, she dealt with her kippers and coffee severely.

Three final-year student nurses scampered into the refectory, late and laughing. Matron frowned, recognising them immediately from their recent poor ward reports. Slapdash – with levels of clinical competence woefully below the desired standards. Matron finished her coffee, grimacing at its bitterness. She had elected to go without sugar forthwith. Soon there would be no choice in matter – the convoys would have more strategic freight to carry – and in this, as in all things, Matron liked to be in control.

Laughter from the gaggle of latecomers rang out as Matron rose from the top table. She descended down to their table and, in a firm voice, reminded them that they were due on their respective wards in four minutes. They nodded in sullen silence and polished off their fried breakfasts. As Matron left the refectory, the sound of their smothered giggling stung her. Wheeling around on her well-polished brogues, she quelled them with her steel-grey stare.

'In my office, all of you, immediately before lunch.'

'Yes, Matron.'

The morning grew unexpectedly warm. Matron finished re-reading the three folders on her desk. A stern frown revisted her cosmetic-free face. Her full lips pursed tightly. Only a month to go before the final exams, perhaps another month, and then the war. The three student nurses were doing badly. Late nights and neglected studies; slovenly ward skills and a poor attitude. No discipline. They could well fail to qualify – just at a time when every nurse would be needed.

The war. Matron closed her eyes and remembered the fierce heat of Spain. Behind the walls of a convent a day's ride by mule from Cuidad Real, she had witnessed the cruel nuns in their black habits punishing two young women from the village suspected of sleeping with enemy soldiers. Dragged squealing out of the shadowed cloisters into the searing sunlight, the two accused had been stripped naked and forced to kneel on the burning sand.

Matron wiped her moistening palms against the pleated uniform skirt at her thighs as she concentrated hard, remembering. Yes. There had been twelve nuns, each holding short, leather straps. Twelve nuns, like predatory ravens – and two naked girls.

First, the nudes had been forced to confess their sins. Scissors had glinted in the sunlight, ready to swoop down and shear the kneeling penitents, should they deny their crimes. Sobbing, they had confessed their unpatriotic sinfulness. The threat of the scissors was removed, and their punishment began. Each had been presented with a little three-legged wooden stool to stretch across, belly-down, buttocks raised up for the lashing straps. Chanting a sonorous '*Confetior*' prayer in unison, each nun had stepped up in turn, strap poised, casting shadows across the pale nudes darker than their black habits. Snap, crack. Each nun had, without pausing in their mournful chant, delivered two blistering strokes across the first bare bottom then almost instantly across the second. Soon the quivering girls were yelling out their pain as the relentless punishment progressed.

Rojo. Matron knew the word for the enemy. *Rojo*. Despite the heat of the Spanish sun, Matron had shivered at the severity of those lashes reddening the bare-bottomed girls. Loud squeals split the dusty air as the straps kissed the proffered cheeks, licking their rounded curves with crimson weals of pain.

The punished nudes were sobbing – Matron recalled – and pleading for mercy. Swish, crack. Swish, crack. The cruel nuns ignored the cries and plied their straps savagely. At length, the twelfth nun had administered two searing strokes to each whipped bottom and returned to join her assembled sisters. All in the courtyard was silent, except for the muffled whimpers from the prostrate penitents.

At her desk, Matron, inching her fingers up along her thighs beneath her pleated skirt, sought and found the wet heat at her pantied pubis. Peeling away the silk, she thumbed her clitoral bud rhythmically and closed her eyes tightly, as if squeezing out the remembered images of that haunting punishment under the Spanish sun.

Four nuns stepped forward from the group and grappled with

their victims, turning the nudes over and spreadeagling them across the three-legged stools: forcing their squirming, whipped buttocks down onto the hard wood. The remaining eight nuns formed a patient single file, their straps flickering impatiently. The fluttering habits approached the pinioned nudes; tiny puffs of dust rose from the sandals as they trod the sand. Each nun administered two more snapping strokes – crack, lash – the first across the helpless breasts, and the second between the splayed thighs of their victims. The two naked girls screamed aloud as the leather kissed their nipples and pink slits, but firm hands pinned them down for their pain. After the strap had visited their slits, the nudes who had slept with *los rojos* had been forced to pay homage to the hide that had just seared their exposed flesh. One, a dyed blonde – her snatch was dark and glistening – tongued each dangling length of leather as they were presented to her mouth. Yes. The blonde had stretched to kiss and frenziedly bite her instruments of stinging torment.

Buckling under the impact of this suddenly remembered delicious detail, Matron gathered up the silk straining at her thighs and deftly finger-forced the panties up between her wet labia, shuddering as the shiny silk rasped her inner fleshfolds. Masturbating expertly as the memories of Spain flooded back, Matron collapsed face-down into the folders of the failing student nurses on her desk. She started to come, the inner walls below her belly contracting violently. Memories of Spain – of punishment under the sun. Discipline and severe punishment. That was how wars were won. Then she came, grinding her heavy buttocks – the silk panties burning at her hot cleft – into her leather chair. She grunted softly, softer than a nun's curse, as her wet thumbnail rasped her clitoral thorn.

A tap at her door announced the arrival of the three backsliders. Ordering them to enter, Matron remained seated at her desk as they lined up before her – like naughty schoolgirls before a slipper-wielding Head.

'I wish to speak to each of you about your recent ward reports and your examination prospects next month.' She flipped open the top folder. After reading it for an agonising three minutes, she raised her steel-grey eyes up. 'Poppy.'

The pert, pony-tailed blonde blushed and shuffled her white pumps uncomfortably. Matron read aloud from the ward report, instancing Poppy's late arrival for duty, unkempt appearance and lack of nursing skills.

'We do not appear to be making the grade, do we, girl?'

Poppy squirmed.

'Too many late nights,' Matron purred, her straightened finger tapping down on the damning evidence. 'And your clinical skills are deficient. Do you entertain any hopes of qualifying next month?'

Poppy's pony-tail flounced as she nodded.

'I don't,' Matron rasped. 'And let me tell you that I cannot and will not tolerate failure. Pull your socks up. No more late nights. Early to bed – and to your studies. Understand?'

'Yes, Matron.'

'Dismissed.'

Poppy scuttled out of the room.

'Henrietta,' Matron continued, flicking open the second file.

The green-eyed girl blushed as she nervously twiddled with her glorious chestnut curls.

'Much the same, I fear. Poor concentration. Listlessness. Untidy work on the wards—' the catalogue of shame was read out tersely. At length, the file was closed. After warning Henrietta in the sharpest of tones to buck her ideas up, Matron dismissed the second student nurse with a curt nod.

'Alice.'

'Matron?' the slender brunette countered evenly, her languid Kensington drawl devoid of contrition.

Matron's grey eyes narrowed. 'Too slapdash. Late for duty. Low marks in your tests. You have clearly been neglecting your duties and your revision for the finals. What have you to say for yourself, girl?'

Alice shrugged her slender shoulders and remained silent.

'Answer me, girl,' Matron thundered. 'I demand an explanation.'

Alice remained unruffled and returned Matron's glare with an insolent defiance.

Matron sighed and tried the reasoned approach. 'Does it not concern you that, within a month or so, we will be at war?'

Alice shrugged once more, her heavy breasts rising beneath her tight, pale-blue-and-white-striped uniform, and remarked that she found all this talk of impending war rather a bore.

Matron's fist pounded the desk top. Rising swiftly from her chair, she approached the student nurse and inspected her closely.

'Your cuff is unbuttoned, your left shoe is scuffed and –' Matron hissed, '– there is a trace of lipstick from last night's little jaunt after curfew.'

'Dancing at the Carlton,' Alice replied, wholly unperturbed.

'Dancing? The Carlton?' Matron spluttered. 'You should have your head in your books, girl—'

'Can't make me,' Alice retorted defiantly. 'If I choose—'

'How dare you, you little brat. "If I choose—" Let me tell you, I have seen war and it can only be waged with determination and discipline. You lack both, girl, but I am going to see to it that you change your attitude this instant. Bend over that desk.'

Alice swallowed – a soft, gulping sound – but remained standing. Matron pounced, grappling the languid girl down across the desktop and pinning her face down by the nape of her neck.

'Lift up your skirt. Right up, girl. Come along. I want your bottom.'

Outraged, Alice wriggled and squealed. Matron dragged the hem of the striped uniform skirt up, revealing the bending girl's black-stockinged thighs and then her snow-white cotton panties. Exposed so suddenly, the rounded cheeks clenched in a reflex of alarm.

'You can't—' Alice protested.

'Oh, but I can – and I damn well will,' Matron snarled. 'Submit to my authority or leave my hospital at once.'

Alice, who planned to make her fortune on the dowager circuit in the Shires to which her cut-glass vowels entitled her, could not risk expulsion. Calculating briskly that even her Kensington pedigree could not gloss over such disgrace, she signalled her submission and ceased writhing, surrendering to Matron's stern authority.

Matron's free right hand dragged the white cotton panties down from the plump cheeks, leaving them at the bending nurse's knees. Alice shivered as she felt Matron palming her bared bottom, and bit her lip. She had escaped the ministrations of the dorm prefects at boarding school and had not had her bottom spanked since Cook had caught her guzzling glazed quail on the night of her parents' reception for the Dutch Ambassador.

Spank. Spank. Cook had been fierce, but Matron proved a ruthless chastiser. Spank. Spank. Sweeping her firm palm down repeatedly, Matron reddened the wobbling cheeks instantly. Alice squeezed her buttocks defensively, her cleft becoming a thin crease of defiance, but Matron's searing palm sought out the outer curves of the naked bottom and blistered them unpityingly. Alice yelped, her left leg raised, her white rump treading the empty air. Spank, spank.

'No – please—' Alice whined.

Spank, spank. Again and yet again, Matron punished the soft cheeks harshly, eliciting a shrill squeal from the punished nurse. Hampered by her panties stretched between her knees and by the pinioning hand at the nape of her neck, Alice could not escape the scalding onslaught. Blubbing now in her pain and shame, she pressed her wet face down into the polished desktop. Spank – and then seven more severe blows in rapid succession – ensured that the creamy cheeks were now ablaze and every soft curve of the plump flesh burnt red.

'That should suffice – for now,' Matron rasped, palming the swell of the spanked cheeks. 'Now stand up, girl,' she barked.

Alice, tears spilling from her eyes, fumbled blindly for her panties, wincing as they returned to cup and stretch across her blistering cheeks.

'Now get along to your room, girl, and open your books and keep your empty head in them until it is filled with enough knowledge to pass your finals.'

After Alice had scampered out of the office, Matron bent down and picked up a stray pubic curl from the desk top – from the spot where the spanked nurse had kissed the polished wood with her exposed pubis.

The rain was falling softly, the droplets rustling the waxy leaves of the rhododendrons. The clouds concealed the moon. At the back of the nurses' quarters – with all the curtains drawn – the darkness was intense.

The rhododendrons rustled more vigorously as three shadowy figures, tiptoeing and giggling, threaded their way through the wet foliage. A soft click was followed instantly by a powerful torch beam. Three startled faces stared guiltily into the shaft of blinding light.

'I thought I told you there were to be no more late nights,' Matron snarled, lowering the torch.

Poppy and Henrietta gasped their alarm; Alice turned and plunged into the wet bushes.

'Alice,' Matron barked out sharply. 'Come back. Come back this instant.'

Alice obeyed, her eyes widening with fear.

'Follow me,' Matron ordered the three shivering girls as she clicked off and pocketed her torch. 'There is no need for you to sneak in through the kitchen window like alley cats. We will use the front door.'

Upstairs, in the communal bathroom, Matron told her captives to strip and get into tepid baths.

'You do not deserve the luxury of hot water. A tepid bath will suffice.'

The three girls groaned but Matron was adamant. Arms folded, she mounted guard and patrolled outside the three cubicles as her captives stripped and bathed.

Matron strode into the first cubicle, entering without knocking.

'I am very angry,' she told Poppy, who drew her knees up modestly to her breasts as she shivered in the lukewarm water. 'Very angry. I specifically said there were to be no more late nights. You should be at your studies. Now get out of that bath and dry yourself quickly,' Matron snapped, showing no sign of leaving the cubicle.

Poppy hesitated, then pulled up the plug and stretched her arm across the rim of the tub for a large, white towel. Wrapping it around her shining nakedness, shielding her breasts and blonde pubic nest from Matron's searching gaze, she patted herself dry.

'Hurry up, girl,' Matron rasped, loosening the leather belt at her waist. 'It's long past eleven and I want you beaten and in bed before midnight.'

'B–beaten?' Poppy stammered, dropping her towel in alarm.

'You've broken the rules and your promises to me, girl. If the only way I can get you through your finals is with this –' Matron snapped the leather belt harshly '– so be it. Touch your toes. No, bend down more, girl. Get your bottom right up.'

Poppy's pony-tail curled down over her right shoulder as she obeyed Matron's instructions. Her slender legs trembled and her plump little cheeks dimpled as they surrendered to the imminent lash.

Matron took a pace back and raised her belt up, snapping it down across the naked buttocks of the bending girl and blistering them with a thin red weal. Poppy's tiny toes scrunched the wet cork tiles. Swish, crack. Poppy gasped and, stumbling forward, collided into the side of the bath tub. Steadying herself with one hand, she swept the other hand protectively against her whipped cheeks.

'Take your hand away at once, girl. At once.'

Whimpering, Poppy shook her head. Her pony-tail danced frantically. Reluctantly, she dropped her hand down to her thigh. 'Please – I'm sorry – Don't—'

Swish, crack. Twice more the leather belt lashed down to bite into her softly rounded cheeks. They tightened, quivering in pain, as the red lines branding the plump flesh deepened into a purplish blue.

Matron shouldered her belt. 'Now get along to your room,' she murmured, dragging her index finger down along the cleft between the striped buttocks. 'Straight to bed, understand?'

Poppy sniffled but managed to reply in a whisper.

'Understand?' Matron demanded.

'Yes, Matron,' Poppy replied, wiping her tears away with the

146

back of her hand, then gathering up her clothes hastily and crushing them to her breast.

'One moment,' Matron whispered fiercely. 'I happen to know that you have hardly any money at the moment. Who paid for your little excursion tonight?'

'Alice,' Poppy murmured, trembling.

'I see,' Matron cut in firmly. 'Off to bed with you.'

As Poppy scuttled out of the cubicle, Matron wound her belt tightly around her right hand.

In the adjacent cubicle, Henrietta had already dried herself and was struggling desperately into her bra and panties. Alarmed by the sounds of punishment – and suffering – quite audible through the thin partition wall, she was determined to escape Matron's wrath.

'Take those off, Henrietta; I'm not done with you yet.'

She turned her pale face, framed by tousled chestnut curls, to find Matron standing in the doorway, her belt unfurling slowly from her hand.

'But Matron, I—'

'Disobeyed me. Bend over,' Matron commanded, tapping the edge of the bath tub with the tip of her belt. 'I am going to see to it that you qualify next month.'

Henrietta's damp curls curtained her face as she bent down over the white porcelain tub, her hands spread wide apart to support her weight. In her confusion and fear, she had neglected to take off her bra and panties. Reaching up awkwardly at her back, she strained to undo the clasp of her bra.

'Leave that alone,' Matron snarled. 'I will attend to you myself.'

Her green eyes widened in fear as the bending girl pressed her thighs together in response to Matron's approach. Inching up against the pantied buttocks, Matron placed her hands dominantly down upon the wide hips, capturing and controlling the girl she was about to beat with her cruel belt.

'Stay absolutely still,' Matron warned, as her nimble fingers undid the clasp and loosened the bra, instantly sweeping around to the bulging breasts to catch the tumbling cups. Matron's thighs scissored and trapped Henrietta's buttocks as the bra was dragged away. The bare-breasted girl hissed as Matron's fingertips briefly caressed her exposed, peaking nipples.

Kneeling, Matron slowly palmed the panties down from the swollen cheeks. She heard the chestnut-curled girl whimper aloud as the cotton was plucked away from her deep cleft. Matron did not leave the panties at the knees but snatched them down over her victim's feet. Pausing, her grey eyes gazed steadily at the curves and shadows of the delicious bottom. The cheeks spasmed, the cleft becoming a fierce crease, as Matron's warm breath grew ever closer to the satin flesh. Matron's nostrils flared as they caught the haunting whiff of carbolic. The kneeling chastiser felt her wet labia tingle. There was nothing quite so intoxicating as the proximity of a freshly washed girl's bare bottom: a bare bottom that was poised for its impending punishment.

'Twelve strokes,' Matron's voice – now a fierce whisper – pronounced. Rising, she picked up the belt and doubled it in her fist. Bending over her victim, she dangled the belt down before Henrietta's green eyes.

'Twelve strokes.'

'No – Please—'

'You have been a wicked, wilful girl,' Matron purred, trailing the leather down Henrietta's shoulder and spine until it tapped the curve of her upturned cheeks. 'Very wicked. If you won't study for your exam as I advised, then perhaps you will learn from this painful lesson.'

Crack. Crack. The chestnut curls flounced as the naked girl twisted and jerked in response to the searing strokes. Crack. Crack. The third and fourth slicing strokes followed almost immediately, striping the gorgeous bottom with pink kisses from the Judas hide. Crack. Crack. Grinding her feet and squealing, Henrietta took her medicine very badly. Her bottom was heavily fleshed, the cheeks full and ripely rounded, offering the leather more flesh to lash. Crack. Crack. The belt swiped down again and again, rocketing the nude into a threshing frenzy. Matron paused and shouldered her belt.

'Spread your legs, girl,' she whispered, her tone as soft as if

148

sharing an intimate secret. 'I want your bottom big and round for the remaining strokes.'

Henrietta sobbed aloud and stubbornly kept her thighs welded together. Leaving her belt at her shoulder, Matron planted her hands – thumbtips touching at the nude's cleft – on the whipped cheeks, then forced the buttocks apart. Deep down in the shadowed cleft, Matron saw the pink sphincter winking wetly.

'I told you to spread your thighs, girl.'

Henrietta obeyed, inching her legs apart. Her cleft widened. Matron raised her left knee up and guided her nyloned shin into the shadowed divide between the whipped cheeks, grunting repeatedly with delight at the heat at her stockinged leg. A sudden thrill ravished the dominant chastiser; she taloned her hands and squeezed Henrietta's captive cheeks viciously as she felt a wet trickle from the nude's sparkling plum. It was unmistakable. Matron glanced down. Dragging her knee deliberately down between the splayed cheeks, she rasped the cleft harshly then withdrew. Yes. A wet stain on the sheen of her nylon betrayed her victim's liquid bubble of arousal. To Matron's mounting excitement, she saw that Henrietta was responding pleasurably to her pain. Something to note for future reference. Something Matron would explore, at leisure, with the girl with the chestnut curls.

In her delicious confusion of the discovery, Matron forgot precisely how many strokes of the belt she had administered. Matron liked to be precise; discipline depended upon exactitude. She fingered the weals across the punished girl's bottom, counting silently, but the thin, red lines had merged into a broad blush of crimson suffering. Snatching her belt down from her shoulder, she swiped the swollen cheeks nine times in swift succession: Henrietta danced and squealed as the leather brought renewed flames of fierce heat to her buttocks. Lowering her belt, Matron adopted a soft tone and instructed the nude to gather up her scanties and go to her bedroom.

Fumbling for her bra and panties – together with the rest of her scattered attire – Henrietta hugged them to her wet slit and dashed out of the communal bathroom, her loud sobs echoing down the corridor.

In the bathroom, Matron carefully released her stocking from its suspender, peeled it down and held it aloft to inspect the wet ooze that had escaped from Henrietta's pouting labia. Moments later, Matron lowered the soiled stocking down to her lips.

Six minutes later, the belt-wielding punisher strode into the third cubicle to whip Alice's bottom. Fully expecting the insolent girl to be shivering anxiously – having heard the punishments in the nearby cubicles – Matron was surprised to find Alice's cubicle empty. The predator snapped her leather belt angrily: her prey had flown.

The door was locked. Matron tried the handle vigorously, then tapped sharply – three times – ordering Alice to open it. Her command was met with silence from beyond the locked door.

'I know you are awake, girl. Very well,' she added as the stubborn silence lengthened, 'I will deal with you in the morning.'

A little later, Matron approached the locked door, her brogues in her left hand, Poppy propelled by her right. Under Matron's orders, Poppy gently tried the handle and then knocked gently.

'Alice, it's me.'

The key turned softly, clicked, and the door inched open. Sweeping Poppy aside, Matron stormed into the bedroom. 'Back to bed, girl,' she barked, dismissing her Trojan horse brusquely. 'Now, Alice,' she murmured, 'I think it's time you and I had a little chat.'

Startled by Matron's sudden – and totally unexpected – appearance, Alice stumbled backwards against her bed.

Matron nodded grimly. 'That's right. On the bed. Face down and kneeling. Bottom up and hands together on the pillow where I can see them.'

'No,' Alice, naked and shivering, hissed defiantly. She grabbed a vest and struggled into it. 'You can't—'

'But I can and I will, my girl. You have flouted my authority and led the other girls astray.'

'I'm going tomorrow,' Alice shouted, 'so you—'

'Will have to punish you tonight. On the bed, now. You may go tomorrow, Alice,' Matron continued suavely, asserting her absolute authority. 'I have not quite decided whether to expel you. You are so very clearly a bad influence. The imminent need for nurses must be acknowledged, however, and so I may allow you to remain. I will punish you now and sleep on the matter.'

Alice gasped but remained silent, not daring to argue with the dominant Matron, whose leather belt gleamed under the light bulb. Head bowed as her defiance ebbed, and fear flooded in, she tugged nervously at the hem of her stretchy vest. As she pulled it down over her proud pubic mound, the fabric moulded and pronounced the swell of her bosom above.

'If,' Matron concluded, snapping the belt, 'I persuade myself to allow you to remain to qualify, in the national interest, it must be clearly understood that you will submit completely to my authority and strict discipline. Now get on the bed and give me your bottom.'

Alice sat down heavily, her bare bottom dimpling the mattress. In a last-minute bid to escape her pain, she bargained frantically. 'I'll study, I promise. Every evening—'

'I know you will. You can depend upon it, girl. Face down; you are to be punished.'

The languid girl suddenly burst into action, making a spirited dash for the door. Matron easily intercepted and mastered her, dragging the wriggling girl back to her bed and forcing her face-down and positioning her for the lash.

'I was going to use my belt,' Matron panted, breathless after the flurry of exertion. 'I see it as fitting. A symbol of my authority. But for you, girl, I think I'll need it to keep you exactly as I want you.'

Binding Alice's wrists together with the band of leather, she dragged the kneeling girl's hips up and arranged the protesting girl's bottom, leaving the peach-cheeks poised for their pain.

'We don't want to disturb all the others, do we?' Matron whispered. 'They have all earned a good night's sleep.' She forced a handkerchief gag into Alice's mouth. 'Now,' Matron mused aloud. 'I think we'll have need of your hairbrush.'

Twisting her wrists in their leather bondage, Alice grunted into her gag as Matron returned from the dressing table, hairbrush in hand. Inverting the stiff bristles so that the smooth pear-wood surface addressed the upturned buttocks, the chastiser tapped the cheeks of the bound nude she proposed to chastise.

'You enjoy so many advantages that Poppy and Henrietta do not,' Matron remarked. 'You have pedigree and privilege, Alice. When the war comes, it is to girls like you that all will turn to for leadership and discipline. Until that moment comes, I will give you all the discipline you both deserve and require.'

The brief sermon ceased – then the pear-wood spoke. Swish, swipe. Swish, swipe. The smooth wood flattened the rounded cheeks each time it cracked down against them, eliciting smothered squeals from the kneeling nurse. Alice struggled and almost broke free, but Matron merely dragged the tight vest up over her victim's head, rendering her completely helpless. Tapping the hairbrush, bristles uppermost, into the spilling breasts, Matron ordered Alice to remain perfectly still while her bottom was being spanked. Alice clenched her cheeks as the bristles rasped her exposed nipples. Matron applied the bristles more firmly, establishing her absolute sovereignty over the kneeling, helpless nude.

Swish, swipe. Swish, swipe. The creamy buttocks reddened quickly as the small room echoed to the harsh swipes of the hairbrush across the upturned bottom.

After the eleventh stroke, Matron applied the bristles up against the bouncing breasts, levelling the cruel spikes at the ravaged nipples. Alice squeezed her thighs together and moaned.

'You will obey me from now on, girl. You will work hard at your studies and improve your ward performance, understand?'

The fingers at the pillow splayed out in a mute gesture of contrition.

'Good. I am prepared to do this every night – if I have to – until you pass your exam.'

Swish, crack. Swish, crack. After the sixteenth stroke – a blistering swipe which left the crimson cheeks jerking in anguish – Matron surreptitiously lifted up her pleated skirt and swiftly dragged the bristled face of the hairbrush against her slit. Administering five more searing strokes, the punisher brought the bristles to her wet heat each time the pear-wood had spanked the bare bottom. Soon the bristles were wet, and Matron was approaching a violent climax. Hurriedly loosening the leather belt from Alice's wrists, Matron snatched it up and left the room in silence.

Closing the door, she gripped the belt in her fist and dashed towards the privacy of her own quarters, her stocking-tops now sticky with the ooze of her urgent arousal. Stumbling towards her door, she sank down to her knees, her face crushed into the linoleum, collapsing under a savage orgasm.

At four o'clock the following afternoon, just when the three student nurses were anticipating slices of buttered bread, strawberry jam, wedges of fruit cake and strong, brown tea, they found themselves summoned from the line of nurses queuing in the refectory and heading for the training block. There, gowned and gloved, they found Matron waiting for them in a clinical practice room.

'You two wait outside. Poppy, get in here and close the door.'

Poppy bit her lower lip and entered the white tiled room.

'Get undressed. I am going to help you with your practical skills. A few useful tips for your finals.'

Poppy stripped obediently, covering her naked breasts and pubis shyly.

'I am going to teach you the finer points of the bed-bath. Up.'

Poppy mounted the bed. A rubber sheet – but no draw sheet – received her soft buttocks with a cold kiss as she eased herself slowly down and stretched out, avoiding Matron's stern gaze. Poppy shivered as Matron became busy with a cold flannel at her face, neck and shoulders.

'More refreshing this way,' Matron murmured. 'Of course, the water would be warm for a patient.'

Cupped and squeezed within the cold cloth, Poppy's nipples peaked painfully. Matron paused, thumbing the nipples tenderly with her gloved thumbtip.

'Observe closely,' she continued, taking a fresh flannel and soaping it vigorously.

Poppy wriggled and squirmed as the soapy cloth massaged her breasts roughly, grinding her buttocks into the rubber sheet. Matron raised her gloved hand warningly, instantly stilling the naked little nurse into passive obedience.

'Turn over. No, girl. Onto your left side. Draw your knees up to your tummy.'

Surrendering her bottom, Poppy whimpered softly but – fearing Matron's promise of punishment – drew her knees up to crush her breasts.

'Hygiene is vitally important here.' Matron fingered Poppy's cleft. 'Hot water is essential.'

Gripped in Matron's gloved fist, the scalding flannel raked up Poppy's cleft twice, causing the naked nurse to clench her cheeks tightly. Removing the cloth, Matron worked her gloved finger between the cheeks and probed the anal whorl within. Poppy squealed.

Spank. Spank. 'I am showing you the importance of washing the patient thoroughly, girl. Do not obstruct me.' Spank. Spank.

Poppy wriggled on the rubber sheet and parted her cheeks, allowing Matron to bend down and examine them intimately.

'Always use a fresh flannel for each part of the patient,' Matron remarked. 'Especially after washing the bottom.'

Poppy murmured a soft response, nodding gently, causing her pony-tail to swish against the rubber sheet.

'Leave the pubic area 'til last. On your back, girl, legs apart.'

The hot cloth – Matron's gloved hand was impervious to the seething heat – was applied firmly to Poppy's pubic mound. 'Not as hot as this, of course,' Matron grunted, ravishing the parted labia and scrubbing the clitoral hood. 'I'm merely making the lesson memorable.' Forcing a corner of the hot cloth in between the labial folds, Matron suddenly pulled it away. Poppy screamed softly and clamped her thighs together, her buttocks hammering the rubber sheet beneath her.

Matron quelled the writhing nude with a pinioning hand. 'You will, of course, never be so inconsiderate towards your patient, girl. I simply deemed it necessary to remind you how it ought not to be done.'

Tossing the soiled flannel aside, she ordered Poppy to roll over onto her belly. Face down into the rubber sheet, Poppy proffered her bare bottom to Matron, who deftly applied talcum powder to the rounded cheeks, massaging the fine white film firmly into the satin-smooth flesh. 'To prevent bedsores, we apply a protective barrier. For long-term bed care, a cream can be used.'

Poppy snuggled down, crushing her breasts into the rubber sheet, and inched her buttocks up for Matron's firm touch.

'What precautions should be taken with a nailbrush, girl?'

Poppy tensed, unable to answer the question.

'I'm waiting.' Matron's index finger tapped the naked left buttock's wobbling swell impatiently. 'Well, girl?'

Poppy clenched her cheeks, fearing Matron's rubber gloved spank.

'I had better remind you.' Taking a small wooden-backed nailbrush, Matron dipped it into warm water and applied it to Poppy's fingernails. 'Do not ever use a nailbrush directly on the patient's flesh,' Matron warned, suddenly raking the sharp bristles down along Poppy's spine – and then between her plump cheeks, ravishing her deep cleft.

Twisting on the rubber sheet, the pony-tailed nurse squealed.

'And that,' Matron murmured, peeling off her rubber gloves, 'is all you need to know about giving a bed-bath. What have we forgotten, girl?'

'Pulse and temperature?' hazarded Poppy, mumbling the response into the rubber sheet at her lips.

'Excellent, Poppy. I'll make a Sister out of you, yet. Pulse and temperature. Turn over.'

Poppy obliged.

'After the bed bath, take advantage of your patient. Naked and relaxed, it will be easy to take the readings required. Pulse first.'

Matron placed two fingers down at the crease of Poppy's pubic delta where it melted into her upper thigh. 'Do not be afraid to press down firmly.' Matron's thumbtip casually swept the tiny clitoris. 'Goodness me, girl. A pulse of eighty-nine, and galloping. We are in an excitable state. Over onto your tummy. I firmly believe in taking a rectal temperature,' she murmured. 'We don't need an actual thermometer, do we girl? My finger will suffice.'

The little pink rosebud resisted at first, but Matron splayed the plump little cheeks apart and forced the small muscle to widen and accept her. A fraction of an inch at a time, she probed the muscled warmth of Poppy's tightness. The little pony-tailed nude lapped the rubber sheet, her eyes closed tightly shut, as Matron dominantly inserted her finger until its full, firm length lay buried between the buttocks.

'How long to take a temperature?' Matron demanded, her voice cool and clinical.

'A minute,' Poppy whispered into the wet rubber at her lips.

'A minute,' Matron nodded, fingering the inverted watch pinned to her bosom.

Sixty seconds later, she slowly withdrew her finger. Poppy involuntarily squeezed her buttocks, as if to capture and contain the firm length inside her.

'Well done, girl. Bed-bath, pulse and rectal temperature reading. I trust you will remember all that I have taught you.'

'Yes, Matron,' Poppy whispered, rising up on her elbows and peeling her bosom and pubis away from the hot rubber sheet. 'I will remember.'

'Henrietta. Will you step inside? Shut the door and lock it, girl. I have no wish to be disturbed,' Matron added, snapping on a fresh pair of rubber gloves. 'I've just given Poppy some clinical tutoring. I note from your ward reports, Henrietta, that you are still unfamiliar with pre-operation preparations. That is remiss of you, girl, with the finals so close. A spell on the surgical ward must be arranged.'

Henrietta, her green eyes wide and wary, merely nodded.

'For now, I had better show you exactly how to conduct a pubic shave. Strip and up on the bed, girl. Hurry up.'

Her chestnut curls tumbled in disarray as, head bowed, Henrietta unbuttoned her striped uniform. Soon she was standing before Matron, scantily sheathed in her bra, suspender belt, shining stockings and panties. As her left knee turned nervously inwards to nuzzle its partner, the whispering nylons kissed.

'Don't be silly, girl. I cannot possibly shave you like that. I need you entirely naked. Now strip at once and get up on this bed, or I'll spank your bottom very severely.' Matron suddenly remembered her own stocking during Henrietta's earlier punishment – and how it had been stained by the green-eyed girl's wet arousal. 'And you wouldn't want that to happen – or would you?' she added, her tone silky and yet stern.

Blushing as if a burning secret had just been shamefully exposed, Henrietta hurriedly unclasped her brassiere. The cups slid away from her heavy bosom and the ripe breasts bounced gently in their freedom. Bending, her exposed breasts now bulging invitingly, she released the stockings from the suspenders and palmed them down. Unfastening her suspender belt, she folded it once and placed it across the back of a chair. Only her panties remained.

'Come along, girl. You'll have to learn to be quicker. Just wait until the sirens start. Take those panties off or I'll come across and pull them down myself. And if I have to,' Matron warned softly, 'you'll regret it.'

Henrietta struggled to step out of her panties, hopping from one foot to the other as her ankles became briefly ensnared in the wisp of silk. Matron sighed impatiently, grappled the staggering nude firmly and spanked her bare bottom.

'Now get up on that bed at once, girl,' Matron thundered.

Gazing down into the wide green eyes, then at the coppery coils of the matted pubic nest, Matron spoke softly. 'There is no time left to study from textbooks. The only way you will learn – and remember – is through experience. Watch me carefully.'

Lathering a small brush, Matron applied it to Henrietta's displayed pubic mound, working the bristles in firmly as she soaped the pubic fuzz. The naked girl squirmed and blushed deeply. The bristles rasped her sensitive labial lips; she squealed and taloned the rubber sheet. The brush swept up against her clitoris: Henrietta moaned gently and pressed her knees together.

'You must remain absolutely still, my girl,' Matron warned. 'It may tickle a little. There's no avoiding that.'

Working the foaming bristles cunningly, Matron quickly had the entire pubic area fully soaped. 'Now. Observe. I take the razor thus—'

Henrietta whimpered and closed her eyes.

'I want you watch me carefully, girl. You'll come to no grief, I promise. I take the razor in these fingers, see?'

Her tummy fluttered as the naked girl nodded.

'Do not grip it tightly. Lightness of touch is what we aim for. Understand?'

The tiny razor skimmed up across the plum of the pubis, neatly peeling away a curl of foamed hairs and leaving a narrow swathe of pink, shaven skin in its wake.

'And again.' Matron guided the razor delicately up across the soaped pubic mound once more. 'And again.'

Holding her breath, and peering down over the swell of her trembling breasts, Henrietta watched spellbound as she was closely shaven. Stroke by stroke, her coppery coils disappeared beneath the glinting blade.

'Be very careful here,' Matron warned, her soft whisper breaking the intense silence. Pinching the labial lips up together – causing the nude to mew like a kitten at its cream – she plied the razor with quick, precise strokes.

'Any stray hairs are better plucked,' Matron remarked, placing the razor down on a towel.

Henrietta shivered.

'All done,' Matron pronounced. 'Almost there.' Taking a swab of cotton wool in the forceps and dipping it in to a small pot of surgical spirit, she wiped the freshly shaven pubic area with firm, upwards sweeps. The spirit stung the pink flesh. Henrietta moaned and then blushed furiously as a silvery bubble peeped out from between her labial folds. Matron tapped the bubble with the swab. It popped silently.

'Now if you look carefully, you'll see that I've missed four stray hairs. These must be plucked out with tweezers. One should, strictly speaking, swab between the buttocks and pluck out any anal hairs – but we have no time for that now. Later, perhaps.'

The last two words hung in the air between them like a delicious threat. Henrietta squeezed her cheeks so hard the rubber sheet became creased up in her cleft.

'Watch carefully,' Matron instructed.

Their heads almost touched as they both gazed down at the shaved pubic mound. Matron guided the tweezers down.

'Ouch.'

'Be quiet or I'll spank you.'

Henrietta hissed softly as the second, then the third, pubic hairs were neatly plucked from her flesh.

'Last one,' Matron murmured, tapping the copper coil with the tip of her tweezers. 'Look. It's just there. Awkward little devil. This might smart.'

'No – please—'

Ignoring Henrietta's piteous whine, Matron teased out the wet coil from the labial crease and plucked it out sharply. Henrietta screamed, her breasts wobbling and her hips jerking in her fleeting spasm of agony.

'Now, my girl,' Matron said, her tone almost affectionate. 'I will wash, dry and powder you. And I will examine you later. In bed, perhaps. Together we will go over the finer points of the pre-surgical pubic shave. I'm sure you've learned your lesson. Hm?'

Henrietta's green eyes flickered up – the tiniest glint of resentment now replaced by her shining devotion.

'Alice,' Matron said, her tone crisp and severe. 'Will you come in here? I am going to give you an enema.'

Alice, her cool reserve crumbling, paled. 'But I don't need—'

'I'll be the better judge of that girl. Get in.'

The door was firmly closed behind the anxious student nurse, who flinched as she heard it being locked. Glancing quickly over her shoulder, she caught Matron pocketing the key.

'Purely in the interests – your interests – of clinical practice. It is my intention to prepare you thoroughly for your finals next month. I will not contemplate the possibility of your failing, and I have a suspicion that the correct procedure for administering an enema will be a feature of your practicals. There is no need to undress, girl. I can have access to your bottom with the minimum of fuss. Just get onto the bed,' Matron ordered. 'I have taken the precaution of spreading a rubber sheet down for any spillage.'

Alice stretched out on her side, then slowly drew her knees up into the prone position.

'The enema,' Matron pronounced. 'We both know what its purpose is, but what equipment do I need?'

Alice, who had forgotten to remove her white pumps, tugged at their laces and kicked them off.

'Well, girl?'

'Warm water, towels, a lubricant, a funnel—' Alice paused.

'And?'

'Soft rubber tubing,' the girl on the bed whispered, her dry throat making her voice husky.

'Very good. Knees up a fraction more. No,' Matron added briskly. 'Leave your skirt and panties alone. I will see to that shortly. I may have to use three lengths of rubber tubing, possibly four.'

'Four?' Alice queried.

'One to administer the enema,' Matron explained, 'one to tie your wrists together, and another to bind your ankles together should you choose to struggle and resist.'

'And the fourth?' Alice murmured.

'To whip your bottom with, should you misbehave.'

Alice shivered and twisted her face up to plead with her uniformed tormentress. At last, Matron saw what she had hoped for – fear, respect and the beginnings of submission in the proud girl's eyes.

'How many rubber tubes do you think I shall need, girl?'

'One,' Alice gasped. 'Just the one, Matron.'

'I am so very glad to hear it, girl. Hands together and up at your face. Now part your thighs a fraction.'

Anxious to obey, Alice huddled down into the rubber sheet and jerked her buttocks back, surrendering them completely to Matron's gloved hands. After dragging Alice's skirt up over her hips and then thumbing her panties down into a tight band just below the swell of the bunched buttocks, Matron lubricated the tip of the soft, brownish-red rubber tube and guided it into the tiny anal whorl. Alice grunted, tightening her cheeks in a reflex.

'Relax your bottom, girl, and accept the tube.'

Whimpering softly, Alice obeyed. The glistening tip of the

rubber tubing slid up between her buttocks.

'Good. A tip for you, my girl. Do not force the tubing at any stage. When you meet resistance, twist it gently. Rotating the tube irritates the anal muscles and they loosen.'

After supervising the slow insertion of five inches of tubing, Matron deftly attached a funnel to the other end and poured two and a half pints of warm water into it.

Alice groaned as the liquid surge burgeoned deep inside her bowels, filling her belly with its warmth. Matron lowered the funnel and, inspecting her inverted watch, observed the passage of a whole minute.

'No, girl. You must not clench your cheeks. The tubing will slip out. If it does, you will be whipped.'

Alice squeezed the rubber sheet between tightening fists as the warm surge bloated her colon.

'Another pint, I think—'

'No—' Alice wailed, shrinking away from Matron.

'I'll be the judge of that. Stay still, girl, or there will be spillage.'

Another pint of warm water rushed down the narrow rubber tubing, causing Alice's anal canal to extend. She jerked and twisted suddenly, dislodging the tubing from her buttocks. The spillage flooded the rubber sheet, drenching her stockings, skirt and panties.

'You wicked, disobedient girl,' Matron hissed. Reaching out for a towel, she stemmed the flood, then, reaching out again, she grasped three more rubber tubes and arranged them lengthways down the prone girl. Taking up the first supple length, she wound it around Alice's ankles and bound them together tightly.

'Please – no—' Alice moaned, writhing in her shame. 'I'm sorry, Matron.'

'You will be, girl, you will be. Now be quiet and give me your wrists.'

'Please don't—'

'Silence. Do I have to tell you again? You seem to deem it necessary to defy me,' Matron grunted, binding the proffered wrists severely with the flexible tubing. 'Don't you?'

As tears glittered on the rubber sheet beneath the bound girl's closed eyes, Matron rolled her over.

161

'Let's see just how arrogant you feel after a taste of this,' she barked, doubling the remaining length of rubber tubing in her right fist. 'Let's see what a dozen or so from my little friend here does, followed by half an hour sitting on the toilet with a whipped bottom.'

With her face pressed down into the rubber sheet, and her hands and feet immobile in strict bondage, Alice was utterly helpless beneath the lash.

Returning from her weekend course at an army burns unit – when the bombers descended upon London spilling their incendiaries, casualties would be very high – Matron ate sardines on toast with those arriving on night duty. She spoke briefly with the Almoner about the purchase of blackout material and then retired to her quarters.

Her wireless was playing Elgar: melancholy but stirring stuff. Matron, who preferred Vaughan Williams, ate a bar of chocolate, then turned to sort out her laundry basket.

Arranging her freshly ironed lingerie in the second drawer of her dresser, she sprinkled a few drops of orange water on the sheer silks and sensual satins. The sweet pungency reminded her of Spain. *Naranja*. In Tudor England, the fruit was called the norange. It was, she recalled, Dr Johnson who had definitively given the swollen citrus from Seville the name orange. Spain. Matron closed her eyes and inhaled the orange water. It reminded her of the fierce Spanish sun: and then, suddenly, of the dyed blonde in the dusty convent courtyard licking and kissing the leather that had just whipped her buttocks and breasts. Yes. The punished nude, her stretched tongue lapping at the leather, her excited eyes sparkling. Sparkling, Matron realised, just like Henrietta's green eyes during and after her humiliation and submission to the razor at her soaped pubic fuzz.

Henrietta. Matron decided upon a brief nocturnal patrol down along the dormitory corridor. Remembering Alice's precautionary habit of sporting a locked bedroom door, Matron picked up her pass key as she kicked off her polished brogues.

* * *

162

Poppy was drifting off to sleep over her studies at her desk. Matron shook the dozing girl gently, noting with approval the chapter on nursing care for the shell-shocked. Poppy sat up, startled.

'Time for bed,' Matron said gently, stroking the pert pony-tail. 'Put your book away now. I am very pleased to find you at your studies.'

She helped the sleepy girl undress. Taking the hem of Poppy's vest in both hands, she drew it up slowly to the breasts above.

'Skin the bunny?' Matron smiled. 'My auntie used to say that to me every night.'

Poppy grinned. The vest swept up over the heavy swell of her naked bosom. They bounced softly in their newfound freedom. Matron's thumbtips captured each nipple briefly – a tenderly dominant touch of authority.

'Tomorrow, I will find time to help you with your splints and bandages,' Matron promised, turning the little nurse around and propelling her towards her bed with a playful spank. 'It is important that the bandages are tied very tightly.'

Henrietta was already in her bed. Matron sat down alongside the green-eyed girl, her heavy buttocks depressing the mattress.

'Let me see my handiwork,' she said, tapping the blanket just below the girl's belly.

Slowly, shyly, Henrietta peeled her blanket away and drew her cotton nightgown up, revealing her shaven delta. Matron, gazing unblinkingly into the wide, green eyes, began to gently massage the exposed flesh with her fingertip. The green eyes widened.

'After you have qualified, would you like to stay here and work for me?'

Tensing, then relaxing as the fingertip described dominant circles at her smooth pubis, Henrietta nodded.

'Excellent. I shall take a very special interest in you, girl. And does pussy miss her sleek coat?'

Henrietta lowered her gaze and blushed.

'Does she?' Matron insisted.

'A little,' the chestnut-curled girl conceded softly.

Matron stood up, inched the hem of her pleated uniform skirt up to her waist and thumbed her panties down. Parting her thighs a little, she inched towards the bed. 'Look at my pussy. She has her winter coat on still.'

Henrietta gasped aloud at Matron's mass of pubic hair.

'Touch pussy. She likes to be stroked.'

Timorously, Henrietta reached out and dabbled her fingertips in Matron's luxuriant growth.

'Tomorrow, if you are very good, I shall let you shave me.'

'Yes, yes please!'

'But now you must get some sleep. Kiss pussy goodnight.'

Wriggling across to the very edge of her bed, Henrietta strained her neck as she brought her lips to the proud pubis before them. Eyes shining – like the whipped nude in the convent courtyard under the fierce Spanish sun – she buried her face between Matron's warm thighs, her pink tongue wet and eager as it licked and lapped devotedly.

Later, approaching Alice's room on stockinged feet, Matron slipped the pass key into the lock and opened the door silently. Alice, naked, was on her bed – not in it – gently masturbating. Eyes closed, her head arched back, she dealt with her slippery labia and clitoris with urgent fingers.

Matron tiptoed up to the bed. 'Wasting precious time on selfish pleasures, I see.'

Alice squealed and attempted to scramble under her blanket but Matron pounced, pinning the squirming nude down firmly to the bed.

'You'll do two hours hard study before you get any sleep tonight, you little slut, but first we'll get this little distraction out of the way. When I see a boil, I lance it. Continue and complete what you were doing.'

'Leave me alone,' Alice wailed, her Kensington composure completely crumbling. Squirming, she looked away, avoiding Matron's stern gaze.

A firm hand clutched her hair and twisted her face upwards. Matron glared down dominantly. 'And you will tell me exactly what naughtiness is going through your mind as your fingers are busy down there. Come along, girl. We haven't got all night.'

Alice stubbornly refused, despite the cruel hand taloning her hair.

'I have a walnut veneer cupboard in my room. In that cupboard, there is a cane. A whippy, bamboo cane. Do you want me to go back to my room and get it? Hm? If I do, your bare bottom will suffer most severely.'

'No—' Alice whispered, shuddering.

'Then continue with what you clearly think is more important than studying for your finals.'

Alice inched her fingers – the tips already wet and shining – back down to where her parted labia greeted them with a wide smile.

'Tell me your most intimate thoughts, girl,' Matron demanded. 'Speak out your flights of wicked fancy.'

Grinding her soft buttocks into the blanket, Alice thumbed her pink clitoris. In exquisitely clipped vowels, she whispered her fantasies aloud.

'I am in that room. The room walled with bright, white tiles. The door is locked. I am naked, except for my ankle socks and white pumps. You are standing over me as I kneel before you. You tell me I am lazy and am not fit to wear the uniform of a nurse. I am only fit to be a wardsmaid, to clean and scrub. To kneel and scrub floors—'

Matron, kneeling down at the bedside, cupped and squeezed Alice's left breast and gazed down at the masturbating girl. 'And?'

'I do not scrub hard enough. You are standing over me, your shoe pressing down upon my bare bottom. You unbuckle your leather belt. It dangles before my eyes; then you tap my buttocks with it.'

'Yes?' Matron hissed, her voice a whisper of gathering excitement.

Alice was now pleasuring herself unselfconsciously, ravishing her wet flesh with frank, unguarded wanton eagerness. 'I shuffle away but you crush me down into the wet linoleum and then whip my bare bottom with your belt—'

Alice closed her eyes and snarled softly as her climax

approached. Inching her hips up, she jerked and writhed as her quicksilver started to spill.

'I whip you,' Matron echoed, savaging the breast in her fierce grip.

'Yes,' Alice screamed softly, now utterly broken and abandoned in her violent orgasm. She hammered her bare bottom into the blanket beneath her, the strong odour of her wet excitement flooding the room.

Matron rose, after the third orgasm had expired, superbly dominant above the shivering nude on the bed.

'By Jove, Alice, I think I'll be able to do something with you yet, my girl. True, I had to bend you to my strap in order to bend you to my will. But we're getting there, girl; we're getting there,' Matron pronounced with proud satisfaction as she unbuckled her leather belt. Gazing down at the arrogant girl from society's top drawer – the girl Matron knew she had dominated and crushed – she raised the leather to her lips and kissed it slowly. 'Turn over, Alice. Give me your bottom. I've only got a month to lick you into shape.'

Severe Mentor

The seagulls wheeling against the clear blue sky were an improvement on the pigeons messing the grimy windows of what used to be his office in Leadenhall Street, EC3. Yes. The move down to Brighton had been a success in every way. What was her name? Samantha. Of course. It all came back to him as he flicked through the glossy photocopier brochure.

Little Samantha, back in the Leadenhall Street days – just the two of them squashed together in that tiny little fifth-floor office, running the claims department for a firm of horticultural insurance brokers. No clients, no new policies, just the treadmill of claims after early winds or late frosts had ravaged the glass-houses from Kent to Cornwall. Just the two of them. The boss and the younger, inexperienced lovely little assistant.

He gazed down at a gleaming new photocopier that could do everything except make the coffee. He grinned, remembering how he had bullied her and shouted at her until she had cried – then made her pull down her panties and sit on the copier in the corridor, the one they shared with the feta cheese import agency in the next cramped office. Enlarging the image of her bottom onto A3 paper, he had obtained a haunting shot of her swollen cheeks. He had kept the picture in the top drawer of his desk. For a week or two afterwards, every time the nervous little thing had made the slightest error, he would force her to stand and watch as he slid the drawer open, took the Xerox out and, smoothing the bottom flat across his desk top, spank it slowly with his right hand.

Spanking her bottom. Another month, and he would have had her warmth across his lap and his hard hand across her peach-cheeks. Yes. He had been close to the point of total domination –

another month and her bare buttocks, more maybe, would have been all his. A pretty little thing but timid. Like a rabbit in a python's tank: easy meat.

Flicking through another glossy brochure – extolling the virtues of the electronic office – he shrugged. Leadenhall Street had been a shambles. Everything was paper, then, with grey metal cabinets jostling for space spilling out their index cards, claim forms and bulging files. Samantha had just started to go to evening classes at Mile End. Computing. No future in that for you, girl, he had warned. Computers were toys for big boys. Stick to what you know, sweetie, and if you are a good girl – a very good girl – I'll see if I can't give you a guiding hand up through the clerical grades.

Then – out of the blue – the axe fell. Canadians. Came and snapped up the horticultural insurance broking arm overnight. Dawn raid, the City called it. Same thing. The Leadenhall Street operation was closed down and, for a bleak fortnight his future was on hold. Came out of it all right, though. The horticultural operation was relocated to Brighton – and, by a judicious mixture of back-stabbing and brown-nosing, he had got the Brighton office and three gorgeous female employees to run. Samantha, he supposed, had got chopped up in the cuts.

The seagulls screamed as they breasted the sharp east wind.

'Good weekend, Susie?'

'Yes, Mr Andrews.' He insisted that his 'girls' always called him by his full, formal name and title. It established the correct tone in the office. Professional and disciplined.

'See anyone interesting? Bet you did. You always do.'

Susie, his part-timer, was an art student. Up to her neck in loans and rent arrears, and sinking fast. He knew she needed her job, even though it included the task of having to invent sexual adventures and recount them every Monday morning to satisfy his prurient appetite – an appetite that fed upon every intimate detail, every moist morsel.

She flushed, took a deep breath and murmured, 'I posed for a sculptress.'

'Naked?' Mr Andrews hissed, his eyes narrowing.

'In my black stockings. But yes. Naked. She made me pose on an automatic washing machine. The round plastic door at the front, you know—'

'I know.' He nodded vigorously.

'It was opened. My stockinged legs framed the large, dark hole.'

His trousers bulged as his cock rose, its length stirring with interest at her words.

Susie spent the next seven and a half minutes entertaining her boss, as she did every Monday morning, with a sizzling account of wholly fictitious weekend adventures. This morning, fingering the tip of his stiffened cock beneath his desk, he listened to her ordeal in the supposed studio of a Belgian sculptress.

'Forty-three. Brown eyes. Wide, wet lips,' she added. Mr Andrews was a stickler for detail. 'She always works in the nude.'

'Go on, Susie.'

Susie obeyed her master's voice. 'When the latex had cooled, she poured it over my breasts. It trickled down my tummy and made my pussy hairs all sticky. She had to wipe my pussy with a soft, yellow sponge.'

'Nice, eh?'

'Very nice, Mr Andrews. She dragged the sponge firmly against my pussy-lips. I squeezed my thighs together and came. She smelt my juices on the sponge and sucked it with her big, wet lips.'

'Tell me about the latex. The latex smothered over your naked breasts.' He was masturbating slowly. His balls ached for release.

Susie told him how the Belgian sculptress had slowly peeled away the clinging second, rubbery skin from the flesh of her bosom. How the dominant sculptress had captured Susie's breasts and examined them intimately for a full six minutes, weighing their passive warmth in her controlling palms before thumbing the nipples up into fierce stubs of pleasurable pain.

'Tell me about the dildo. Quickly,' he rasped.

Susie described how the Belgian had teased the nude poser perched on top of the washing machine with a wicked little black ebony shaft.

'She made me go belly-down across the automatic and slid it up my—'

He grunted as he came. She gazed out of the window, watching the seagulls soar and dive.

Hands busy with tissues beneath his desk, Mr Andrews recovered his composure. 'Tell your landlord to give me a call, Susie. I'll see if fifty quid can block that eviction notice.'

'Oh, would you, Mr Andrews? Thanks. Thanks ever so much.'

'I'll have a coffee now. Nip down the road and get me some biscuits. Anything chocolaty. You know what I like.'

'Yes, Mr Andrews.'

He was lucky to be in Brighton. The Canadians left him alone to run things his way. No prying auditors querying his idiosyncratic use of company funds and, better still, no prying personnel managers from 'human resources and staff development' to offer a shoulder for his 'girls' to cry on and shout harassment. No. Relocating away from head office down here in Brighton had dealt him a very good hand. He held all the aces.

'Can I see you for a minute, Mr Andrews?'

Annie, a trim blonde, was a twenty-nine-year-old single parent. When she asked for a minute, it was usually to ask for an hour. An hour off early to pick up the kid from school. She hovered in the doorway, biting her lower lip. He made her wait while he flicked through an empty file, relishing her anxiety. Her breasts – braless, as he had instructed – bounced gently.

'Well? I suppose you want to go early. Again.'

'Yes, please, Mr Andrews.'

Annie worked a sort of flexi-time which allowed her to be at the school gates when other arrangements broke down. Mr Andrews always agreed, providing Annie proved flexible enough.

'Are those stockings or tights?'

'Stockings, Mr Andrews,' she whispered.

'Seamed?'

'Just as you suggested, Mr Andrews. And very smart for the office, like you said they would be, don't you think? They're self-support. No suspender belt.'

The pretty young woman closed the door behind her and stepped into his office. Turning her bottom towards him, she inched up her camel skirt over her thighs until the hem rode her hips. Waggling her pantied buttocks, she allowed him a long, lingering look at her stockinged legs. Slender and shapely, they were sheathed in a light tan sheen up to the softness of her thighs where darker bands bit into the flesh below the swell of her buttocks.

'Come closer,' he commanded.

She shuffled back towards him with mincing steps, her cheeks joggling deliciously.

'I can't let you go until three forty-five, I'm afraid, Annie.'

She tugged at her panties, dragging the thin silk up into her cleft.

'Three-thirty, at a stretch.'

She yanked her panties down, allowing him to feast upon her swollen cheeks as they wobbled before him in naked splendour.

'Let me see the jewel,' he grunted thickly. 'The jewel in the crown.'

Her fingers appeared at her buttocks, taloning the soft peaches and spreading them apart. Deep in the cleft, her tiny pink anus glistened.

'Better make it three o'clock.'

'Thank you Mr Andrews,' she whispered, choking down her tears.

The great thing about Brighton was that he could just shuffle everything over to other branches, and head office never twigged. All queries were sent straight across to Basingstoke and new claims were stamped 'insufficient data' and palmed off on Croydon. This left him all the time he needed to enjoy his 'girls' and his computer. He could empty his in-tray by ten every morning, then settle down for a couple of hours downloading porn from East European web sites.

Mary, his office manageress, did everything. Thirty-two, heavily breasted and superbly buttocked, she was now the breadwinner, since her husband had been made redundant. The mortgage was heavy and his severance money light. Every penny counted – and Mary had to ask for a sub before her salary every month.

'Take sixty out of the petty cash,' he would instruct her.

'Thank you, Mr Andrews,' she would reply, undoing a second – then a third – blouse button, offering his greedy eyes her cleavage. The underwired cups, deliberately selected for the push-up effect, held her bulging breasts in submissive bondage – just like her cash shortage kept her under his firm control.

The soft curves of her bosom would collide and shudder as she deliberately bent down across his desk towards him, slowly tidying away his paperwork. When he carelessly dropped paperclips on the floor, she knelt down on all fours to gather them up, surrendering her tightly skirted bottom up to his gaze.

'Did I say sixty?'

She flinched as his hand stroked her left buttock, staying at her ripe flesh to cup and squeeze.

'Better make it a round hundred, Mary.'

'Just as you like, Mr Andrews.'

When he returned from his two hour pub lunch – ice-cold Guinness, sausages and a stripper with baby-oiled breasts – his e-mail advised him that the Canadians were sending down one of their consultants to evaluate the Brighton branch. Management mentorship, as the jargon put it. Mr Andrews summoned Mary into his office.

'We're getting a visit tomorrow. Some snooper coming down from head office to assess our operation here. Jobs-on-the-line time, Mary. We'd better look busy. See to it.'

'Are they looking for a redundancy?' she murmured, paling.

'Downsizing is the name of the game.'

She stood behind him, placing her slender hands down upon his shoulders. 'I serve you well, Mr Andrews,' she whispered, massaging away the tension of his stress brought on by the e-mail.

'Nobody's indispensable. Look what happened to your bloke.'

'I'll fill up all the in-trays with outstanding claims.'

'See to it that the "girls" are hard at it.'

'Relax,' she said softly, lowering her bosom down to pillow his head. 'You mustn't get stressed, Mr Andrews. It's bad for you to get upset.'

Kneeling, she slipped her hand inside his shirt, fingernailing his nipple. He grunted, his trousers bulging in response.

'We don't want any changes here, do we?' he reasoned, spreading his hands out expansively. 'Everything's just fine as it is.'

'Just as you want it, Mr Andrews,' her moistened lips whispered as she unzipped him. She closed her eyes and saw the unpaid bills stacking up behind the toaster in the kitchen. Opening her eyes, she managed a forced smile as she dragged out his erection, enclosing the hot length in a fist of fingers, and started to pump rhythmically.

'Get us two coffees,' Mr Andrews barked out to Susie as he ushered the head office consultant into his office. 'Take a seat.'

She took one – his. He scowled and pulled up a chair alongside his desk, barely able to conceal his resentment at the cool young blonde who oozed efficiency, self-possession and an assurance that he found maddening. From her razor-cut blonde fringe to her black, kitten-heeled court shoes, the consultant projected executive success. The suit, a Louis Feraud, was severely chic and expensive. Her metal briefcase matched her silver nail varnish. The mobile phone was fashioned into an ivory dildo. Impudently ironic. He blushed as she absently fingered it candidly.

There were no polite preliminaries. No how-was-your-journey-down. She got stuck into him straight away.

'I've been running audits on you over the past few weeks. And—'

'Audits?' he echoed. 'But—'

'I can scan you from HQ and track everything that goes on here through your computer.'

'I had no idea.' He looked at her closely, as if troubled by an elusive thought.

'Yep,' she nodded. 'Our software can trace every transaction.' Her voice was crisp and assured, but he seemed to be recollecting a memory from the past.

'So you've been watching me—'

'Every move you make.'

He stared at her, a flash of recognition in his widening eyes. Surely not. No. It couldn't be. He shook his head, convinced he was mistaken.

'For instance,' she continued, 'I would like to hear your reasons for the petty cash account being –' she consulted a print-out '– over two hundred pounds short this month. Why is that, Mr Andrews?'

Advances to Mary, rent arrears for Susie, lingerie for Annie and a couple of crisp fivers down that stripper's cleavage yesterday lunchtime. But Mr Andrews had better answers prepared for the question.

'Donations to local charities. Essential PR. Generates goodwill and business. I have the receipts here somewhere,' he countered smoothly, opening his top drawer and producing the bogus paperwork.

She had to swing her legs away to let him get access to his desk. His knuckles grazed her glossily stockinged knees.

Her hand brushed his away sharply. 'Keep anything else in your top drawer these days, Andrews?' she snapped.

He froze, alert to her authority. No 'Mr': just 'Andrews'. Only somebody well in with senior management would express themselves so dominantly.

'Any Xeroxed bottoms, perhaps?' she asked, her tone as hard as cold steel.

Swallowing noisily, he slumped back down in his chair. Memories of Leadenhall Street flooded his swirling brain. Samantha. The sharply spoken, severely attired blonde sitting across the desk – in his chair – was Samantha.

Her voice broke into his confusion. 'As I suspected, these figures do not tally with the figures downloaded from your computer to mine. Substantial amounts, Andrews,' she murmured. 'I've been monitoring you very closely. Watching you milk the company on a petty but regular basis. It soon mounts up. And I also know you've been accessing porn.' Her silver fingernail tapped a blue floppy disc. 'State-of-the-art memory search facility. I've got all your web sites visited. Dates and times.'

Mary tapped politely on the door and entered, bringing the

coffees in. Samantha noted the unbuttoned cleavage and the anxious eyes.

'Thanks for coming in a little earlier. I needed to see you before Andrews comes.' Samantha invited the three 'girls' to sit.

'Is it bad news?' Susie asked.

'Our jobs?' Mary echoed.

'You can all be assured that your jobs are secure,' she replied, smiling. 'No, it's nothing like that. I'm down here to fine-tune things here at Brighton. Andrews needs a little tweaking. I know him of old. Nasty piece of work. It's time he was taught a lesson. Susie.'

The young art student looked up quickly.

'I'll get our legal department onto your lease. As a valuable employee, we will take care of that. Annie,' she continued briskly, 'I know you need to go early at short notice. From now on, consider yourself on flexi-time. Work your hours to your own schedule, as long as they match the contract, OK?'

Annie beamed.

'As for you, Mary, I will set up an interest-free loan, with a repayment spread you'll hardly notice. The company can afford it. It can't afford to lose you.'

The three employees chorused their thanks.

'Now you can all do something for me. Andrews. I don't know what you've had to endure, but I can guess. I'll need your help sorting him out.'

'You've got it.' The three women spoke with one voice.

'Half an hour late, Andrews. A regular bad habit?'

He flushed and muttered something about parking problems as he swept past Samantha into his office.

'Get back out here at once,' she barked.

He came out of his office, open-mouthed.

'Over by the photocopier, please.'

He strode across to the copier and, lifting the rubber cover, peered down into the dark glass plate. Shrugging, he turned to her.

'Seems all right. What's the problem? Paper jam? No need to get into a state about it—'

'Shut up,' Samantha thundered. 'Unzip. Unzip and get it on the glass.'

The three 'girls' stopped working and giggled as they enjoyed his outrage. Crimsoning, he spluttered angrily.

'At once, Andrews. Unless,' Samantha continued distinctly, 'you want me to suspend you immediately – and prosecute you subsequently for fraud and embezzlement?'

Andrews paled.

'I'm waiting. Waiting for you to unzip and slap it on the glass.'

He obeyed, his trembling fingers struggling with his zip. Up on tiptoe, he eased his flaccid penis onto the copier and closed the lid on it gingerly.

Samantha strode across to the machine. Stabbing the buttons with her silvernailed fingertip, she produced a hugely magnified image on A3 paper. Extracting it, she flourished it aloft.

'This is what Andrews thinks he's like. Potent. A masculine menace. A well-hung wolf.'

Jabbing the buttons once more, she produced a diminutive image on a small A5 sheet, the penis diminished by 200 per cent. She made six more copies. He squirmed as she pinned the cover down firmly, his naked thighs glowing eerily each time the green light flashed.

Abstracting the derisory images from the tray, she handed one to each of the three laughing women. 'This is what Andrews really is,' she snarled, blue-tacking the other images up on the walls around the office. 'In case you ever forget, just look up and remember that he is, after all, only a little prick.'

Ribald and scornful laughter drowned out his angry protest.

'You can't—' he exploded, stumbling in his loose trousers as he lurched to snatch down the taunting pictures of his unmanhood.

'Leave those alone,' Samantha warned him, her tone one of icy contempt. In a brighter voice, she asked the three women if they were ready for coffee.

'Yes, please,' they replied, just about able to manage the words through their giggling.

'That'll be just the four coffees, then, Andrews. You've forfeited yours by arriving late. Be a good little boy, won't you, and when you've put the kettle on and washed the cups from yesterday, slip out for some cakes. I rather fancy a Bakewell. They can have what they want. They'll give you their orders.'

Finally managing to master his zip, Andrews stumbled out of the office, his face a blaze of anger and shame.

'That certainly taught him,' Annie remarked.

Susie and Mary grinned.

'Andrews has a lot to learn,' Samantha murmured. 'That was merely lesson one.'

When he had returned and served them coffee in his own office, Samantha ordered him to bend across his desk. Protesting at first, he quickly obeyed when she picked up her silver mobile – fingering the smooth phallic shape slowly – and started to press the number for head office.

She invited the three watching women to gather around the desk as she yanked down his trousers and shorts and spanked his bare buttocks with a long, plastic ruler. He yelped as his buttocks reddened under her savage chastisement. After a blistering twenty-six strokes, she placed the ruler down on the desk and taloned his hot cheeks, digging her silver nails into his crimson flesh.

'Kneel,' she ordered. 'No: keep your trousers down and your red bottom where we can all see it.'

They resumed their seats and their coffee as he remained on all fours, the plate of cakes perched on his hot bottom. As they sipped their coffee and chatted, he shuffled between their chairs, offering them cakes from the plate balanced on his buttocks. Mary selected a chocolate eclair and was just about to bite into it when, with an impish grin, she jammed it between his cheeks. They collapsed in raucous laughter as he shuffled around in a circle.

Annie kicked off her sandal and guided her stockinged toes up to torment his sac, scrunching his balls savagely.

Samantha shook her head. 'Patience, Annie. You'll each get your turn with him over the next few days. I promise. I have a working brief to be his mentor. He's long overdue for a spot of training. You can each help me correct his faults and reconstruct his management style.'

At two o'clock, they amicably tossed a coin in front of him to see which of them would enjoy having Andrews at their mercy first. Susie, the art student, won. She led him into his office by his tie, inviting her two colleagues and Samantha in to witness his humiliation.

Kneeling down before her, Andrews begged: but she merely gagged him with her panties before baring his groin. After binding his hands tightly behind his back with one of Susie's seamed stockings – making sure the shining nylon burnt at his wrists – she produced a can of pink paint and a stiffly bristled twenty-centimetre brush. His eyes widened in mute appeal above the gag as she snapped on a pair of yellow rubber gloves.

'Heard of Jackson Pollock? Well, now you're going to see an original Jackson Bollock.' She dipped the bristles into the gleaming pink paint and wiped them against the lip of the can. 'He always wants to know what I get up to every weekend. I'm a painter. I paint.' She dabbed the brush at his balls, deliberately guiding the cruel bristles home harshly. His squeal was audible despite the panties binding his mouth. 'God, they'll have a laugh when they clean him up in casualty tonight.' She drew the dripping brush along the length of his shaft. Jabbing at his balls, she produced an erection – more 'canvas', she joked, for her to work on. 'It'll sting like hell.'

Mary frowned, despite her grin. 'Sting?'

'Oil-based. They'll have to use turps and an astringent.'

Andrews wriggled to evade the deft brush-strokes but Susie was resolutely firm, covering every tiny inch of his buttocks, balls and extended, nodding cock with the glutinous pink paint.

He did not show up for work the next day.

'He'll be in,' Samantha reassured them. 'He's got no choice.'

As she predicted, Andrews slunk into the office the next day. He blustered, his violent indignation soon collapsing into a whimpering appeal for mercy. Samantha silenced him abruptly, then handed him over to Annie, the single parent.

'Sorry, girls.' She shrugged, pushing him into his own office, 'I want to do this alone.'

'We promise not to listen or peep,' they lied.

'Strip,' she commanded, closing then locking the office door.

'Now look here, Annie, I'm ordering you—'

'Get undressed, you obnoxious little toad. I'm going to teach you a lesson. A lesson you'll never forget. Now strip.'

He struggled out of his clothes and threw them down onto the floor. Moments later, he cowered before her, shivering in his vest, pants and dark socks.

'Pick up your clothes and fold them neatly,' she instructed in a tone normally reserved for naughty boys.

Flushing, he obeyed, bending down and scrabbling to retrieve his clothing. She dragged his underpants down over his buttocks and spanked him harshly, twice.

'I want you naked,' she ordered. 'Vest and pants off for your punishment.'

As he struggled out of his underwear Annie pulled her cashmere jumper up over her head. Her naked breasts were round, ripe and heavily swollen. They wobbled as she tossed the cashmere jumper aside and, taking a seat, ordered him to sit on her lap.

Cradling him like a baby, she cupped her left breast and forced it into his mouth. Andrews withdrew his lips from her erect nipple but quickly returned his mouth as she dropped her hands down and squeezed his balls.

'Suck.'

Closing his eyes, he mouthed her slavishly. She breast-fed him dominantly, smothering him until he spluttered and gasped for air. Her tweaking fingertips at his naked balls ensured that she made him suffer to her complete and utter satisfaction. Annie grew wet, so exciting was her absolute revenge. She ordered him to stretch out, belly down, across her lap.

Spanking him was delicious. He squealed as she hammered her hot left palm, savagely cracking it across his seething cheeks. All the weeks – months – of pent-up anger and humiliation poured out in the vengeful spate of furious punishment. He howled, but the heavily breasted young woman merely renewed her vicious onslaught. Spilling him down onto the carpet, she knelt over his reddened buttocks, straddling him between her thighs.

'You've made me all wet and sticky,' she murmured, dragging her skirt up and her panties down. 'I'd better dry myself.'

He moaned as she raked her wet plum down over his hot cheeks repeatedly, buckling face down into the carpet as he suffered this gross humiliation. Annie rode him until she came, squealing out her joy as she climaxed contemptuously against his spanked bottom.

Breathless, she remained astride him, then slowly rose – to tread on his red buttocks, dominantly pinning him down.

'You told me that I didn't need a bra, didn't you?' she demanded.

He remained silent as she trod him ruthlessly into the carpet.

'Didn't you?'

'Yes, no, I'm sorry—' he spluttered.

'You were wrong,' she whispered, flourishing a white cotton sports bra. 'I do need a bra. To whip you with.'

Whipping it down a dozen times, she lashed his bare cheeks mercilessly, striping his helpless buttocks with cruel crimson weals.

The following day, Mary held the entire office in suspense until late in the afternoon. Andrews was kept busy dealing with the backlog of neglected claims – a task broken only to attend to his colleagues with cups of tea, coffee and total obedience. Samantha timed his twenty-minute ham sandwich lunch at his desk and hounded him tirelessly, checking his output and berating him for his slowness.

At three-fifteen, Mary invited the others to accompany her into his office. She surprised them by addressing Andrews as William.

'William. Willie,' she laughed. 'How appropriate that the vicar named a little prick like you Willie.'

Andrews paled with anger. The girls giggled, enjoying the joke.

'Well, Willie,' Mary continued softly, 'all work and no play is no good. No good at all. So I want to see you come out from behind that desk and play, Willie. With yourself.'

Remaining behind the desk, he appealed to her, but Mary was adamant. She ordered him to come and stand before them.

'No need to get it out, Willie. We don't particularly want to see the wretched thing,' she added, piling on the humiliation. 'Just knuckle yourself through your trousers. Commence.'

Andrews crimsoned under their expectant gaze. Clenching his right hand into a fist, he dragged it down against himself half-heartedly.

'Faster, Willie. Come, come, we know you can do better than that,' she snarled. 'Faster – unless, of course, you really want to suffer.'

At the promise of pain, his fist rasped the front of his trousers, conjuring up a prominent bulge. Closing his eyes and planting his feet wider apart, he savaged himself until, moments later, he moaned – staggering back against his desk and shuddering. He came, to their ragged cheer, the dark stain spreading across his lap.

'Good boy, Willie,' Mary crowed, clapping her hands. The others clapped vigorously, their sporadic applause echoing around the office. Mary held her hand up for silence.

'Again, Willie. Do it again,' she instructed.

'I can't—' he pleaded, shaking his head.

'You'd better, Willie. I think you'll find you can.'

The watching circle of women nodded vehemently and brayed for another orgasm.

Twenty-six minutes later, Andrews knelt in a crumpled heap on the carpet. Obeying Mary's stern instructions, he had climaxed four times. His trousers and the knuckles of his right hand were soaking.

Mary hitched her skirt up and, leaving her dark bronze tights in place, straddled his face and forced him down onto the carpet with her heavy buttocks. Kneeling astride him as he lay stretched out beneath her, his face smothered by the weight of her warm bottom, she rocked gently to and fro, burying him completely. His hands taloned the carpet desperately as he struggled to breathe, but Mary ignored the muffled screams of her mount and rode him ruthlessly.

Squeezing her thighs together, she bent forwards to unzip him. His little wet cock proved elusive but she finally managed to tease it out. The spent penis was wet, pink and shrivelled. She toyed with it contemptuously for several minutes, to the delight of the onlookers. Still riding him with her splayed cheeks – her dark bronze tights rasping his upturned face painfully – she asked for a tissue. Samantha supplied one. Mary dried the tiny penis carefully, then held it dominantly in a finger-and-thumb pincer.

'Little Willie,' she remarked, flicking the tip of his pathetic specimen. 'We are drying you now and putting you back where you belong. And we don't want to see you ever again.'

Stuffing his penis back into his wet underpants and then zipping Andrews up, Mary carefully planted her hands down onto the carpet before angling her rump directly down onto his face. She started bouncing her bottom slowly at first, then with gathering momentum and increasing violence, she commenced the queening of the dethroned office king.

'I think I've done all that there is to be done here,' Samantha announced the following lunchtime. 'Almost.'

Outside, the grey sky darkened ominously as Brighton braced itself for the impending storm. Driven on shore by the violent winds, the seagulls appeared as tiny white flecks against the storm clouds.

The stern mentor from head office slipped into the small kitchen at the rear and emerged grasping the white electric flex from the jug kettle. 'Come with me, please. I'm going to say *au revoir* to Andrews.'

Samantha rationed them to two strokes apiece. After her departure, things would return to normal at the office – so they enjoyed themselves thoroughly, making every slicing stripe count. The whippy flex kissed his pale buttocks six times, leaving them criss-crossed with livid red lines. Andrews, spread face down across his desk, whimpered.

'From now on, his bottom is yours. Absolutely. But I think he's learnt his lesson. You shouldn't have any more problems with him.'

The three women nodded.

'And don't forget,' Samantha murmured, producing her thin, phallic mobile, 'with this, I can plug into a modem and track his every move.'

Outside, the wind moaned loudly. Up in the boiling clouds, the seagulls mewed and squalled. Inside the office, Samantha approached the whipped cheeks and stroked the tip of her slender mobile down between them. Andrews grunted as she forced the tip into his sphincter and gently probed his anus.

'Andrews said there was no future in computers,' she told the watching women. 'Thanks to this and my modem, I'd say his future is programmed. It's as good as having him electronically tagged.'

'You can control him from your desk in head office,' Mary replied enthusiastically. 'Remote control.'

'Exactly,' Samantha whispered. 'Andrews said that the electronic office would be a nightmare. In his case, he was right.'

Samantha drove the slender phallus deep into his anus. He opened his mouth wide, to plead and protest: but all they heard was the scream of the gulls circling above in the storm.

Strict Mistress

Miranda stretched out in her bed, spreading her thighs wide. Naked – it was a warm night – she relished the crisp linen at her skin. The freshly laundered sheets rasped her nakedness deliciously. It had been another busy day. Demanding. Teaching Greek and maths at the Jakob Institute was challenging. The young ladies – opting for the Jakob Institute instead of Oxbridge – were reluctant to learn. In return for astronomical fees, the Institute promised a régime of academic excellence coupled with strict discipline. Daughters of the rich and privileged, their wild behaviour excluded them from attending conventional colleges. Their despairing parents firmly approved of the strict code of discipline imposed by the Institute.

Discipline. Miranda shivered with pleasure as her nipples tightened then thickened up into peaks of pleasureable pain. Discipline. She swept her fingertips down across her belly and gently stroked the fuzz at her dark pubic nest.

A shrill bell rang out twice, the sharp bursts signalling lights out in the four dorms at the rear of the rambling Queen Anne mansion. Miranda knew that the thirty-two young ladies would be scrambling into their spartan beds, no doubt clutching lipsticks, chocolates and other forbidden luxuries. Miranda closed her eyes and strummed her pussy rhythmically, knowing that soon the silent footfalls of the Head would haunt the corridors. Every night, after lights out, the Head would prowl the dark silence of the dorms, swooping instantly on any torch light under tented bedclothes. The girl caught breaking the rules would be dealt with instantly. Miranda's fingers punished her sticky labia as she imagined the Head pulling away the bedclothes and ordering the naked miscreant to turn tummy-down into her bed, then swiping the bare-bottomed girl severely with her supple slipper. It was usually four strokes. Miranda slowly tweaked her clitoris four times, then gently knuckled her wet heat.

The Head had made it perfectly plain at Miranda's interview, six months ago, that all members of staff were expected – indeed, encouraged – to promote the strict principles laid down by Dr Jakob, the founder of the Institute.

'Strap or cane?' the Head had asked, raising her voice against the winter rain lashing the windows of her study.

Miranda, clutching her certificates to her breast, had merely stared back across the polished desk.

'Which do you prefer? For punishment?' the Head had insisted.

Miranda, who had presumed that 'punishments' meant setting an extra Greek translation task for evening prep, mumbled an incoherent reply.

'I prefer the cane,' the Head had continued, momentarily closing her eyes, as if savouring the word as one savours a superb wine. 'The cane.'

The interview had been touch and go – but Miranda rallied. The Head seemed to be more interested in Miranda's own experience of discipline at the hands of the strict nuns who had schooled her so rigorously. An awkward silence filled the room. Miranda, reading the stern face of the Head – the iron-grey cropped hair, pale-pink lips and unblinking blue eyes – sensed the right thing to say. She launched into a hymn in praise of Dr Jakob and the benefits of discipline.

'Punishment—' she blurted out.

'Yes?' the Head encouraged, her eyes widening a fraction.

'The thing about punishment I most remember is that it forms a close bond. A very close bond—'

'Between the whipper and the whipped?'

Miranda nodded.

'Tell me more about this bond between the chastiser and the chastised,' the Head continued, sensing at last that Miranda might well be the right candidate to appoint.

'There was a nun,' Miranda confessed, her voice no more than a troubled whisper. 'A very strict nun. When she punished me, she placed her hand down across my bottom, letting it rest there for several minutes before the spanking commenced. She would speak to me in a severe tone, but squeeze my bottom tenderly.'

'Yes?' the Head hissed.

'I can remember her cool palm resting lightly across the swell of my bare bottom. I can remember the delicious promise of pain – and the dreadful threat of pleasure – to come.'

'Exactly.' The Head nodded.

'And of course I would do anything for that nun, afterwards. I adored her. I'm sure I owe my first in Greek to her – efforts.'

Miranda got the job.

Since her appointment, Miranda had not spanked, strapped or caned a single lady at the Jakob Institute. To the amazement of her pupils – and the growing concern of her fellow tutors – Miranda taught the torments of Greek and the miseries of maths with patience and persistence, never once resorting to punishment to promote learning. Her leniency was commented upon openly and her reluctance to chastise became the focus of the Common Room gossip.

When the winter snow was still blanketing the manicured lawns surrounding the Institute, the murmurs of discontent reached the ears of the Head. Miranda was summoned to the study. On the polished desk, the Punishment Book lay open, the entries neatly penned. Miranda watched as the Head dragged her forefinger down along the signature column, tapping it from time to time. As Miranda gazed at the lines of red ink, she felt the silent eloquence with which each entry attested to the punished pupil's suffering – just as the cane stripes across the punished pupil's buttocks betrayed her burning pain. The Head raised her finger up from the page and pointed it directly at Miranda.

'You appear to be the only member of my staff who has not entered a punishment in the records. I think it would be instructive for you to witness more experienced tutors administering discipline. Look, and learn. When I appointed you, I believed that I was engaging the services of someone who would rigorously uphold the standards of discipline laid down by Dr Jakob. I believed you to be a strict mistress. Do not disappoint me.'

The next day, in the late afternoon when the sun had set and the neon lights burned brightly, Miranda sat in the music room. The French music mistress was tutoring four stubborn girls in vocal harmonic technique. Pages of Schumann's *Frauenliebe und leben* littered the top of the highly polished piano, which reflected the swelling breasts of the four girls standing around it. Miranda watched the reflected bosoms rise and fall as the students struggled to sing a perfect A sharp.

'*Non, non, non. Quel horreur,*' the French mistress exclaimed. Chic in a black poloneck and tight pencil skirt, she sat with her pert bottom perched on the edge of the piano stool, one slender hand held aloft, the other at the black and white keys, fingering them expertly. Miranda saw that the music mistress was growing increasingly impatient.

'*Lah,*' the French mistress trilled, opening her red lips wide and letting her pink tongue-tip quiver on the tremolo. As her own clear note died, she stabbed her finger down on the keyboard, making the piano sing.

'*Lah,*' came the ragged response – missing A sharp completely – as the four pupils attempted to harmonise with the clear note.

Miranda held her breath as she watched the angry music mistress order each girl to drag up her pleated skirt and hold it up at her hips. Deftly yanking the girls' panties down, the French mistress severely spanked each bare bottom in turn, to a ringing A sharp freshly fingered from the piano.

'*Lah.*'

Spank.

A squeal, followed by a tearful attempt at A sharp. '*L-lah.*'

Within eight minutes, and twenty-four spanks, three of the whimpering, red-bottomed young ladies had achieved the desired pitch. The spanking hand hovered over the crimson-buttocked girl who could only manage to sing a flat note off key. Miranda felt her throat tighten as the French mistress insinuated her free hand down between the girl's parted thighs, taking a tuft of her exposed pubic fuzz in a cruel finger and thumb pincer.

The piano was struck, producing the A sharp. The fingers tweaked and tugged, bringing the gasping girl up on her toes to produce a poignant vibrato.

Miranda gazed out through the classroom window. Two robins were bullying a blackbird for cake crumbs in the snow. She smiled – a clever starling in speckled splendour had hopped down to join the fracas – but the crisp tone of the Geography mistress drew her attention back to the blackboard.

The Geography mistress was feared and respected by all her students. She had a collection of bamboo canes and used them to illustrate variations in global climate and vegetation patterns. Selecting a short, whippy specimen – some fourteen inches of silvery lemon malice – she held it aloft and instructed a dark-haired girl to identify it.

'Rattan,' the girl replied promptly.

'From?'

'The rain forests of Indonesia, particularly Borneo. It prefers the lowlands, never found above a treeline of 2,000 metres and requires an annual rainfall of 82 inches with an ambient temperature of 42°C.'

'Giving it a supple core and a pliant casing. Excellent. You, girl,' the mistress continued, selecting another length of yellow cane. The thin rod shivered as the mistress flexed it with her supple wrist, swishing it twice and filling the classroom with its eerie thrumm.

'Malaccan.'

'Good. The darker wood that grows beneath dense tree canopies in tropical jungles. Growing on lighter soil, it absorbs less water but compensates for this by retaining moisture in its fibres. A surprisingly supple specimen. Observe how it bends.' She gave a brief but memorable demonstration, bending the rod in her strong, slender hands. Several of the girls, Miranda observed, squirmed on their hard wooden stools.

'And this?' the mistress purred, producing a slender wand that glinted under the electric light. 'You, girl.'

The blonde, pony-tailed girl remained silent.

'Well?' demanded the mistress, tapping her open palm with the cane.

'I forget—'

'Then I must help you to remember.'

Miranda watched spellbound as the Geography mistress ordered the blonde pupil to stand and then bend over across her desk. The wooden stool squeaked as it was pushed aside. The blonde's heavy breasts kissed the surface of her desk and then squashed down into it as she bent down, surrendering her buttocks up to the approaching mistress. Flipping the hem of the short, pleated uniform skirt up over the bending girl's buttocks with a neat flick of her cane tip, the mistress tapped the navy blue knickers dominantly.

'Down,' she ordered crisply.

Miranda felt her tingling labia part and pout, the sticky hot lips of her arousal puckering up to kiss the cotton of her satin panties.

'Quickly, girl.' The tip of the cane tapped the rounded cheeks impatiently.

With trembling fingers, the bending blonde slowly inched her navy knickers down to her knees, drawing her legs together and binding them tightly as she revealed the perfect peaches of the bared bottom.

Miranda felt the soft plucking at her wet heat, then the warm scald as she juiced freely.

'This,' the Geography mistress barked, guiding the cane to the blonde's lips, 'is a species of bambusa. Taste it.'

The obedient blonde licked the shining cane gently, and mewed aloud as it was pressed against her lips. Miranda started to come, soaking herself.

'What is it?' the mistress demanded, flourishing her bamboo.

'Bambusa,' chorused the entire class – Miranda was surprised to hear her own voice among them.

'Bambusa,' whispered the blonde girl, clenching her soft cheeks anxiously.

Spelling out the seven letters aloud, the Geography mistress swished the cane down across the upturned buttocks, striping them severely and bequeathing seven thin red lines across their luscious swell. Miranda saw the pony-tail flounce as the bending, bare bottomed girl jerked across her desk. The mistress, having administered the painful instruction, grasped the pony-tail and twisted it, dragging the snivelling girl's head up.

'The name,' the mistress demanded, waving the cruel rod slowly before her captive's tear-blurred gaze.

'Bambusa,' mumbled the punished blonde.

'A sharp lesson. I trust you won't forget.'

The class then launched into the strategic development of light engineering in the aftermath of the collapsed 'Tiger' economies. Miranda withdrew, her own instruction completed.

Miss Peterson (known as 'Peters' throughout the Institute) used chastisement as encouragement, incorporating it into every aspect of her gym sessions – from the rigorous work-outs to the steaming shower room afterwards. A trim-buttocked, lithe brunette, Peters palmed the dimpled rubber surface of a table tennis bat as she stood beside the vaulting horse.

'Lazy little hounds,' the gym mistress remarked to Miranda, who had been sent into the gym by the Head to observe. 'Come to us here at the Jakob after years of pampering and indolence. Champagne suppers, late nights, jacuzzis,' she snarled contemptuously, betraying her jealous, envious anger towards the decadence of her young charges. 'I soon lick 'em into shape.'

Eight young ladies – for whom champagne suppers were now a mere, half-forgotten memory – in white vests and tiny black shorts trod the polished wooden floor with squeaky pumps. It was February. A hard frost overnight had left the glass roof of the gym clouded and opaque. The huddled girls shivered, arms crossed against their bulging breasts. It was chilly in the gym. Miranda discerned the peaking nipples behind the tight, white vests.

'Soon warm 'em up,' Peters promised, cracking the rubber-coated bat down across the dull hide of the leather vaulting-horse.

Calling each girl forward, the gym mistress instructed them to vault. Hammering their pumps into the floor, they took turns to sprint up towards the horse, spring and vault clear. The first three girls were successful; the fourth stumbled slightly on her approach run, falteringly lost momentum and failed. She landed astride the scuffed leather, breasts bouncing and buttocks splayed. Peters sprang like a cat, pouncing mercilessly to pin the unfortunate girl face and breasts down into the horse.

Crack. Crack. Crack. The triple echo reverberated around the spacious gym as the bat bit into the bunched buttocks sheathed within the thin black shorts. Miranda shuddered as the punished gymnast squealed aloud in torment. Peters controlled the delicious rump with the surface of the bat which had just blazed down upon it.

'Again,' she commanded.

The hot-bottomed girl peeled her breasts and tummy away from the dull hide and slipped down from the horse. Returning to make her approach five yards away, the girl rubbed her buttocks resentfully. Peters cracked the bat down onto the hide. The girl's hands fell from her cheeks and she dutifully took up her stance.

'Approach,' came the command.

Breasts bouncing within the stretch of her white vest and pumps pounding the polished wood, the girl ran, sprang and vaulted high. A superb effort.

'See?' Peters remarked, thumbing the dimpled rubber of her bat. 'All they need is a little strict encouragement. A firm touch on the tiller. Next,' she barked, raising the bat.

Spring brought the dancing daffodils to the manicured lawns surrounding the Queen Anne mansion – and panting, mottle-thighed hockey players onto the pitch down by the spinney. The Jakob Institute insisted on a vigourous régime of sports for all the pupils. Long-distance running through the spinney in blue track suits, followed by steaming showers in which the squealing girls jostled and squabbled in their shining nakedness. Hockey before tea – just as the chill wind gathered strength to whip the short pleated skirts of the girls up over their buttocks as they bent down to bully off. Divided into two teams representing their respective 'house colours', blue for Spartans and green for Corinthians, they played a mean game. The losing team went supperless – and spanked – to an early bed. There was, Miranda discovered, all to play for.

The tackling was hard, the fouls increasingly blatant. Squealing girls, pony-tailed hair streaming out behind them, collided bosom to bosom, thigh to soft thigh. Punishments were administered on the spot by Peters, whose table-tennis bat never left her hand, playing an unorthodox role on the hockey field. For the more flagrant offenders, punishment meant a more intimate appointment with the dimpled rubber in the changing rooms after a compulsory cold shower.

With the spring came an addition to the curriculum.

'Dance is such a disciplined activity,' the Head beamed, catching Miranda firmly by the elbow after prep. 'Go down and watch Emily putting our naughty girls through their paces.'

Miranda joined Emily, the Institute's drama and dance tutor, in the windowless studio fashioned out of the mansion's cavernous wine cellarage. Unaccustomed to the spotlights, the twelve young ladies appeared to Miranda to be utterly naked as they twirled and pranced – but she saw that they were in fact clad in tight, pale cream body-stockings. The sheer second skins of satin revealed more than they were designed to conceal of the lissome young dancers' firm bodies. Miranda gazed wide-eyed as breasts thrust out from the sheaths of sheen, and swallowed at the shadowed clefts between rounded buttocks deliciously sculpted within the stretchy fabric. The satin paid full homage, Miranda decided, to the perfection of the girls' buttocks, capturing and controlling the swelling contours so tightly.

Emily, twenty-seven, dark eyed and severe, darted between the dancers wielding a brutal leather tawse. The cruel hide snapped repeatedly across proffered bottoms, its harsh staccato echoing around the dance studio. Up on tiptoe, arms above their heads, the pirouetting girls were completely defenceless as Emily prowled between them, tawse in hand.

One girl proved sullenly reluctant and quickly became the focus of Emily's attention – and her tawse. Miranda was perusing the girl's long, slender legs and chubbily pert cheeks when Emily pounced. The tawse flickered, lashing the softness of the upper thighs, then snapped twice, biting into the flesh of the twin peaches above. Miranda thrilled to the haunting crack-lash of the leather and secretly longed to hug the whipped dancer's buttocks, pressing her face into the punished cheeks. Emily demonstrated a more prosaic interest in the stubborn girl's bottom. Her sole desire was to make the blistering cheeks hotter with her unerring lash.

Suddenly, the music stopped. The perspiring girls stood in a bewitching gaggle, plucking their damp satin from their breasts, clefts and moist labia. Their tousled hair spilled down in a wanton tumble, clinging to their faces and necks as if they had just been caught in a spring shower. Emily's dark eyes flashed dangerously.

'I am not satisfied. Not satisfied at all. And I am far from convinced that any of you are even trying. Everyone get down and do a dozen press-ups.'

The girls groaned their protest. The tawse snapped harshly. Seconds later, Miranda was treated to the vision of a dozen bosoms flattening as they kissed the dance floor and a dozen perfectly poised bottoms looming up as the girls obediently executed the press-ups. Weaving between the stretched thighs of her pupils, Emily admonished them with sharp strokes of the tawse across their clenched cheeks. The soft sound of the struggling girls' panting was punctuated by shrill yips as the leather licked their upturned buttocks.

Miranda stole her fingers down to her pussy and thumbed it covertly. She closed her eyes, storing up the images for later – later, when, alone in her bed, she would masturbate furiously, feeding from her memory bank loaded with the sounds and sights of strict discipline.

Crack. Crack. The straining girls powered themselves towards the target of a dozen press-ups. Some were already wobbling on unsteady arms. Crack. Crack. As Miranda slipped out of the dance studio, she heard the tawse encouraging some unlucky pupil who had just slumped down onto the polished wood.

Summer came early. Blossom burgeoned on the apple trees in the walled kitchen gardens, but Miranda's name had yet to make an appearance in the pages of the Punishment Book. Brimstone butterflies fluttered in the flower-beds and a cuckoo called each evening from the spinney.

The Head, eager to complete Miranda's induction to discipline, sent her to Miss Bannermann's lesson to observe the mature teacher's methods. Miss Bannermann taught economics, and carried a polished pear-wood paddle with her in a red velvet bag. It seemed to remain in the red bag, Miranda thought, hidden away – just like the Chancellor's statement on the eve of the Budget.

The lecture and subsequent question and answer session was tedious, the subject matter dry and the girls openly bored. Yawns were smothered and chins propped up on hands. Pens and pencils lay still on empty notepads. But Miss Bannermann had only to fleetingly touch the red velvet bag with her caressing fingertips and suddenly the entire class, Miranda noted, became animated with copious note-taking and eager responses to the teacher's questions. Just a touch of her fingertips against the red velvet. The pear-wood paddle was not actually produced, remaining out of sight but vivid in the girls' imaginations as a potent threat.

Miss Bannermann did not, Miranda realised, allow poor performance to go unchallenged. Three girls who displeased their tutor were ordered to step forward from their desks and place their hand briefly on the red bag. Miranda frowned – but noticed that when they had returned to their desks, the three culprits sat white-faced and shivering throughout the rest of the lesson. When the bell sounded, the class rose and filed out in silence. Miranda was about to thank Miss Bannermann and depart when she saw that the three girls who had been ordered to approach and touch the red velvet remained seated at their desks.

'One moment, Miranda. Observe,' Miss Bannermann said, picking up the red bag and striding down between a row of desks. 'Observe how I dispense discipline. Economically.'

Taking the pear-wood paddle out of its velvet bag, Miss Bannermann offered it to the first girl. Taking it in her trembling hand, the girl promptly rounded on the second miscreant, bent her over and administered a stinging six strokes. Miranda saw that, though it was not a bare-bottomed chastisement, it was a blistering business. The second girl, rubbing her buttocks, accepted the paddle from the hand that had just beaten her and approached the third penitent, who shivered in silence at her desk.

'They beat each other. It is a method which instils both fear and respect in the girls. Fear and respect for me. And it extols the virtues of capitalist enterprise. I get what I want – I remain absolutely in control but get others to do all the work. An excellent grounding in economics for the girls, don't you think?'

Deeply impressed, Miranda nodded.

The evening that the first swallows swooped low over the elm trees, confirming that summer had truly arrived, Miranda was instructed to attend an interview with the Head. As she entered the study, she saw Prism, the secretary, in urgent conference with the Head. There was much remonstration, shrugging and gesticulation. Prism looked up, frowned at Miranda and left.

'My secretary tells me that the staff are anxious about my judgement, Miranda. There appears to be something of a whispering campaign against me.'

'Judgement?' Miranda echoed.

'In appointing you. Despite the fact that you have been privileged to witness at close quarters every method and example of administering discipline you have, to date, singularly failed to dispense discipline yourself. And your failure,' the Head continued tersely, 'is being deemed by the Staff Common Room gossip to be my failure.'

Miranda looked down at the carpet, avoiding the Head's searching gaze.

'In two and a half minutes, Pastora will be coming into this study to be chastised. I caught her using a mobile phone. Strictly against the rules. I am going to give you the opportunity to administer a severe spanking. The young lady's misbehaviour has been grave and her punishment must be commensurate with the gravity of her offence.'

'Who was she phoning?'

'The details need not concern you. Her need for strict discipline does. I trust you will spank her good and hard. Understood?'

Miranda nodded.

'Here she is. Come, girl,' the Head commanded.

Pastora, sallow-skinned and spoiling her pretty face with a scowl, entered the study. Like all those summoned for punishment, she wore only her vest and panties. The unbrassiered breasts were proud and thrusting, the buttocks ripe and round. Miranda felt the pulse at her throat quicken, and the flesh at her slit tingle.

The Head rose up from behind her desk and approached the sullen young Portuguese girl.

'Ah, Pastora, I'm afraid I am too busy to attend to your naughty little bottom—'

Pastora's eyes flashed wide as she sensed the possibility of a reprieve.

'I'll leave it in the very capable hands of our Greek tutor.'

Glimpsing her doom, Pastora automatically shielded her buttocks with protectively cupped hands at their swell. She bowed her head. The light shone on her dark, oiled hair.

The Head dragged Pastora's hands away from her bottom and turned her around, presenting the young Portuguese girl's buttocks to Miranda. 'Her bottom is yours. Do your duty,' the Head commanded. Pushing Pastora towards Miranda, the Head abruptly left the study, closing the door firmly behind her.

Miranda wasted no time, realising from what she had observed and learnt of discipline that it was essential to establish absolute authority over the victim immediately. To hesitate was to lose the advantage – the upper hand.

Even before the Head had joined Prism in the secretary's office to eavesdrop on the proceedings over the intercom, Pastora was bare-bottomed across Miranda's lap. Pinning the wriggling Portuguese beauty down firmly at the nape of her neck, Miranda placed her spanking hand palm down across the tempting swell of the upturned cheeks.

'You have, I believe, been very naughty, Pastora,' Miranda said sternly, firmly squeezing the softness of the girl's outer cheek. 'Very naughty.'

'I'm sorry,' Pastora whispered. 'I used the mobile to phone Isobel. I lied. I said I was phoning my aunt. I said my aunt was ill.'

'So,' Miranda repeated, beginning to understand. 'You

lied. You phoned Isobel. And she is?'

'My lover. I miss her.'

'Using a mobile is forbidden, as you well know,' Miranda said, her tone still severely sharp. 'And lying deserves to be harshly punished. Doesn't it? Hm?'

Pastora remained silent. Wriggling gently, she buried her breasts into Miranda's stockings, crushing her nipples into their nylon sheen.

'Doesn't it?' Miranda repeated.

'Yes.' The sulky whisper was barely audible – but both the Head and Prism, crouched over the intercom, heard the important admission.

'Yes,' echoed Miranda. She squeezed both buttocks fiercely, causing Pastora to squeak in anguish and jerk her hips in an effort to escape.

'Are you truly sorry?'

'Yes, I'm sorry,' Pastora hissed, threshing her small feet as she writhed.

Miranda relaxed her fierce grip on the rubbery flesh and soothingly palmed the crown of the buttocks in her absolute thrall. 'Tell me a little about Isobel before I punish you.'

'About Isobel?' Pastora replied in surprise.

'Tell me,' Miranda whispered, dragging her straightened forefinger dominantly down along the darkly shadowed cleft.

Inching her cheeks up a fraction to receive the fingertip more fully, Pastora confessed her love for the girl left behind in Lisbon. She spoke of her loneliness at the Institute and of the bitter tears she shed each night on her pillow. Miranda – and the Head at the intercom – listened in silence to this important revelation. It did not excuse Pastora's misbehaviour, but it certainly explained it.

'I see.' Miranda stroked the warm cleft more dominantly, allowing her fingertip to trace down the increasingly sticky flesh-creases to Pastora's warm, pouting plum.

'After what you have told me, your offence appears to be less grave. I will spank you, though. I will spank you because you broke the rules and you lied. But I will not punish you too severely. What I want you to do is promise me that you will work harder

198

and obey all the rules. If you do so, you will be successful here at the Institute. And if you are successful, your parents will allow you to return to Lisbon – and Isobel.'

'I promise—' Pastora gasped hastily.

'No, no promises. Not yet. Promises made under the shadow of impending punishment and pain are easily made – and all too easily broken. Thighs apart please, and get your bottom up.'

Pastora obeyed, inching her soft thighs apart a fraction so that her wet plum-lips smiled their sticky welcome. Snuggling down into her chastiser's lap, the bare-bottomed girl jerked her cheeks up for their pleasurable pain. Miranda gazed down, drinking in every detail of the beautiful Portuguese girl at her mercy. The tumble of dark, glistening hair curtaining the penitent's sorrow-shadowed eyes. The slender neck firmly in her pinioning grasp. The swell of the naked cheeks, occasionally dimpled by a spasm of expectancy. The neat little feet pressed together as if making a mute contrition. The sight, the sheer sensation, juiced Miranda urgently. Her hot quim perfumed the air of the study, the feral perfume of arousal as heavy as over-ripe medlars oozing their sweetness.

Crack, smack. The spanking was slow, deliberate and searching, each measured swipe of palm across plump cheek echoing around the study. After every third resounding blow, Miranda paused to thumb Pastora's cleft, dragging her thumbtip down to torment and pleasure the punished girl's clitoris. After eighteen spanks across each crimsoning cheek, Miranda paused again – for a full, delicious minute – then used two firm fingers to probe Pastora's slit deeply. The Portuguese girl clamped her thighs together as she rocked gently back and forth across her punisher's lap.

'Don't stop – please—' she begged, her voice a choking whimper. 'Spank me. Spank me hard. I was bad. I must be punished—'

'Silence, girl. I am in control of your bottom. I and I alone will decide whether you deserve to be spanked any more.'

'I promise to obey you. Spank me. I will do as you say. I will work hard. Obey all the rules. Spank me. Spank me, please—'

In the secretary's office, huddled over the intercom, the Head gripped Prism's arm tightly. Both faces bore the broad smile of delight.

'Listen to that. She's actually pleading for more punishment. I knew I was right. I knew it. She is an exceptional teacher – and disciplinarian. She got the whole story out of the girl: and how many of our wayward young madams actually whimper for more chastisement? Hmm? My new appointment,' the head concluded, 'is a triumph.'

Wincing at the fierce grip at her arm, Prism agreed enthusiastically.

In her bed, Miranda had just enjoyed her second climax. Her pubic fuzz and inner thighs were soaking wet. Beneath the warm weight of her clenched buttocks, her crisp white sheet was stained. The orgasms, fuelled by images of the Head prowling the dorms, slipper in hand, had been powerful. Powerful and exquisite. Loosening her limbs, she slumped into her mattress.

The Head had been very kind and fulsome in her praise. Miranda had arranged for Pastora to have two compassionate phone calls to Isobel every week – and already the Portuguese girl's work and behaviour had improved.

Miranda was very tired. After teasing her clitoris until it pulsed and tingled with raw pleasure, she inserted her thumb into her bottom, jabbing it deep into the tightly muscled warmth. All was quiet now. The Jakob Institute was in darkness. The Head was probably taking a shower before retiring to bed. The image of the Head palming perfumed gel into her heavy breasts drove Miranda's thumb deeper into her anus. Though very tired, she still had the appetite for one more orgasm.

Closing her eyes, she rolled over onto her belly and dug deeper between her tightly squeezed cheeks. As the climax gathered itself up into a clenched velvet fist in the pit of her belly, Miranda rasped her clitoral thorn against the wet patch on her sheet. As she jerked into the mattress, bright lights exploded behind her tightly shut eyes – green, blue, red and gold. She stiffened, trembling on the brink of her climax then tumbled headlong into its silent explosion of delight.

The crimson, gold and blue lights behind her eyes faded slowly until only the pulsing blue light flashed. Sighing deeply, Miranda removed her thumb, easing it out from her hot sphincter, and opened her eyes. The blue light continued to flash intermittently, raking the pale walls of her darkened bedroom. Miranda sat up in bed, alert. Shaking off her lust-drowsiness, she scrambled across to her window. Down on the gravel drive, a white ambulance waited with open rear doors, its emergency lights flashing eerily in the night.

Grabbing a robe, Miranda hurried down to the front hall, taking the sweeping stairs three at a time in her nimble stride. Several members of staff were at the open door before her. Prism, Miss Bannermann and Peters were looking on anxiously as a stretcher-trolley was being guided over the gravel. Miranda joined the anxious group just in time to glimpse the pale face of the Head lolling on a pillow. She was clearly naked. Beneath the red blanket, her proud breasts joggled.

'Slipped in her shower,' Peters whispered.

Miranda expressed her concern.

'Severe wrist sprain. Probably a hairline fracture.'

'Who do you wish to deputise for you?' Prism asked, fussing over the stretcher.

Miss Bannermann, imperiously robed in a vivid peacock blue gown, started to speak. 'Rest assured, I will—'

'Miranda,' came the distinct reply from the stretcher, cutting Bannermann short. 'Miranda is in charge in my absence.'

Knowing that she would be the focus of intense scrutiny and interest that morning at breakfast, Miranda dressed carefully for her new role as deputy Head. Naked before her full-length looking glass, she examined herself appraisingly. Beneath their superb swell, her ripe breasts smothered the rapid heartbeat of her mounting excitement. She selected a white cotton sports bra and, after capturing her warm bosom in its cool cups, snapped the straps firmly at her back. She fingered each cup delicately, smoothing the cotton trim at her soft flesh. Every detail must be perfect this morning, she thought. All the eyes of the Institute would be upon her. The white panties bit into her pubis and cleft deeply; in her excitement, Miranda had dragged them up too severely. She thumbed the tight satin away from her warmth, leaving them tight, but comfortably so. She chose chocolate-coloured leather trousers. Unorthodox, perhaps, but quite distinctive. Skin-tight and shining, they bestowed upon her youthfulness a chic sophistication, an air of cool authority and competence.

Miranda palmed her buttocks beneath the sleek second skin. Perfect. Her white shirt-blouse was finished off with a thin, dark leather tie, which she knotted loosely at her collar, leaving the top two buttons at her throat casually undone. Among the tweeds and twin-sets at the staff breakfast table, she knew she would appear devastatingly dominant and clearly in command.

At the staff common-room door, Miranda paused. It was ajar. Through it, she heard her own name being repeated twice. Once, in a tone of surprise. Again, disapprovingly, in an echo of dismay.

'But surely not Miranda—'

'It's true. The Head said so herself,' Prism confirmed.

'Impossible,' a voice of doubt chimed in.

'I simply can't believe it,' Miss Bannermann broke in waspishly. 'In the absence of the Head, what the Institute needs is a strict mistress.'

Miranda retreated, her eyes clouding with apprehension.

The refectory was buzzing with speculation at breakfast time.

All the pupils were sitting at their long wooden tables, heads together in loud whispering. The staff, who took their places at the high table, sat in dignified silence, gazing occasionally at the empty place reserved for the Head.

The pupils ate frugally, enjoying their weak tea, toast and fresh fruit. The staff had to make do with deliciously aromatic coffee, kippers, flaky croissants and home-made raspberry preserve. Peters, in from a two-mile jog, braced herself for bacon, sausage and eggs.

The whispering rose an octave to a murmur of surprise as Miranda entered the refectory and assumed her place at the high table. Her hand grasped the small bell and shook it briskly as she exercised her prerogative – as Head – to let breakfast commence. The excited murmur remained in the air. Miranda held up her hand, gesturing for silence, and was relieved when it was instantly achieved. The girls adored Miranda and were eager to give her loyal support.

After a brief announcement, outlining details of the day's activities, Miranda said grace impeccably, and took a fork to her glistening kippers. Around her, the refectory was filled with the barely audible sounds of tea being poured and toast being buttered. Smiling, Miranda talked easily with her staff, with a sympathetic and generous word for each of them. Miss Bannermann doggedly refused to be drawn into conversation, stolidly munching a croissant. Miranda noted the sullen scowl on the economics teacher's face. With her seniority, she had clearly expected to be appointed the Head's deputy.

A shrill squeal rang out. All the girls stopped eating and stared as a petite brunette stood up abruptly, sneezing violently. A cloud of pepper hung in the air where she had shaken out her napkin.

'Silence,' Miranda barked. 'What is going on?'

The brunette was incapable of speech. Several girls sitting beside her attempted to explain. Miranda rose from her chair and strode towards the sneezing girl.

'Go and wash your face in cold water,' she said, her gentle tone comforting the tearful girl. 'You, girl,' Miranda pointed to an adjacent blonde. 'Take her to the bathroom.'

The blonde steered the snivelling brunette out of the refectory. An expectant hush filled the room. Turning to address the silent pupils, Miranda maintained a quiet tone – all the more menacing because of its cool control.

'Who is responsible for this stupidity?'

The question was greeted in silence, but Miranda noticed that none of the girls avoided her searching gaze. There was no evidence of concealed guilt on their upturned, anxious faces. Puzzled, she quickly sought her own solution. Breakfast was prepared by a domestic – a treasure from the neighbouring village – before the pupils arrived. They arrived together. For Miranda, it was as clear as a Greek translation in which every word fell into place. None of the pupils could possibly have sabotaged the napkin.

Glancing across to the staff table, Miranda caught the ghost of a mocking smile on Miss Bannermann's face. There was malice in her smile. No. More than malice. There was a challenge.

'The foolish girl responsible for this outrage will come to my study before noon for punishment. If not, I will personally administer a bare-bottomed caning to every girl after lunch. Dismissed.'

The girls filed out in silence as Miranda rejoined the top table.

'Excellent,' Peters murmured, tackling her bacon and eggs. 'I think you handled that episode very well.'

Others agreed, nodding vigorously as they chorused their approval.

'Very firm. Fair, to give the stupid culprit a chance, but firm.'

'A sensible decision. Stern, but sensible—'

'Just a spot of house rivalry,' Miss Bannermann observed, licking raspberry jam from her thumbtip. 'I am sure of it. That girl was a Corinthian. A Spartan did it. No doubt about it. Cane the Spartans,' she pronounced judiciously.

And blunder into your little trap, Miranda thought, sipping her coffee noncommittally. Blunder into your cunning little trap, Bannermann. To do so would be to alienate half the girls at a stroke – and earn the contempt of the rest.

'Do you think the girl responsible will own up and take her stripes?' Emily asked, absently fingering the leather belt at her trim waist.

'Depend on it,' Miranda replied in a tone of finality. 'I will have whipped the culprit before noon.'

Miranda sent a message to Miss Bannermann's class at eleven-forty, requesting the economics teacher to call into the study at the end of the session.

'You sent for me?' Miss Bannermann said rather impatiently, juggling an armful of text books. 'I am extremely busy but,' she condescended, 'I am prepared to help you, of course.'

'Yes, I need your help,' Miranda replied. 'I'll need all the help I can get to keep the Institute running smoothly in the absence of the Head. The hospital said that it may be a couple of weeks.'

'Has the guilty girl come to confess? Or are you going to cane all the Spartans?'

'I propose to punish the culprit,' Miranda replied softly, closing the door behind Miss Bannermann and locking it. 'That is why I sent for you.'

'I don't think I quite understand you. Do you need my help when it comes to chastising the guilty party?'

'Up to a point, yes. I need you to undress, completely, Miss Bannermann, and present your bottom for my strap.'

The text books clattered to the floor. Miss Bannermann's blustering outburst was quickly checked by Miranda – who had produced a leather strap and snapped it harshly.

'Silence,' she commanded. 'Strip and get across that desk, Bannermann. No,' she continued, her sharp tone rising, 'don't deny it. I know it was you. And I have all the proof I need.'

'Proof? Preposterous—'

'Proof which I am fully prepared to put before the staff common room, if you insist,' Miranda purred, fingering her length of supple hide.

She was calling Bannermann's bluff. The mistress could not bear the indignity before her colleagues, Miranda calculated. It worked.

'There is no need for all this,' the economics teacher blurted out quickly. 'I – I was merely testing you. Put you on your mettle.'

'Across the desk, Bannermann. I promised the entire Institute that the guilty party would be punished before noon and I intend to keep my word. Or do you want me to summon the rest of the staff?'

Broken, Bannermann started to wheedle and plead. Miranda remained resolute, toying with her strap. Moments later, she was rewarded with the sight of her economics tutor bending, bare-bottomed, across the polished surface of the desk.

Levelling the strap, which she held doubled up in her firm grasp,

Miranda ordered Bannermann to spread her thighs wider apart. The soft cheeks wobbled as Bannermann reluctantly obeyed, proffering her rounded buttocks up for the bite of the leather and exposing her dark fig.

Crack. Crack. Miranda lashed the leather down, searing each cheek with vertical strokes that striped the swollen globes of creamy flesh with a vicious weal. Naked across the desk, Bannermann crushed her breasts into the desk top, raking her stubby nipples into its polished wood. She grunted aloud at each stroke.

Swish. After the second scalding stripe, Miranda flicked the strap upwards, kissing the exposed slit with the cruel hide. Bannermann gasped aloud. Crack. Crack. Swish. For a full eight minutes, Miranda continued to whip the reddening cheeks, bringing the leather up after each double lash to sting the wet labia of the writhing nude.

Bannermann's lips mouthed silent obscenities into the polished wood as she groaned and squirmed, her blazing cheeks dancing in agony under the lash and her wet slit throbbing on the verge of orgasm. Miranda tossed her strap down and, pressing herself into the punished nude, finger-stroked the weeping fig, instantly propelling Bannermann into a loud climax.

'Am I strict enough for you?' Miranda whispered.

The economics mistress hammered her belly and hips into the desk as she came.

'Now that you have the measure of my mettle, are you prepared to be my assistant? Be my deputy? I need you, Bannermann. So does the Jakob Institute. Will you serve?'

'Yes,' moaned the sweetly suffering nude as she threshed in her hot-bottomed ecstasy. 'Yes,' she hissed, parting her thighs painfully wide as Miranda drove three fingers into the hot wetness of the whipped nude. 'I will serve you.'

Spanking Memoirs

The waiters moved silently between the tables, like ushers at a funeral service. Afternoon tea at the Royal was always a sombre occasion, conducted in hushed tones and full solemnity. At her customary window table, from which Regents Park could be fully appreciated, Nanny Stevens was entertaining Nanny Pearse to egg and cress sandwiches, a madeira cake and a moist chocolate sponge, together with endless cups of Gunpowder tea.

'Of course, ' Nanny Stevens reminisced, 'spanking is a more intimate punishment. One can actually feel the bottom growing hotter.'

Chivvying some stray cress with her tonguetip, Nanny Pearse countered with her confession that she preferred the cane.

'They shiver at the swish and then shudder at the stroke,' she affirmed. 'And there is nothing quite so satisfying as counting the thin, red lines across the punished cheeks. Touching them with the cane tip and counting out each stroke aloud.'

'Flesh upon flesh,' rejoined Nanny Stevens. 'Nature fashioned the buttocks to receive the curved palm of the spanking hand. A perfect fit.'

The waiter at the nearby table adjusted his white cloth to conceal his gathering erection. An Austrian learning the arts of silver service, he did not fully understand these strange English nannies, but he liked what he heard.

'It was frequently the master of the household that caused the most problems.'

Reaching the cake stage, Nanny Pearse bit into her Victoria sponge with vigorous relish only partly restrained by the dictates of decorum. Crumbs tumbled down upon her proud bosom, which bounced as she swept them away, nodding her agreement with the last statement.

'Men,' she sighed. 'Always more trouble to a nanny than the rest of the household.'

'In my post at Holland Park—'

'With Lady Bellingham?' Nanny Pearse queried.

'Just so. Lord Bellingham was in Hong Kong most of the time, but her brother was in residence.'

The talk turned to the perverse habits of the aristocratic male in general and his intense interest in 'Nanny' in particular. Nanny Stevens was celebrating her fiftieth birthday at the Royal. Her iron-grey hair was flecked with silver but her strong face remained free from the tell-tale lines of age. It was a face that had been scrubbed every morning and every evening and had never known creams, cosmetics or lipstick. The skin was soft and translucent. She was striking rather than beautiful. The mouth was always pursed in grim resolve. Nursing her china cup, she recounted the buttocks she had blistered with slipper, crop and cane.

Her companion and lifelong friend was equally handsome. Nanny Pearse had a stern face, her severity sharpened by a hint of red lipstick on her full mouth. Both nannies were trim-waisted, broad-hipped and heavily bosomed. They wore their authority gracefully, exuding a natural dominance. Shopgirls, cabbies and those they had chastised across their knees shivered in their wake.

'He was the brother, you say, of Lady Bellingham?' Nanny Pearse asked, catching up a loose thread of conversation and weaving it seamlessly into the flow.

Nanny Stevens sighed and helped herself to chocolate cake. Dabbing her lips daintily, she launched into an account of her experiences above stairs in Holland Park.

He would hover around on the landing, she recalled, or lie in wait at the top of the stairs. 'Skulking in the shadows, hoping to corner me.'

'Bed?' Nanny Pearse tilted her head slightly.

'No. The usual. Punishment. Surprising how many of them seek discipline. No, no,' Nanny Stevens said briskly. 'He simply wanted to have his bottom smacked. I was quite safe from . . . the other problem.'

Nanny Pearse nodded understandingly – mentally brushing aside the occasion when her employer, a lusty race-horse owner, had bedded her on the eve of The Oaks twelve years ago. The way he used his crop would have caused comment in the Jockey Club, she remembered, shivering pleasurably.

'–in the bathroom,' Nanny Stevens was saying, breaking into her companion's distraction. 'And wearing nothing but his socks. The hot tap was running, the soap dish was a mess and there was toothpaste on the linoleum.'

'Dear, dear,' chimed Nanny Pearse. 'I trust you chastised him.'

'After a stern lecture—'

'For such slovenly behaviour—'

'Bent him over the bathtub for a good, hard spanking.'

The waiter hovered, agog, as Nanny Stevens gave a detailed recollection of the severe chastisement: how the man had howled, how his bottom had reddened, how his semen had squirted up and slithered down the perspiring tiles.

'Ah,' her companion responded, alert to the last detail. 'So he responded.'

'Copiously. I made him wipe it all up with a flannel.'

'My dear, I'm so glad you made the wicked man wipe up his own mess,' Nanny Pearse replied fastidiously.

'I made him kneel and draped the flannel over his spanked bottom – and the bounder had the temerity to relieve himself once more. All over the linoleum.'

The Austrian waiter jumped as he poured hot tea over his hand instead of into a cup at the adjoining table. Excusing himself profusely, he whimpered as he scuttled away to the double swing doors leading to the kitchens.

'Happy birthday,' Nanny Pearse beamed, raising her cup.

'Bottoms up,' Nanny Stevens replied, accepting the toast. 'Now, do tell me all about little Alice.'

Nanny Pearse frowned. Little Alice, her niece, was a twenty-two-year-old blonde currently nannying in Bath.

'Something in your manner tells me that Alice is not entirely

209

happy with her new post. They are in electronics, aren't they?'

'I never can quite think of the Quantocks as "silicon valley", can you? Yes. The family fortune was made in chips.'

'Do you mean to say Alice is employed by a fried fish empire?'

'Microchips, dear,' Nanny Pearse hastened to assure her companion. 'The house is splendid. Nash, of course.'

'Of course.'

'And the family are quite manageable. Nanny is in charge of the youngest two and tutors the elder girl.'

'How very enterprising. But?'

'There is a difficulty. The husband—'

'Bed?'

'I think not. No, no direct advances in that direction.'

'Discipline?'

'Exactly. Wanders into her bedroom at night and talks. Sometimes in his shirt tails.'

'Underpants? ' interjected Nanny Stevens shrewdly.

'Not always.'

'Then it's chastisement he wants, depend upon it.'

'He certainly seems to be hoping for a little stern nannying,' Nanny Pearse continued, disclosing that the young and inexperienced Alice was finding the situation increasingly difficult to manage.

At this point, the young Austrian waiter returned, solicitously inquiring if more hot water was required for the Gunpowder tea. Nanny Stevens sniffed suspiciously, catching the whiff of lavender soap masking the ranker tang of semen. Odours familiar to all experienced nannies.

'You'll be in hot water, young man, if you slope off to masturbate in the middle of serving afternoon tea,' she rasped.

At a nearby table, a rural dean was tackling a buttered muffin. His eyes widened at the overheard words, he coughed, then his coughing turned to a choking splutter.

'Just the bill, please,' Nanny Stevens said curtly, frowning across at the cleric, who had turned as purple as his vest.

The telephone rang. Nanny Stevens switched off her vibrator –

but left it buried up inside her muscled warmth between clamped thighs – and plucked up the receiver.

'He's getting more persistent,' the voice of Nanny Pearse barked, dispensing with the preliminaries. 'I'm going down to Bath.'

'Alice finding it all a bit too much?'

'He's leaving her little presents. Rubber-wear and black leather bras. And little notes, saying how he thinks about her wearing them under her starched white blouse and—'

'Yes, yes. Will the two o'clock from Paddington be a safe bet?'

'Are you proposing to join me?'

'Wouldn't miss it for the world, old girl. Tally ho.'

A little after two, the train glided out of Paddington. In their first-class seclusion, the two nannies settled down to doze.

Nanny Stevens dreamed of a young man she had occasion to punish. She recalled, in her sleeping memories, the Easter when all the eggs had been wolfed by a certain young gentleman down from Eton, while the rest of the family had been piously at morning prayers. Tears and tantrums greeted the scraps of silver and gold wrapping paper as the younger ones loudly mourned the loss of the chocolate eggs. Papa had Daimlered off to his golf club and Mama had hidden behind a migraine. Settling the grieving children down with colouring books and crayons, Nanny had stalked the gardens until she cornered the miscreant in the redcurrant bushes. He was seventeen – but Nanny had owned his bottom for many years and he followed her meekly up to his bedroom, where she ordered him to remove his shoes and stockings and then present himself, trousers down, bare-bottomed for chastisement.

'Shan't,' he shouted rudely.

In her sleep, Nanny Stevens smiled. The young Turk had been very rude and outspoken in his derisive refusal to comply with Nanny's stern instructions. She became very cross – and he weakened, fiddling with his shoelaces as he knelt at her feet.

'You simply can't, Nanny. I'll be at Sandhurst, soon—'

Nanny was firm. 'Too old to be spanked, I suppose?'

'Yes,' he replied sulkily.

'Very well then, young man, it shall have to be the cane. Go down at once to the potting shed and bring me back a length of bamboo cane. This season's, mind. Nice and springy. I want to be able to hear it swish, understand? Take one from the bundle on the top shelf by the lawn food and phosphate.'

He reached down to pick up his trousers.

'Never mind about those. I want you bare-bottomed for the cane—'

'But Nanny,' he protested, his voice a rising whine. 'Cook may see me – or the new maid.'

'And if they do, then they'll know that Nanny is going to beat your bare bottom, won't they? Now go and fetch the cane.'

He raced off, returning red-faced – the new maid had squeaked her surprise at catching the young master naked – carrying the short length of whippy bamboo. Moments later, face down across the duvet, Nanny was tap-tapping his bunched cheeks, smiling as they suddenly clenched in a responsive anxious reflex.

Stepping back a pace, and judging the distance expertly with the cane's length, she planted her dark brogues into the carpet. He buried his face in the duvet, whimpering his apologies.

'Too late for sorry, young man. You know you deserve to be punished – and punished you shall be.'

She lashed him eight times, pausing between each stroke to let the searing pain soak in, and the dread of the next swipe build up to haunt his imagination. Swish, stripe. Swish, stripe. Each measured stroke lashed the thin cane down across his jerking buttocks. Soon the pink weals were deepening to a darker shade of pain. Between the fifth and the sixth stroke, she tamed him with her cane by depressing it at the nape of his neck. Dominating him superbly, she quelled his wriggling and writhing. The concluding strokes were vicious, planting crimson stripes across the roundest curve of his helpless cheeks. He squealed aloud, clamping his pale thighs together until his cleft became a mere crease.

'There,' she murmured, resting the cane across his punished rump. 'Nanny has chastised you. And what do you say to Nanny after our punishment?'

'Thank you, Nanny,' he whispered thickly.

'Good little boy.'

Prodding him gently with the tip of the cruel cane, she rolled him over. His erection flickered up, saluting her smartly. She teased its glistening snout with the cane. He blushed furiously – his face almost as red as his bottom – and scrabbled his hands to cover his proud shaft.

'Don't be silly, young man,' Nanny purred, sweeping his fingers away from his throbbing cock deftly with her bamboo. 'No secrets from Nanny. After all, I've bathed you and owned your bottom for many a long year, haven't I?'

He closed his eyes tightly, burning in his shame. She began to tap his balls, flicking her wrist so that the cane jerked up into them softly, maddening the heat in his sac. Grunting softly, he thrust his hips up and came, splattering his tummy and chest as he gripped and taloned the duvet in exquisite torment.

'Now run along to the bathroom and wash yourself thoroughly,' she said crisply, wiping the wet tip of her glistening cane in her skirt. 'I will be along shortly to apply a cold flannel to your hot bottom. And,' she concluded sternly, 'Nanny hopes that she has taught you not to be such a greedy, selfish little piggy. Really, eating the young ones' Easter eggs like that. Has Nanny taught you a lesson?'

'Yes, thank you, Nanny,' he mumbled, wiping the semen from his chest hairs with a flattened palm. 'How – how did you know it was me who ate the eggs, Nanny?'

'Nanny knows everything,' she replied tersely. 'And, above all, Nanny knows best. Aren't you glad I chose to cane you rather than spank your bottom over my knee? Hm?'

'Yes, Nanny.'

'Of course you are. You wouldn't have wanted to be spanked across my knee and splash my nylon stockings with your sticky wickedness, would you?'

'No, Nanny.'

'And why not?'

He lowered his head and remained stubbornly silent.

'Because,' she whispered, 'Nanny would have had to spank

213

your sore bottom very hard until you had licked her nylons clean.'

Wet from her reverie, Nanny Stevens rose from her seat and swayed down the carriage towards the loo. In it, she used a fistful of tissues to dry her excitement.

The train sliced through the countryside, scattering crows and cows.

In her seat, awake behind closed eyes, Nanny Pearse enjoyed her spanking memories, her wet lips parted in a carnal smile. She recalled her time in a Suffolk manor farmhouse. The cook, a young Welsh girl with large, brown eyes, had been very temperamental over Christmas. The turkey had survived, but the pudding had been ruined. Cook remained out of sight, clattering and crashing angrily in the kitchen. Eight years younger than Nanny Pearse, the tempestuous Welsh beauty refused to be consoled.

After a supper of cold meats and relish on Boxing Day, when the children of the household were safely asleep and the adults had gone out for drinks, Nanny Pearse had discovered the young cook kneeling at the Christmas tree in the drawing room, weeping gently. A broken heart, Nanny had diagnosed. Correctly – for the large brown eyes brimmed with tears as, in her soft Welsh lilt, the sad girl had spoken of her love for the village schoolmistress. Their affair had been broken up by the arrival of a new, pretty librarian.

'I do miss her so, Nanny. She had a severe way with her. Such a sweet, severe way. I miss that savage tenderness so much.'

Nanny Pearse had used the switch of mistletoe to whip the cook's eagerly upturned bare bottom. The whipped girl had smothered her squeals of delicious anguish in a large crimson cushion; soon, her bare cheeks were criss-crossed with crimson from the strict kiss of the mistletoe's lash.

'Oh, Nanny,' the punished cook had moaned, scrambling to plant her mouth between her chastiser's parted thighs – licking the pantied pubis adoringly – and spilling out her gratitude, 'You've made my Christmas come.'

A taxi took them from the station to the fine Nash mansion in an exclusive part of Bath. Alice received them both and gave them a supper of sardines on toast. They retired to her room upstairs and undressed, remaining in their lingerie. Nanny Stevens sported a ribbed, cream pantie-girdle with dark brown stockings snapped up tightly at the suspenders. The sheer stockings sheathed her legs superbly. She wore a balconette bra to bunch her heavy breasts in strict bondage, the semi-cupped support thrusting her bosom up in plump provocation. Nanny Pearse had selected an underwired basque cut high at her thighs and buttocks, and pearl-grey tights of a cotton and lycra mix.

After inspecting them, and stooping to straighten Nanny Stevens' seams, Alice left, taking a taxi to the cinema. Both nannies sat in silence on the bed in the darkened room.

At a little after ten, the bedroom door handle rattled softly. The door inched open and the blonde head of a young businessman – Alice's employer – peered into the darkness.

'Nanny,' he whispered. 'It's me. Don't be alarmed.'

'Come right in, young man,' both nannies boomed. The light was snapped on. He froze.

He smothered his startled cry at the sight of the two splendid matrons in their delicious underwear. His cock stiffened in response to the swollen promise of Nanny Stevens' breasts wobbling in their balconette – and twitched painfully against his shorts at Nanny Pearse's heavy buttocks. In his sac, his tightening balls churned at the glimpse of her sleek thighs sheathed in the sheen of her pearl-grey tights. Behind their sheer stretch, her pubis fuzz showed darkly.

'Not a sound,' Nanny Stevens warned, 'unless you want to explain the presence of a couple of tarts under your roof to the board of directors tomorrow.'

He stumbled into the bedroom. 'Were's Alice?'

Ignoring him, they closed the door and quickly gagged him, then stripped him naked. With hands buried in blue rubber gloves donned for the purpose, they toyed with and tweaked the tip of his straining shaft. His pre-come made their rubbered fingertips shine.

'We gather that you have been persistently pestering Alice for

215

a taste of nanny domination,' Nanny Pearse whispered, masturbating him but pinching his foreskin in a bid to deny him his liquid release.

Gagged, he could only manage a muffled denial.

'If it's nanny domination and discipline you want, young man, nanny domination and discipline you shall most certainly have. Bend over.'

She spanked him severely, her flattened palm sweeping down crisply across his bare bottom, reddening it instantly. After the thirteenth swipe of her spanking hand, he came, soaking her pearly grey tights with a spreading dark stain.

'Naughty boy,' Nanny Pearse whispered venomously. 'Now you're really going to suffer.'

His eyes widened above his tight gag as they bound his wrists and ankles together using a pair of Alice's black stockings for the impromptu bondage. The stocking at his wrists was bound so tight it bit and burnt the whitened flesh.

Forced to kneel, his sweating face now buried completely in Nanny Stevens's bosom, he shivered and groaned into his gag as Nanny Pearse mounted his bottom from behind, raking her pubic mound repeatedly and dominatingly down against his hot cheeks, the sheen of her wet tights stretched across her plum-pubis, rasping his punished buttocks savagely.

Biting into his gag in ecstasy, he came: lurching drunkenly and splashing Nanny Stevens' girdle with a prolonged, pumping squirt of hot liquid joy. Imprisoning his cheeks between her straddling thighs, Nanny Pearse expertly milked and drained the last drop out of him.

They worked on him ruthlessly 'til well past midnight, leaving him pale and spent – having come six times at their cruel command. Straining in his bondage, he wriggled and threshed in a vain attempt to escape their intimate attentions, but there was no hiding place in the small bedroom from their capable, nannying hands. Although the polished leather sheath of a riding crop glistened on the bed, it had not been used upon his bottom.

'A little treat for later,' the nannies had whispered.

Apart from the occasional staccato bark of a crisp spanking –

and the sticky smear of both nannies' wetness – his cheeks remained virginally creamy.

Alice returned, and gasped aloud at the scene that greeted her wide eyes as she entered her bedroom.

'We've prepared him for you, Alice. Warmed him up a bit. I'm sure, after you've dealt with him,' Nanny Pearse murmured, picking up the cruel crop, 'you won't be having any more trouble from him.'

Both nannies dragged him, still bound and gagged, before Alice.

'Get into your nanny's uniform quickly,' Nanny Pearse told her.

Alice obeyed, stripping then dressing gingerly from nakedness to pert, starched nanny in a pinstriped uniform – allowing her employer a tantalising, teasing feast.

'Hold him fast,' Nanny Stevens advised her companion. 'I'll use the crop now.'

Taking the crop from Nanny Pearse, she swished it. 'Better keep his gag on. They squeal a bit under the lash.'

'No, he won't. Too much at stake if his wife came to see what was going on. Besides,' Nanny Pearse reasoned as she undid his gag, 'we want him to taste his domination, don't we?'

Nanny Stevens grinned and nodded.

The bound man, now ungagged, shrank back but Nanny Pearse forced his face in between Alice's thighs. Alice raised the hem of her uniform skirt and peeled her panties down to receive his nose, lips and tongue.

'Look at Nanny,' came the first strict command.

Opening his eyes, he gazed adoringly into Alice's pubic nest.

Swish, crack. The crop seared his buttocks.

'Smell Nanny,' came the second stern injunction.

He dug his nose into her moist warmth.

'Inhale her fragrance.'

He obeyed, his striped cheeks spasming.

Swish, crack. The crop sliced down again.

'Taste Nanny.'

His tongue worked busily at the labia, then probed them.

Swish, crack. He screamed softly, mouthing his agony into the wet pussy.

'Worship Nanny.'

Kneeling, he bowed down in abject reverence before the adored one.

Swish, swish, swish. He came at her feet. Literally, ejaculating over Alice's stockings. Treading his head down with her prinked foot, Alice drove his face down into his own warm mess – as Nanny Stevens plied the short leather-sheathed crop again and again in a stinging rain of pain.